In 2012 I began a holiday tradition of writing Christmas codas for some of my — and your — favorite stories. I ran the codas on my blog and left them up there for readers to enjoy all year round.

At the end of 2013 I collected those first two years' worth of novellas, edited them, expanded a few of them, added in recipes that were either featured in the original works or seem to add some final comment or insight into the era or the characters or their relationship and made them available in a collection titled Merry Christmas, Darling!

In 2016 I did it all again with the latest batch of codas and called the collection Christmas Waltz.

Over the years readers have requested that I make the collections available in print, so here are both of them together -- all codas written up to this date -- in one print volume.

Happiest of Holidays to you all. May this season be filled with love and laughter, and may the New Year bring you health and happiness.

D1127858

ALL I WANT FOR CHRISTMAS

COMPRISING

HOLIDAY CODAS 1:
MERRY CHRISTMAS, DARLING!

&

HOLIDAY CODAS 2:
CHRISTMAS WALTZ

JOSH LANYON

ALL I WANT FOR CHRISTMAS (HOLIDAY CODAS 1 and 2)
Collecting MERRY CHRISTMAS, DARLING! and CHRISTMAS WALTZ

Copyright (c) 2017 by Josh Lanyon
Cover and book design by Kevin Burton Smith
Cover art by Johanna Ollila
Edited by Keren Reed

ISBN: 978-1-945802-18-8
Published in the United States of America

JustJoshin Publishing, Inc.
3053 Rancho Vista Blvd.
Suite 116
Palmdale, CA 93551
www.joshlanyon.com

This is a work of fiction. Any resemblance to persons living or dead is entirely coincidental.

Merry Christmas, Darling!

CHRISTMAS WALTZ

MERRY CHRISTMAS, DARLING!

HOLIDAY CODAS 1:

JOSH LANYON

NICK & PERRY

THE GHOST WORE YELLOW SOCKS

"You'll like California." Nick turned his head on the pillow and caught the shine of Perry's eyes in the muted light, the gleam of his smile. His blond hair was still damp and spiky from the snow.

"I think so." Perry sounded content. "I want to paint the beach."

"There's plenty of beach in California."

"Yeah."

They had dug the sheets out of the box Nick had packed a couple of hours earlier and made up the bed. Nick's sleeping bag was unzipped, spread out over them like a quilt. It was comfortable. Probably the most comfortable bed Nick could remember, though that had more to do with Perry lying next to him than clean sheets and a good mattress.

The snow, which had started falling while they were otherwise occupied, made a soothing shushing sound against the bedroom window.

"It'll be good for you. California, I mean. The climate and everything."

"Yep." Perry still sounded supremely untroubled. Untroubled and young.

"You…don't think you'll be homesick?"

Perry chuckled. "Nope." He wrapped his good arm around Nick's waist and settled his head more comfortably on Nick's shoulder. "It's like my mom used to say. Home is where the heart is."

Nick's own heart seemed to swell with another surge of that unfamiliar emotion. He bent his head, his mouth seeking Perry's, and Perry responded with that easy enthusiasm.

When their lips reluctantly parted he said astonishingly, "Don't worry, Nick. I'll be fine. *We*'ll be fine."

"I know that," Nick said gruffly.

"And I promise I won't get in the way or disrupt your work."

"The hell you won't." Nick was smiling as his mouth found Perry's once more.

GLEN AND NASH

In Plain Sight

Nash did not have any holiday traditions. He had holiday habits. Christmas dinner with his parents every couple of years. New Year's parties with work colleagues. Gifts of booze to male colleagues and gifts of coffee to female colleagues. He probably hadn't bought a Christmas tree since he'd had college roommates to help decorate it.

So that had been the first question. "Should we get a Christmas tree?"

Well, not the *first* question. The first questions had taken place while Glen was still in the hospital recovering. Those had been the big questions: where are we going to live and who's giving up his job? A two-part question really. And he'd known the answer before he asked.

He would transfer to the Salt Lake Division and work out of Pocatello. He told himself Glen required every penny of his health insurance right now, so that meant Glen needed his job more, but the fact was, Nash was embarking on a new life and that meant from now on his job was just that, a job. He'd sell his house in Fredericksburg and move in with Glen.

"Are you sure?" Glen had asked more than once. As happy as he was, he was afraid Nash was making a mistake. And if Nash was honest, he occasionally wondered too. But then he would think of that terrible, terrible time when he had not known whether Glen was alive or dead, and everything seemed clear again.

His house was still on the market — it was not a good time to try and sell — and it had taken six months for his transfer to go into effect, so he and Glen had been living together for less than two months by the time the holidays rolled around.

They were still getting to know each other so they were a little careful with each other. Well, a lot careful.

Glen had admitted once, revealingly, "It's like we're doing this backwards."

"Do you mind?"

"Compared to the alternative?"

That was exactly right. They were starting from the standpoint of knowing they loved each other and wanted to be together. But could you really love someone you didn't know?

It seemed the answer was yes, because Nash did believe he loved Glen. More than he had ever loved anyone in his life. Every morning that he woke up beside Glen was a good morning. It just felt right. It felt like he was finally home. It didn't matter who technically owned the real estate. He felt Glen's smiles in his chest. He felt at peace listening to Glen's quiet breathing in the night. And his not quiet breathing made him smile. He liked talking to Glen over breakfast and not talking to him over breakfast. They didn't have enough dinners together, but he enjoyed those too.

He was regularly adding to the small store of everything he knew about Glen. He now knew that Glen liked basketball and photography and fishing and camping. He was an Independent, a non-church-going Protestant, and he did not want children. He did not care about marriage, but he cared very much about commitment. He was close to his family and generally spent the holidays he didn't work with them.

Which brought them full circle.

"A Christmas tree? Sure," Glen had said. And then, "I don't have any decorations or anything. But if you want a tree…"

"I just thought maybe you would," Nash said hastily. Now he felt silly. He never bothered with this kind of holiday stuff.

Glen had looked undecided, and then he'd said, "Well…"

Nash joked, "Are we the kind of guys who get a Christmas tree?"

Glen stared at him and then he'd seemed to relax. "I think we are. I think we should…" Then he'd stopped looking self-conscious.

"Should get a tree?" Nash said.

Glen had said, "Should start building our own traditions." He'd looked so serious and hopeful that it had been all Nash could do not to grab him then and there.

That was it exactly. They needed to build traditions together. Their own traditions.

And just the process of picking their first tree was instructive.

"Real or fake?" Nash had asked.

"Real." Glen had been definite.

"Do we chop our own or —?"

"What do you think?"

"I'm not a lumberjack."

Glen had laughed. "That's okay. I've had my fill of lumberjacks."

Nash had spluttered, but moved on. "Flocked or unflocked?"

"It kills the scent."

Nash had volunteered, "But it is pretty."

"Flocked it is," Glen had said easily.

"So. The important question. How big?"

Glen had met Nash's eyes and started to laugh. Nash *had* grabbed him then.

Glen's mother had supplied a handful of family ornaments that probably qualified as heirlooms. They had bought the rest themselves at the drug store. Pretty, frosted gold balls, ropes of shiny red beads, and a few silly things — glass balls with bewildered-looking moose and nervous reindeer.

Not every decision would be made as quickly, and not all the compromises would be as easy, but as Nash sat on the sofa in front of the fire that night, arm around Glen's shoulders as they admired their handiwork, he felt truly at peace.

"God rest ye merry gentleman," sang Josh Groban from the media cabinet. *"Let nothing you dismay."*

Until that moment Nash had always imagined joy as something big and bright and noisy. But in fact joy was also as small as the gleam of firelight on two pairs of slippers, obscure as the reasons for love, and quiet as two people who did not need words.

DREW AND FRASER

Mummy Dearest

"What was that?"

"Thunder."

"That didn't sound like thunder to me."

"It's thunder."

"We should have stayed at the monastery."

"No, we should not have." Fraser's hazel gaze met mine and I cleared my throat.

"Mm. Possibly not." I was not about to let that smug look sit on his face one second longer than I had to. "Why do I let you talk me into these things?" My moan could barely be heard over that of the icy wind outside our tent. Our tent in northern Nepal. You know: the Himalayas. Home to Meh-Teh. AKA the Yeti. AKA the Abominable Snowman.

Fraser grinned at me over the rim of his mug. His red-rimmed eyes sparkled in his ruddy, wind-burned face. His teeth were white in the gold frame of his beard. "You always say that, but you know you love every minute."

"Love every minute!" I spluttered.

"You have loved every minute of the past five years."

"You're starting to hallucinate. Move closer so we can conserve body heat."

Not that we could really get any closer. "Here." Fraser held out the thermos and I let him top up my mug. "You have to admit, it's a lot better than garden parties and the opera."

"No I don't."

"I took you away from all that."

"I'm not forgetting whose fault this is."

"I saved you from a life of boredom."

"I wasn't all that bored."

"Yes you were. And you'll thank me for this in the end."

"Which will be any minute now. They'll find our mummified remains in an ice cavern. Beneath an avalanche."

"Locked in each other's arms." Fraser continued to beam at me while I slurped my steaming cocoa.

Not bad. The cocoa, I mean. Although the other was alright too. In fact...

I took another cautious slurp and frowned suspiciously. "What's in here?"

"Peppermint schnapps."

"Schnapps? Are you trying to get me drunk?"

"Of course. Drunk and debauched."

"Let's just skip to the debauched part. The hangover isn't so bad."

He touched his plastic mug to mine. "Cheers, Drew. Merry Christmas."

"Merry Christ —" I nearly dropped my cup at the boom of sound bouncing off the mountains around us. Fraser's blazing look of joy told me all I needed to know. "Hey. That was *not* thunder!"

PERFECT CUP OF COCOA

INGREDIENTS

⅓ cup unsweetened cocoa powder

¾ cup sugar

Pinch salt

⅓ cup boiling water

3 ½ cups milk

¾ teaspoon vanilla extract

½ cup half-and-half cream

OPTIONAL: 1 ½ ounces of Peppermint Schnapps

DIRECTIONS

Begin by combining the cocoa, sugar and salt in a saucepan.

Blend in the boiling water. Bring to easy boil while stirring.

Simmer and stir for about 2 minutes, being careful that the mixture does not scorch. Stir in the 3 ½ cups milk and heat until very hot, but DO NOT BOIL.

Remove from heat. Add vanilla.

Divide between four mugs. Add the cream to each of the mugs.

ARCHER & RAKE FROM "GREEN GLASS BEADS"

SONG FOR A WINTER'S NIGHT

It was a stupid argument.

Not least because it served to bring about the very thing Archer did not want. Now he was on his own for Solstice AND Christmas. And perhaps for the foreseeable future.

"You're not an Irregular anymore," he had protested, when Rake first brought up the subject of the Christmas party.

"I served with the Irregulars for four decades."

"But you're not an Irregular *now*." This was an important point for Archer because he hated the Irregulars. Rake excepted. It was the only thing about Rake he didn't like. His past with the Irregulars.

Rake, who understood him very well, had started out trying to be patient. "I still have friends there. Good friends. I'd like to see them again."

"Good friends like Sergeant Orly who tried to have me thrown in prison for thirty years? Can't you see your good friends another time? Does it have to be Solstice Night?"

"It's a party. Everyone will be in one place. That's the point of inviting me."

"It's Solstice Night!"

"I know, sweeting. And I'm sorry for that. But we'll have *Réveillon* and Christmas together." Rake nibbled delicately on the upswept point of Archer's nearest ear. He teased, "And Boxing Day and Feast of St. Stephen and New Year's and First Footing and Three Kings Day. We'll celebrate Chinese New Year, if you like. We'll spend every single holiday you please together. We'll spend them any way you choose."

Archer pulled his head away. "None of those mean as much to me as Solstice!"

Which was quite true. Solstice was the festival that mattered to the Fae. The Solstices and the Equinoxes. And yet…and yet… He wasn't five years old, after all. Archer had spent plenty of Solstices on his own — and without the promise of sharing every other holiday on the calendar with someone he loved — someone who loved him. He knew he was being unreasonable. Even —

"You're being childish," Rake had said.

And the conversation had gone from precariously balanced to a headlong plummet into the abyss.

"Is it childish to expect loyalty? Is it childish to expect that I would come first with my-my chosen consort?"

"It's childish to imagine I would abandon all other alliances and obligations simply because we're now together."

"Alliances and obligations to people who are my enemies."

"Enemies?" Rake had laughed.

The laughter was a grave mistake because Archer already knew he was being foolish. The laughter stung him on the quick, and he had reacted accordingly.

At one point — the point where Archer had said, "I oppose everything the Irregulars stand for. If it was up to me they'd be disbanded and destroyed!" — Rake's demon side had shown briefly in red eyes and very sharp incisors. He had ended the conversation, conversation being a polite word for what was now a slanging match, and gone for a walk, slamming the door to the cottage so hard Mikhail Alexandrovich Vrubel's painting of the demon surrounded by green moths fell from the wall, landing face first in front of the stone fireplace.

An hour later Rake had phoned to say he was in San Francisco and that Archer should expect him back in Saint-Malo when he saw him.

Seven long and lovely months they'd had together, but now it appeared to be over.

A stupid, pointless, useless argument.

Archer was alone again, the thing he dreaded most. And not just for the holidays.

Disconsolately, he wandered through the crowded winter garden inside the Château, investigating the chalet-style stalls of the Christmas market. There were holiday delicacies to sample, handmade toys and old-fashioned ornaments to admire, choirs to listen to. The wet grass glittered, the cobblestones were dark with rain, and the fairy lights gleamed in the bare bones of the trees, like fireflies flickering through an army of skeletons. The scents of wonderful cooking mingled in the frosty air with jovial French voices and music. Much of the music was traditional Breton and French folk songs, but Archer recognized a familiar melody: "Song for a Winter's Night," made popular by Sarah McLachlan during the years he'd lived in Canada. The choir sang in French, but he knew the words and they made his heart ache.

If I could know within my heart
That you were lonely too
I would be happy just to hold the hands I love
On this winter night with you

He was homesick, that was the trouble. But he was not homesick for Canada. Nor any place he had lived in in his much-traveled life. No, he was homesick for Rake.

Why had he said such stupid things to Rake? Why had he gone out of his way to make Rake angry? He didn't even mean most of it. He didn't agree with some of the aims and some of the tactics of the NATO Irregular Affairs Division, but he knew they were a necessary evil. Not even an evil, really. Nuisance? He didn't wish any Irregulars harm. He didn't wish anyone harm. It was just…

Just what?

Archer walked on through the merry crowd. The Christmas market was packed this night, and so it would continue to Christmas day. He stopped to buy a bag of roasted chestnuts and drink a cup of Christmas coffee. The strong coffee hinted at cinnamon and allspice and cloves and peppercorns, reminding him of Rake's kisses. You wouldn't expect a demon to taste so sweet. Sweet and smoky, that was the flavor of Rake's kisses.

Archer's eyes blurred, his breath catching in his throat as he realized he might never taste Rake's kisses again. Demons weren't famous for their steadfast affections, after all. Wasn't this sudden decision to go see his old comrades proof that Rake was growing bored with sharing Archer's banishment?

Archer sniffed miserably and walked on past laughing people in folk costumes performing traditional folk dances.

Very pretty and festive in the lantern light. If you liked that kind of thing.

The real festivities, for Archer at least, were outside the walls of the city. Solstice celebrations would be held up and down the coast and on the small island of Grand Bé. There would be bonfires in isolated coves and fields and the Fae would gather to drink and feast before the Procession of Light began. Archer would not attend the festivities. He was not generally welcomed by the local *fée*. Not because he was half-blood, but because he was a foreigner. A foreigner with an ancient Sumerian demon for a boyfriend. But even if he didn't attend the feast and the procession, the holiday was still important to him. He had looked forward to spending his first ever Winter Solstice with Rake. It would be the first time he'd belonged to someone, that someone had belonged to him.

But in fact, what was Winter Solstice but a celebration of the shortest day of the year? And the sooner this one — and all the rest of them without Rake — were over, the better.

Archer stopped at another stall. It had been a busy day in the shop and he had not found time to eat. He bought *galettes*, a kind of buck-wheat pancake, spread thickly with honey, and washed them down with two beers.

It was starting to rain again. The crowd didn't seem to mind, but Archer suddenly had no heart for it.

He finished his beer and left the winter garden and the Christmas market, walking back through the narrow cobbled streets. The rain was in his eyes the whole way, blurring his vision.

This was all his own fault for being insecure and jealous and possessive. Of course Rake had no patience for such nonsense. Even if it was typical faerie behavior. Well, the jealousy and possessiveness. The insecurity was all human.

Archer reached the cottage he shared with Rake. He hoped against hope the door would swing open and Rake would be there.

But no. The door was still fastened with its protective wards, and when it opened for Archer, the rooms were dark and cold. Aunt Esmeralda's cloisonné clock sweetly chimed the hour. It was late.

Too late.

He stood for a moment, struggling to contain all the emotion threatening to tear out of his chest. He was not a child, and faeries, despite the cute pictures and YouTube videos, did not cry.

He took off his scarf, his Burberry, and hung them by the door. No point in building a fire or fixing supper. He'd eaten enough at the Christmas market and no fire would warm him now. Instead he went upstairs, undressed, and climbed in the enormous bed he shared with Rake. The green glass beads were draped over the tall headboard post, and he slipped them free and looped them around his neck. They were cool against his hot face, glimmering mysteriously in the darkness and whispering comfortingly to him.

The beads spoke of green things, of soft moss and silky grass and sparkling jade and glittering emeralds and spicy pines and splashing water and hopping frogs and rustling leaves and celadon bowls and smiling waves…

They had done delightfully naughty things with these beads, things that made Archer blush and shiver now as the beads reminded him, reassured him that all was not lost.

When Archer woke a few hours later the room was alight with the gentle glow of dozens of floating will-o'-the-wisps. He blinked sleepily as they drifted down around him, landing on the velvet coverlet and disappearing like pinched out candles. He sat up. He was alone, but the bedroom door was open and he could see by the way the shadows moved in the hallway that the fireplace in the living room was lit.

Archer threw back the blankets and stumbled downstairs.

A small feast for two had been set out before the blazing hearth. There were apple tarts and blackberries and cream, mince pie and little amber cakes that looked exactly like butter and honey cakes from his favorite bakery in Vancouver. Brown bottles of honey ale glistened in the firelight.

"I was beginning to think I would have to jump up and down on the bed to wake you up," Rake remarked. He sat in front of the fire wearing only a pair of scarlet Paisley silk pajama bottoms. The hard planes of his muscular chest gleamed like bronze in the golden light. His eyes were black and unfathomable.

Archer chuckled uncertainly and wiped the sleep from his eyes. He approached the little feast hesitantly. "I didn't think I would see you so soon."

"Disappointed?" Rake was smiling.

Archer shook his head.

"No? You weren't looking forward to a nice, long, undisturbed night? A few days peace and quiet?"

It was such a lovely little feast — and yes, the cakes were the very ones he used to love.

Archer's eyes filled with tears. Through the blur he saw Rake's rugged features alter, grow aghast. "Archer?"

"I thought you weren't coming back. I thought I'd spoiled it all."

Rake rose and scooped him up, returning to his place by the fire and cuddling Archer against his broad chest. His eyes glowed red with emotion, his incisors showed very white as he delivered little punishing love bites over Archer's throat and shoulders. His silken wings folded protectively, creating a little cocoon for them.

"Not coming back! I said I was coming back!"

"You said I would see you when I saw you."

"But…then you would be seeing me, right?"

"Maybe a century from now."

"A century! But it's only four days till Christmas."

Archer gave a watery chuckle and wiped his eyes. Tonight Rake's kisses tasted of vanilla. "You've been eating cookies."

"Yes, I have. I brought you some. And Barry Littlechurch sent you those little cakes. He said they were your favorite."

"You saw Barry?"

"I stopped in to say hello. He's thinking about coming out here in the summer for a visit."

"Is he really?"

"Yes. He misses you."

Archer sighed and rested his head on Rake's chest listening to the boom of his eight-chambered heart. "I miss him too. Did you have a nice time at your party?"

He felt Rake's smile. "I did. It was nice seeing old friends. And it was nicer still coming home."

"I'm sorry I was so bad-tempered."

Rake laughed. "It was pretty frightening." He kissed Archer and nipped his lip.

"Ouch." Archer touched his mouth, but there was no blood. Rake never drew blood.

"Did you really think I wouldn't come back?"

Archer closed his eyes. "I thought you might not."

The wings folded more closely about him with a heavy rustle. Rake bent his head and said softly, "But I'll always come back. Do you know why?"

Archer opened his eyes. Rake's eyes glowed warm and golden into his.

"Because I love you." Rake teased gently, "Better than stars or water, better than voices of winds that sing, better than any man's fair daughter, or your green glass beads on that silver ring." He wound the green beads around his fist and drew Archer's face to his for another kiss. "Happy Solstice, sweeting."

BUCKWHEAT GALETTES

INGREDIENTS

BATTER:

2 eggs

¾ cup buckwheat flour

1 cup + 1 teaspoon whole wheat flour

½ teaspoon salt

1 tablespoon canola oil

3 tablespoons salted butter

FILLING:

Raclette cheese

Button mushrooms sliced

Red bell peppers sliced

DIRECTIONS

Using a handheld mixer, whisk the eggs until foamy.

Combine the flours and salt in a bowl. Sift the dry ingredients. Form a well in the center of the bowl. Pour in the eggs and ½ cup of water. Mix by hand for about 3-4 minutes until the batter is smooth. Do NOT over-mix. Add the oil.

Let the crêpe batter rest for at least 2-3 hours (I let it rest overnight).

Thin the crêpe batter with about ⅓ cup of water (up to ⅔ cup).

Place your crêpe pan (or any flat pan) over medium heat. Grease it with a little butter using a silicone brush. Pour about ½ cup of the batter in the center of the pan. Lift the pan and then tilt and rotate it until the batter is evenly spread and forms a nice thin disk. Put it back on the stove. It should start bubbling after a few seconds. Lower the heat to low. Place a slice of raclette cheese and add a little bit of the button mushroom and red bell pepper filling. Fold the crêpe and let the cheese melt for 1-2 minutes. The traditional method is to fold the edges of the crêpes in on all 4 sides by about 2 to 3 inches; this leaves the filling exposed.

Repeat until all the ingredients are used. Stir the crêpe batter as you go for uniform consistency.

Yields: 18-21 crêpes.

These can be eaten with butter and honey or jam. Or with thin slices of a favorite cheese. Or they can be filled with button mushrooms and roasted red bell peppers.

INDIAN CARDAMOM TEA

INGREDIENTS

5 cardamom pods, slightly crushed

2 teabags

4 tablespoons sugar

Milk

DIRECTIONS

Put about 7 cups water into a large pan, add the cardamom and bring to the boil.

Once boiling, add the teabags and sugar.

Add enough milk to turn a milky tea-color.

Bring to the boil again and before it bubbles over, take off the heat.

Pour through a strainer into cups.

BRETT AND RAFFERTY

THIS ROUGH MAGIC

Rafferty told himself he didn't expect Brett to show.

Christmas Eve? Nah. There would be some swell Snob Hill party he was expected to attend or some wingding at the old plantation he'd feel it his duty to soldier through. And it wasn't like Rafferty was ten years old and still believed in Santy Claus. It was a long time since he'd knelt by his cot praying for a pony or a long lost uncle. He was a big boy now and this was just another night in foggy old San Francisco. A little colder, a little darker than some — but Rafferty'd known colder and darker.

It was well after midnight when he poured a stiff drink, his second of the evening, and turned out the lights in the front of the house. He was lying in bed reading *White Fang* by Jack London when he heard the faint, familiar scratching at his bedroom window.

His heart sprang into life. He threw the book aside, unfolded from the bed, and shoved open the window. Brett stood in the alley. He grinned at Rafferty and held up a bottle of Dom Perignon.

"I thought I heard the click click click of reindeer hooves," Rafferty drawled.

"Merry Christmas." Brett handed over the champagne and climbed through the window with considerable agility, given that he was wearing evening clothes beneath a dark ulster. The ulster had a Persian lamb collar, so Rafferty had guessed right. A night on the town for young Master Sheridan.

He shoved the window closed behind Brett, yanked the curtains shut. "I wasn't expecting you."

Brett gave him a level look, his eyes as green as spring. "I can leave if you've got other plans."

"Of course I don't have plans and of course I don't want you to leave." Rafferty took him in his arms. Brett's eyes were shining and happy, his flushed face cold from the bitter night air. He tasted like champagne.

"I got away as soon as I could."

"You should have told me you were coming. I'd have…" What? Fixed Brett a meal? He'd have had plenty to eat and plenty to drink wherever he'd been.

"I wasn't sure I'd be able to make it. I didn't want to disappoint you."

Rafferty was touched — and embarrassed. He would have been disappointed, sure, though he'd like to think he was better at hiding his feelings. "I'm glad you made it."

Brett treated him to one of those rare, unguarded smiles. Six months they'd been…whatever they were, and those smiles still made Rafferty's breath catch in his throat.

"Did you have a nice evening?" he asked, and he genuinely hoped Brett had because there weren't nearly enough nice evenings in Brett's life.

"Not particularly." Brett reached deep into his coat pocket and pulled out a small parcel, a flat blue box with a white ribbon.

"What's this?" Rafferty took the box.

Brett shrugged out of his ulster and draped it over the bed post. The first time he'd done that, Rafferty had woken during the night and, thinking someone was looming over them, nearly shot the coat. "Open it," Brett said, and turned his attention to the champagne.

Rafferty recognized that blue box and he wondered uneasily where the hell Brett had found the money to buy whatever was inside. Hopefully Brett and Kitty weren't back to pawning family heirlooms.

By the time Rafferty had fumbled open the box, Brett had uncorked the champagne and poured it into the only two clean coffee cups left in the house.

"Hell." Rafferty stared down at the gold pocket watch. He swallowed hard. "I got you a book."

Brett laughed. "Did you? What book?"

Rafferty's face felt hot. It had seemed like a good idea at the time, but really what the hell had he been thinking? "Shakespeare's sonnets."

Brett laughed again, an indulgent chuckle. He had placed his mug of champagne on the steamer trunk that served as Rafferty's bedside table and was shedding his clothes with quick, unselfconscious grace. His skin was pale and smooth like warm marble. He said, "You're a romantic, Neil."

Maybe. He was Irish. It was pretty much the same thing.

Rafferty removed the pocket watch from the fancy box. It was a beauty. The nicest thing he'd ever had in his life. He glanced at Brett now climbing into his bed, and mentally corrected himself. The second nicest thing he'd ever had in his life.

"Thank you," he said, and he wasn't talking to Brett.

THE ORANGE BLOSSOM

INGREDIENTS

¾ ounce gin

¾ ounce Italian / sweet vermouth

¾ ounce orange juice

DIRECTIONS

Combine ingredients in a cocktail shaker, shake and strain into a cocktail glass.

Garnish with an orange zest if desired.

WHITE HOUSE COFFEE SOUFFLE

BY FIRST LADY GRACE COOLIDGE

INGREDIENTS

1 ⅓ cups brewed coffee

1 tablespoon plain gelatin powder

⅔ cup granulated sugar

½ cup milk

3 egg yolks, slightly beaten

¼ teaspoon salt

3 egg whites, beaten stiff (use pasteurized egg whites)

½ teaspoon vanilla

Whipped cream for garnish

DIRECTIONS

Mix brewed coffee, gelatin powder, ⅓ cup sugar and milk.

Heat in a double boiler, add beaten egg yolks, ⅓ cup more of sugar and salt.

Cook until it thickens.

Add the whites of the eggs, beaten stiff, and vanilla. Pour in gelatin mold, chill and serve with whipped cream.

MITCH AND WEB

LONE STAR

"How's that?" Web asked.

Mitch moaned his pleasure.

"Yeah?" There was a smile in Web's voice. "How about there?"

"Good…"

"How about right here?"

"Yeaaa — Ouch!"

"Sorry."

"No, don't stop! It's all good." Mitch pleaded, "Harder, Web…"

Web said with amused exasperation, "I prod any harder and I'm goin' to puncture your calf muscle."

Mitch opened his eyes and grinned at Web, and Web's lean, tanned cheek creased in response. Even in the soft, multi-colored light from the very tall — Texas-sized — Christmas tree, his gaze was very blue, very bright, very tender.

They were lying on the wide, comfortable couch in the front room of the ranch house where Mitch had grown up. Not that it bore a lot of resemblance to that house, not after Web had got done with it. This was their home now, though it was still hard for Mitch to believe it. Seven months since he'd left the American Ballet Theater. Two years since he and Web had first made this plan. There had been times he'd believed they would never make it. And, to be honest, a few times he'd thought they were crazy for trying. But he was here now. Lock, stock, and barrel. For better, for worse; for richer, for poorer; in sickness and in health and in leg cramps.

"How's that?" Web asked. "Any better?"

Mitch nodded seriously. "Thank you." He was generally in pain, one way or the other — that was the reality of life as a premier ballet dancer — so he sincerely appreciated physical relief, let alone pleasure.

Web smiled again, as though nothing gave him more satisfaction than to take away Mitch's aches and pains. He went back to rubbing Mitch's battered and bruised feet. Mitch sighed his enjoyment. "This is heaven."

"It'll do for starters."

"Someday I'm going to get a pedicure," Mitch murmured, closing his eyes again.

"You're off for a week. Get one."

"Can't. Maybe when I retire some day. Not while I'm still performing. I need my calluses." Though not this week. His mouth curved, thinking about the luxury of having a week — an entire week — off. This was one of the advantages of working with a smaller dance company. This afternoon's Christmas Eve performance had been his final one of the season. He was actually going to have a vacation. A week with Web. Heaven. They hadn't had a chance to spend this kind of time together since he'd come back to sell the ranch two years ago. It was going to be like a honeymoon.

"You look mighty pleased with yourself," Web commented.

Mitch laughed. He opened his eyes and sat up, swinging his legs off the couch. "You sure it's okay about tonight? Nobody's going to be disappointed if we don't show up at your parents'? *You're* not going to be disappointed to spend Christmas Eve here, just the two of us?"

Web reached over and smoothed the crease between Mitch's brows with the edge of his thumb. "I wouldn't have suggested it if it was a problem for anybody."

"Yes, you would have," Mitch said. "You think I'm tired and stressed-out and need a break from people. Or people need a break from me."

Web nodded. "Well, sure. That's all true, Mitchell. But the fact is, I want this time with you. *I* want your undivided attention for a few hours."

Mitch leaned in for a kiss. "Oh you do, do you?"

Web kissed him back with unexpected hunger, and Mitch's heart did a happy little flip. Sometimes he still had trouble believing things were going to work out, but so far, so good. Because of Web. Because Web made it possible. Made it — almost — easy.

"We're goin' to have our own little party tonight. I've got a bottle of champagne chilling, supper in the fridge, a dessert that will make you fat just lookin' at it, and silk sheets on the bed," Web told him.

"*Silk sheets?*" Mitch started to laugh.

"Cross my heart."

"I've never had silk sheets. What color are they?"

Web looked reflective. "Not sure. They might be pale green or they might be gray. Maybe you should come and check them out?"

"I'm pretty tired," Mitch said regretfully. "I think you'd have to car —" His breath whooshed out as Web stood, grabbed his arm, and hoisted him over his shoulder in a fireman's carry.

Mitch began to laugh. "You crazy cowpoke…"

Web was laughing too. He swatted Mitch's ass. "What do you call this lift again? A press lift?"

"It might be a lifestyle lift…"

"It might at that, Mitchell. It might at that."

As Web bore him away down the hall, Mitch had a final upside down view of the Christmas tree with its gold and glittering star.

WARM CHOCOLATE CAKES
WITH MASCARPONE CREAM

INGREDIENTS

8 ounces bittersweet chocolate, chopped, plus shavings for garnish (optional)

1 ½ sticks (6 ounces) unsalted butter

3 large eggs, plus 3 large egg yolks, at room temperature

½ cup sugar

¼ cup cake flour

½ cup heavy cream

½ vanilla bean, split and seeds scraped 2 tablespoons light brown sugar

½ teaspoon finely grated lemon zest

1 cup mascarpone (8 ounces)

1 teaspoon fresh lemon juice

About ½ cup brandied cherries or kirsch-soaked sour cherries

DIRECTIONS

Preheat the oven to 375°F.

Coat six 6-ounce ramekins with butter, and dust lightly with flour. Set the ramekins on a sturdy baking sheet. In a microwave-safe bowl, melt the chocolate with the butter; let cool.

In the bowl of a standing electric mixer fitted with the whisk, beat the eggs, yolks and sugar on high speed until pale and fluffy, about 4 minutes. Using a rubber spatula, gently fold in the chocolate, then fold in the cake flour just until no streaks remain.

Spoon the batter into the prepared ramekins and bake for 15 minutes, until the cakes have risen, the tops are dry and the centers are slightly jiggly. Let stand for 5 minutes.

In a bowl, beat the cream with the vanilla seeds, brown sugar and lemon zest until soft peaks form. Add the mascarpone and lemon juice and beat until blended.

Run the tip of a small knife around each cake to loosen it, then unmold onto plates. Spoon the mascarpone cream onto the cakes and garnish with the brandied cherries and chocolate shavings.

FORD AND JACOB

HEART TROUBLE

It was a little white house on a quiet residential street.

Nothing to strike fear into a man's heart.

Christmas lights were strung along the roof and through the neatly pruned trees, a large wreath with red ribbons and pine cones hung on the front door, solar candy cane lights lined the cement walk.

Bad things did not happen in houses that looked like that. I knew because I had grown up in a house like that. In fact, I should be walking into a house like that right now. My parents' house in Cotati where my sisters and aunts and uncles and cousins and grandparents would all be sitting down to Christmas dinner any minute.

But instead, I was sitting in my car outside a strange house. A house that belonged to the parents of my...boyfriend.

The boyfriend my parents and all the rest of my family didn't know about because I hadn't told them. And because I hadn't told them, instead of going home to spend Christmas with my own family, I was spending it with Jacob's.

No. That wasn't fair. I was having Christmas dinner with Jacob's family because I wanted to spend Christmas with Jacob. And because it would be hard to do that at the home of my parents until I came out. So…Jacob's family.

"We'd trade off anyway, right?" Jacob had been his usual kind, supportive self, finding excuses for me when he should have told me to grow a pair. "Next year we'll go to your parents."

Right.

A red VW pulled up and parked in front of the Hoyles' house, and Rob, Jacob's brother, got out and went around to open the passenger door for a dark-haired girl in a white rabbit fur coat. That would be Karin, Rob's new girlfriend. Her family was back east, so this was her first Christmas with the Hoyles too.

I watched Rob and Karin walk up the candy cane lined walk. Karin was carrying a bottle of Blue Nun. I glanced at the bottle of Blue Nun on the seat beside me. They knocked on the front door, the door opened, and Jacob greeted them with a big, warm smile.

Just that little glimpse of him made my heart do a happy handspring.

It was worth it. Worth anything because if I didn't love Jacob, I was closer to it than I'd ever been in my life…

I watched him lean out the doorway and glance up and down the street before ducking back in and closing the door.

I wondered why I was sitting in my car working myself into an anxiety attack when I could be saying hello to Jacob right now.

I could be kissing Jacob hello.

I got out of my car.

ETHAN AND MICHAEL

SORT OF STRANGER THAN FICTION

"Merry Christmas, darling," sang Karen Carpenter. *"We're apart, that's true…"*

It was the first Christmas Ethan had ever had a boyfriend, so it was only reasonable that he'd hoped he and Michael might spend the holiday, at least part of the holiday together. He was pretty sure Michael had at least been open to the idea — he hadn't mentioned any other plans when Ethan had dropped hints about holiday dinners and so forth — but then when Ethan had finally got around to actually inviting him, Michael had looked vaguely regretful and said he had already agreed to spend Christmas day at his father's in La Crescenta.

"He's got a new fiancée," Michael had said. "He wants me to meet her."

"Oh." Ethan had tried to hide his disappointment.

He wasn't good at hiding his feelings though, and Michael had added a curt and belated, "Sorry."

Ethan blushed hotly. "No! Of course you'd go to your dad's. I only meant…if you didn't have anywhere else to go, you could spend it with us."

Maybe he was taking too much for granted anyway. It wasn't like he and Michael had any formal agreement. It wasn't like Michael had ever said Ethan was his boyfriend. They saw each other regularly, exclusively, but that was probably — on Michael's side, anyway — because there really wasn't another gay person within five hundred miles of Peabody. Even Karl Hagar had moved away to enter an MFA Writing Program at the University of San Francisco.

"It was nice of you to ask," Michael said politely.

"Oh no," Ethan said quickly and awkwardly. "You're always welcome. It's awful to be alone at the holidays. I'd have asked sooner, but I assumed you had somewhere to go."

Oh my God. He couldn't stop. He couldn't shut up! He couldn't stop making it sound like he was only asking out of politeness — and the worst part was, he sort of *wanted* it to sound like he was only asking out of politeness since Michael was rejecting his invitation anyway.

Michael let him babble to a stop, then he said, "Thanks anyway."

They finished their sandwiches in silence — they were having lunch at The Sandwich Shop — and parted ways.

Parted ways for real because Michael did not ask Ethan out that night — or the next — and by noon on Wednesday, Christmas Eve, Michael was driving south to La Crescenta, wherever that was. Ethan only knew because Erin told him. Michael had not even looked in on Red Bird Books to say goodbye and wish Ethan a Merry Christmas.

So instead of spending Christmas with his first boyfriend, it looked like Ethan was maybe breaking up with his first boyfriend over Christmas.

Every time he thought of the two gaily wrapped parcels hidden beneath his bed, he wanted to burst into tears. Not that a Timex watch, even a nice Timex watch, or a bottle of good Scotch were such amazing gifts, but he'd chosen them with care. He'd bought the very best he could afford. He knew what Michael liked and he'd wanted to please him. It wasn't about the gifts. It was about what the gifts represented, the promise of something more between them…

He was behaving like his nine-year-old self upon learning Santa wasn't real. Boo-fucking-hoo. That's what Michael would say to him, if he'd had any idea Ethan was such a big baby. Happily he had no idea. Had probably not given a thought to Ethan since he'd left Peabody.

"So I guess we take the turkey out now?" Erin was repeating patiently.

"Huh?"

"We have to take the turkey out early so we can bake the stuffing and the green bean casserole, right?"

"Right. I guess."

This was the blind leading the blind. They'd never tried to cook a whole turkey before. Not for just the two of them. They'd done Cornish hens a couple of times. Erin had tried to cook a duck once — that was better forgotten. Usually the McCartys invited them to Thanksgiving and Christmas dinner. But Erin had a new boyfriend this year. She was back together with her high school sweetheart Tony Guinn, and out of kindness to Tony, Ethan was doing his best to keep his twin sister from killing them all. It was at his insistence they were baking the stuffing in a casserole instead of flouting the possibility of ptomaine poisoning by packing clams and celery and nuts and bacon and bread cubes into a raw turkey.

"But then do we put the turkey back in?" Erin asked.

They both doubtfully studied the sallow looking turkey in its large roasting pan.

"Probably." Ethan said. "Right?"

"But then the casseroles will be cold."

"We could try keeping them warm on Mom's old heating plate," Ethan suggested. He wasn't sure that was a good idea. The heating plate had been a wedding gift to their parents and it had always been a little persnickety. They were liable to burn the house down. They were still weighing merits against risk when the doorbell chimed.

"That's Tony!" Erin exclaimed. She bustled away, flushed and pretty in their mom's old, violet-sprigged apron. The apron reminded Ethan of happier times, holidays when their parents were still alive, when the world had seemed a safe place and love had been something he had taken for granted.

He desultorily stirred the gravy and listened to the harmonious blend of Erin and Tony's voices from the front room.

"Oh, the music stopped!" Erin said clearly.

A minute later Karen Carpenter was back. *"Merry Christmas, darling..."*

Ethan sighed. But then a moment later he heard Tony's deep voice say something, heard Erin giggle, and he smiled.

At least one of his Christmas wishes was granted. His beautiful, funny, awful cook of a little sister finally had someone to love and to love her back. Right there, that made this one of the best Christmases ever.

After dinner — the edible parts were surprisingly delicious — Tony invited Erin for a walk.

"Ethan, let's leave the dishes and go for a walk!" Erin urged happily.

Ethan caught Tony's gaze. Tony was medium height, dark-haired and square-jawed. He still looked a lot like he had in high school, only more sure of himself. Except he didn't look sure of himself just then. He looked self-conscious and slightly dismayed.

Oh.

"You two go ahead," Ethan said. "I'm just going to put some of this food away. I'll catch up to you."

Tony looked relieved and grateful as he dragged Erin out the front door.

Ethan swapped the Carpenters for the Mills Brothers and busied himself putting all the leftover food away, rinsing the dishes for the dishwasher, scrubbing burnt pans. By the time he finished, Erin and Tony were back. Erin was wearing a small solitaire diamond on her left hand and her eyes as well as her nose were red.

"Guess what!" she said to Ethan. "You'll *never* believe it."

"You're engaged?"

"Well yes, but that's not it. Pete McCarty just invited us all over for pumpkin pie!" Erin's eyes were sparkling with happiness. She actually clasped her hands together like a little girl. Like Ebenezer

Scrooge's sister when she came to take him away from school to spend Christmas at home.

"He invited me too?" Ethan asked. "Are you sure?"

"I'm sure. He said, *Tell that brother of yours Anna made a pecan pie just for him.*"

Ethan's throat closed. Well, that was a Christmas miracle right there. After two years, he'd given up hoping Pete McCarty would ever stop being mad at him. It just proved that you should never stop hoping.

"Hey," Erin added, frowning. "Why would you believe I could *never* get engaged?"

Ethan and Tony both laughed. Tony hugged her. It was so great to see that open affection, to see Erin appreciated. Even kind of adored, if appearances were anything to go by. Ethan was truly happy for her and he refused to think about Michael or his own situation. Or lack of situation.

He congratulated Tony and they shook hands with unexpected solemnity. Then they all toasted the engagement with a bottle of sparkling cider because Erin, having no clue of Tony's plans, had insisted on serving the champagne he'd brought, at dinner.

So it was turning out to be a very good day, and Ethan wished he could stop wondering all the time what Michael's Christmas day was like. Hopefully Michael was having a good day too, and maybe the next time they saw each other, things would be back to normal. It was probably just the pressure of the holidays making them both awkward.

It couldn't really be over. Could it? Because Ethan really did love Michael, and it wasn't just because Michael was his first boyfriend.

It was because Michael was Michael. And up until the holidays had made everything uncomfortable, he'd been pretty sure that Michael felt the same. Even if Michael was not the expressive type.

At all.

Ever.

But maybe it *was* over and Ethan was soon going to be living in this house on his own. He'd be going to Christmas dinners at Tony and Erin's, and bringing presents to their cute little moppets. He'd be Uncle Ethan the Lifelong Bachelor.

Michael would not be anyone's lifelong bachelor uncle. Or even the special friend of anyone's lifelong bachelor uncle. Michael had been places and done things. And he would eventually — maybe already had — find someone like himself to share his life with. Someone who took what he wanted, instead of always waiting to be told what he was allowed to have.

Anyway, there were a lot worse fates than spending the holiday with family who loved you and sharing pie with neighbors you were no longer feuding with. So Ethan grabbed his jacket and the three of them started across the frost-covered field to the McCartys'.

Erin was singing, "But I can dream, and in my dreams…"

Tony's baritone joined in, "I'm Christmasing with you."

Even their voices blended perfectly. Even so. *Christmasing?* What kind of a verb was that?

"Hey," Erin broke off. "Isn't that Michael's pickup?"

The three of them stopped walking. Sure enough a familiar white pickup truck was trundling down the long dirt road to their house.

Ethan gulped, "I'll meet you at the McCartys'," and started walking back. Then he got worried that Michael might knock, find nobody home, and leave, so he began to run. He flew across the field, scrambled over the fence and raced up the walk.

Michael was holding a grocery store pie box in one hand and was raising his other to the doorbell. He turned at the pound of Ethan's feet. Ethan slid to a stop.

"Uh, hey," Michael said, sounding uncharacteristically self-conscious. And then, "Something wrong?"

Ethan shook his head vigorously, hand to his chest. "Half a mile. Two seconds." He leaned against the side of the house, wheezing, "You're...back!"

"Yeah." Michael shrugged. "I was hoping..." His gaze dropped to the pie box. He handed it to Ethan. "It's pecan."

"I love pecan!"

"I know."

Ethan smiled down at the pie box and then, shyly, at Michael. "Did you...want to come in?"

No, Ethan. I want to stand here in the freezing evening air and talk about pies. But Michael nodded gravely, almost as though the invitation had been in doubt.

Ethan opened the door and they went inside the house which was redolent of wonderful smells: apples and cinnamon and Christmas tree and turkey dinner with all the trimmings (most of them not burnt too badly). He carried the pie into the kitchen and set the box on the breadboard. By then he had his breath back.

"Would you like a piece of pie?" he asked.

"No."

"Oh. Okay." Maybe Michael simply intended to drop off the pie and go? Ethan didn't want that. He said desperately, "How's your dad? How was your Christmas?"

Michael was studying the sink full of soaking blackened pans. He wore charcoal dress trousers, a tailored pale gray shirt, and a red tie. Ethan had never seen him in anything but jeans and T-shirts or flannel shirts — or his boxers. He felt shy with this new formal looking Michael. He smiled uncertainly as Michael turned his cool gaze his way.

"Fine. The new girlfriend is fine too. My father's been married five times already, so I'm not sure why it was so important I meet this one." Michael stopped. His eyes were very blue as they studied Ethan, his expression grave. Sort of pained. "Look, Ethan. I'm not sure how to say this."

Ethan felt winded all over again. Like he had just made another run across the meadow.

Please don't say it. Please don't do it. Not today. Not on Christmas. Not ever.

But of course this was it. Michael was trying to be as nice as he could about it. Heck, he'd even brought pie. They would still be friends. Ethan closed his eyes, bracing for it.

"What's the matter?" Michael asked.

Ethan opened his eyes. "Nothing. Go ahead."

Michael said uncomfortably, "I'm sorry if it seemed like I was —"

"Wait," Ethan said. His voice sounded choked even to his own ears.

Michael stopped, looking confused.

Ethan blurted, "Are you breaking up with me? Yes or no?"

Michael's mouth opened. He seemed to run through all the possible responses before saying cautiously, "I wasn't going to, no. Do you want me to?"

All at once the tightness eased from Ethan's chest and he could draw a full breath again. He said weakly, "I thought maybe you were — I thought maybe we broke up."

Michael didn't laugh. He didn't say he didn't know what Ethan meant. He was silent for a moment, frowning, then he said, "I thought maybe we did too. But I wasn't sure. And I wasn't sure why we would. I thought I'd like to know."

Relief washed through Ethan, leaving him unexpectedly weak in the knees. He leaned back against the counter. "I don't know what happened," he admitted. "I was thinking you would come to Christmas. But then you didn't." It sounded idiotic, put like that, but that was pretty much the gist of it.

"I thought I would too, but then you never asked. Until…"

It was too late. Yes. And then Ethan had taken great pains to make sure Michael understood he was being invited out of politeness.

"I wasn't sure you wanted to be invited," Ethan admitted.

"Why wouldn't I want to be invited to Christmas?"

"Maybe you had plans."

"With who?"

"Well, you *did* have plans," Ethan pointed out.

"At the last minute I did, yeah. I didn't before."

"Well, you didn't say anything," Ethan said. "So I didn't know for sure."

Michael frowned. "I can't invite myself. Not to Christmas. Anyway, I don't want to always invite myself. I don't want to feel like the only reason we get together is because I push for it."

"Is that how it seems?"

"Yes," Michael said bluntly.

Ethan flushed. "I'm just never sure if you really want to get together or if I'm just bothering you."

Michael stopped himself from saying whatever he nearly answered. He raked a hand through his long, pale hair and said, carefully, "Ethan, do I really seem like someone who would spend five minutes with you if I didn't feel like spending five minutes with you?"

No. No, Michael was polite, but not overly so. He was not the suffer-fools-gladly type, that was for sure.

"Er…no."

Michael's hard, blue gaze softened. "We have coffee together every morning. We have lunch together every other day. We're together more nights than we're apart. Wouldn't that be a hint that I like to be with you?"

"Yes. But."

"But what?"

Ethan felt himself coloring. "It's just that you're hard to read and I still don't know how this works."

Michael's mouth twisted. He turned the scarred half of his face to Ethan. It was funny that Ethan never noticed Michael's scars anymore. He only noticed now because he could tell Michael was struggling with some unfamiliar emotion.

"I know I'm really bad at this," Ethan admitted humbly.

Michael turned back to face him. "Well, at least you have the excuse of inexperience. I'm really bad at this too, and I've had my share of relationships."

"Right. I guess." Ethan hated thinking that maybe he was just one more in a series of relationships in Michael's life. But even if that was true, Michael had cared enough to come here today to find out what the situation was between them. That took courage. It wasn't fair not to try to meet that straight on.

Ethan gathered his nerve. "I guess the problem is I don't know how you feel, and I really, *really* li —"

"I love you, Ethan," Michael said.

"Y-you do?"

"Yes." Michael spoke with such quiet, simple sincerity it brought tears to Ethan's eyes. "I think I loved you from the moment I saw you. I figured you knew that."

Ethan swallowed. "Sometimes I think maybe you do. But then other times I think maybe you don't."

"I do," Michael said firmly. He gave one of his rare, beautiful smiles. "Hasn't it crossed your mind that maybe I was waiting for *you* to say something?"

"Me?"

"Yes, you!"

No. It really had not. But now that he understood? He was probably never going to shut up about how much he loved Michael. Michael would be wishing he'd kept his mouth shut. Or maybe not. Because Michael did suddenly look a lot happier and relaxed.

It was going to be all right after all. Somehow it was going to be happy endings for everyone tonight.

Ethan said mischievously, "Hm. What would you like me to say?"

"Anything!"

Ethan reached for Michael, who met him halfway. There were many things he wanted, needed to tell Michael, and now he knew for sure they would be welcome. The little things and the big things both. He started with something small.

"Okay. Well," Ethan hugged Michael back with all his strength. "Merry Christmas, darling..."

TINY PECAN TARTS

INGREDIENTS

1 cup butter

6 ounces cream cheese, softened

2 cups all-purpose flour

4 eggs

3 cups packed brown sugar

4 tablespoons melted butter

Pinch salt

1 teaspoon vanilla extract

1 cup chopped pecans

DIRECTIONS

TO MAKE PASTRY:

Cream butter or margarine and cream cheese. Add flour and mix well. Make into 48 balls; place one ball in each cup of a mini tart pan. Use your fingers or a tart tamper to press out into a tart shell.

TO MAKE FILLING:

Break the eggs, but do not beat. Add sugar, melted butter, salt, vanilla and pecans. Mix well. Fill the tart shells. Bake at 350°F for about 30 minutes or until delicately browned.

ELLIOT AND TUCKER

FAIR GAME

The stuffing in the sweet potato roulade was made with parmesan and cheddar cheese, crushed garlic, nut bread crumbs, sage and parsley. The moussaka was made with portobello mushrooms and seitan. There were Provencal stuffed tomatoes, buttermilk biscuits, and ginger-brandy cheesecake for dessert. There was a lot of food. A lot of wonderful food.

What there was not, was a turkey.

But there was plenty to drink, and Elliot kept Tucker's glass topped up — and his own.

They had sailed across that morning on Tucker's boat. The biting cold wind off the Sound had turned their hands red and their faces ruddy in the early morning light, but every time they caught each other's gazes, they'd grinned. Their first Christmas.

They were spending the day with Roland, but they would sail back that night. Tomorrow they would have all day to themselves.

Tucker was dealing manfully with the absence of turkey, stuffing, and mashed potatoes at Christmas dinner. But then Tucker had a small turkey all prepped and ready to go into the oven when they got home to Goose Island that night.

Roland, who had also had his share of alcoholic beverages, was saying, "When you look at it that way, when you consider how much money is spent on stuff that people don't want and don't need, it makes sense to skip buying presents and just donate to the person's charity of choice."

Tucker and Elliot had exchanged gifts last night. Elliot had given Tucker a top of the line stainless steel thermos and Coffee Joulies. Tucker took his coffee seriously, and Elliot remembered how often it was hard to get hot coffee, let alone good coffee on the job. Tucker had given Elliot a tactical fountain pen ("Never hurts to be prepared"), a copy of *Photography and the American Civil War*, and a very expensive watch.

"Hey, I thought we agreed we weren't going crazy buying gifts," Elliot had protested as Tucker had fastened the watch on his left wrist. Elliot's right arm was still in a cast.

Tucker had ignored the reproach, leaning in to shut Elliot up with a kiss.

Now Tucker drawled, "What charity were you thinking of donating to on my behalf?"

Roland stroked his beard thoughtfully. "Hmmm. I guess the NRA doesn't really qualify as a charity, does it?"

Elliot laughed and popped a stuffed olive in his mouth. His two favorite people in the world and they couldn't be more unlike each other. But they were making an effort. They were all making an effort. And you couldn't ask for more than that.

Tucker glanced across the table. His blue eyes gleamed in his tanned, freckled face. He gave Elliot a slow, deliberate wink.

TUCKER'S CEDAR PLANK-GRILLED SALMON WITH GARLIC, LEMON AND DILL

INGREDIENTS

1 (3 pound) whole filet of salmon, skin on, scored

(up to but not through the skin) into serving pieces

6 tablespoons extra-virgin olive oil

4 large garlic cloves, minced

¼ cup minced fresh dill

2 teaspoons sea salt

1 teaspoon ground black pepper

1 teaspoon lemon zest, plus lemon wedges for serving

DIRECTIONS

Soak an untreated cedar plank (or planks) large enough to hold a side of salmon (5 to 7 inches wide and 16 to 20 inches long) in water, weighting it with something heavy, like a brick, so it stays submerged 30 minutes to 24 hours.

When ready to grill, either build a charcoal fire in half the grill or turn grill burners on high for 10 minutes.

Meanwhile, mix oil, garlic, dill, sea salt, pepper and lemon zest; rub over salmon and into scored areas to coat.

Place soaked cedar on hot grill grate, close lid, and watch until wood starts to smoke, about 5 minutes. Transfer salmon to hot plank, move salmon off direct charcoal heat or turn burners to low, and cook covered until salmon is just opaque throughout (130 on a meat thermometer inserted in the thickest section), 20 to 25 minutes or longer, depending on thickness and grill temperature.

Let sit 5 minutes; serve with lemon wedges.

ROLAND'S CAULIFLOWER
WITH MUSTARD-LEMON BUTTER

INGREDIENTS

1 small head of cauliflower (about 1 ¾ pounds)

1 teaspoon coarse kosher salt

6 tablespoons (¾ stick) butter

2 tablespoons fresh lemon juice

2 tablespoons whole grain Dijon mustard

1 ½ teaspoons finely grated lemon peel

1 tablespoon chopped fresh parsley

DIRECTIONS

Preheat oven to 400°F.

Butter rimmed baking sheet.

Cut cauliflower in half, then cut crosswise into ¼-inch-thick slices. Arrange slices in single layer on prepared baking sheet; sprinkle with salt.

Roast until cauliflower is slightly softened, about 15 minutes.

Meanwhile, melt butter in small saucepan over medium heat. Whisk in lemon juice, mustard, and lemon peel.

Spoon mustard-lemon butter evenly over cauliflower and roast until crisp-tender, about 10 minutes longer.

DO AHEAD. Can be made 2 hours ahead. Let stand at room temperature. If desired, re-warm in 350°F oven until heated through, about 10 minutes.

Transfer cauliflower to platter. Sprinkle with parsley and serve warm or at room temperature.

SWEET & SPICY MOROCCAN CARROT SALAD*

INGREDIENTS

1 lb. carrots, peeled and cooked until just tender, cooking liquid reserved

2 tablespoons vegetable oil

2 garlic cloves, peeled and finely chopped

1 teaspoon salt

1 ½ teaspoons cumin

½ teaspoon cayenne pepper

1 teaspoon sugar

2 to 3 tablespoons chopped fresh parsley

3 to 4 tablespoons lemon juice

Fresh parsley sprigs for garnish

DIRECTIONS

Grate carrots into a large bowl.

In a medium frying pan, over medium-low heat, heat oil.

Add chopped garlic and cook until garlic begins to soften and color, 2-3 minutes.

Add salt, cumin, cayenne and sugar, stirring to blend.

Stir in chopped parsley and lemon juice. Slowly pour in 125 to 175 ml/4 to 6 fl oz of the carrot cooking liquid.

Bring to a boil and simmer 3 to 5 minutes.

Pour over carrots. Cool to room temperature.

Cover and refrigerate 6 to 8 hours or overnight.

Spoon into a serving bowl and garnish with parsley sprigs.

Serves 4 to 6.

*Recipe from Harper Fox

SWIFT AND MAX

COME UNTO THESE YELLOW SANDS

*P*olice chiefs don't get Christmas Eve off.

But Swift was used to that. He had been used to it even before the relationship between him and Max had become official. Being a night owl, it was no hardship to wait up for Max. He took his time preparing every detail of what felt like their first Christmas Eve together, although it was not technically their first. Not at all.

He wound a few Christmas lights around the bookshelves and statuary, lit the strategically placed red and white candles, and set up the Christmas tree. The latter took all of five minutes. It was a small artificial tree from the 1960s which he'd picked up at a flea market the first winter he'd spent at Stone Coast. The tree was white, as were the star-shaped lights. The scratched and faded bulbs were red and silver. It was about as kitschy as Christmas could get, and Swift dearly loved it.

He spent the rest of the evening cooking and listening to music. Mostly *Christmas Time with Motown*, Max's favorite holiday record. It took a fair bit of time to get their midnight repast ready and prepare for the following day's meal. Not that Max would have Christmas day off either, but they would get to spend a portion of it together and Swift had learned to make every minute count.

Swift could not sing to save his life, but that didn't stop him humming along with Smokey Robinson.

Well I wish it could be Christmas every day
When the kids start singing and the band begins to play
Oh I wish it could be Christmas every day
So let the bells ring out for Christmas

Tomorrow he was doing a full-on traditional feast with a small roasted goose stuffed with chestnuts and cranberries, among other goodies, as the centerpiece. He was even doing a figgy pudding which he had attempted just for laughs, but the pudding had turned out to be astonishingly delicious after a liberal dosing of cognac and rum. That was tomorrow taken care of — and probably a number of nights to follow because there would be a ridiculous amount of leftovers.

Tonight's meal would be relatively light: bacon-wrapped scallops, spinach, fennel and citrus salad, and wild rice, all set off to perfection by a nice white wine.

After the cooking and clean-up was done, Swift had a glass of the nice wine while he sat in front of the fire and jotted down some notes.

At a quarter after eleven, Max's key scraped in the front door lock, and Max let himself in. Snow dusted his dark hair and the wide shoulders of his sheepskin coat.

"You're early."

"Doesn't feel early to me," Max said, bending over the sofa to drop a kiss on Swift's neck. "Working?"

Swift shook his head and tossed the legal pad aside.

"Something smells great."

"Hungry?"

"Starving."

Max followed him into the kitchen, talking about what had been a relatively crime free Christmas Eve and watched Swift dish out the food.

"Do you want to eat at the table or in front of the fire?" Swift asked.

"Fire."

They returned with their plates to the warmth of the fireplace.

Max stopped talking and devoted himself to the food. Swift watched him, smiling. He enjoyed Max's heartfelt appreciation of his cooking.

At last Max set his empty plate aside, heaved a deep sigh of relief and smiled back at Swift. "Christ, it's good to be home. I thought the night would never end."

"Maybe we'll get snowed in."

"Maybe we will." Max's gaze grew thoughtful. "Are you sorry you didn't go to your mother's?"

"No. I wanted to spend Christmas with you."

"If I could have gotten away?"

"No." It wasn't easy to explain without sounding hardhearted, but if anyone understood, Max did. "Too many memories. I want more new memories, new…traditions to balance against the old before I try that. I'll see her in the spring."

Max nodded.

"You want another glass of wine?"

"I'll switch to beer."

Swift rose to refill his glass and get Max a beer from the fridge. When he returned to the couch Max was looking at the legal pad. Swift resisted the instinct to take the pad from Max. They had no secrets from each other.

Max looked up and there was something in his expression, a softness, a light. It took Swift aback, that funny regard.

"Are you writing again?"

Swift's face warmed, though that could have been the wine. "I don't know. Maybe. Just playing around with words right now."

Max looked down at the page. "'The first bell is winter. Frozen breath of cold blue streets.' What's it mean?"

Swift laughed. "Probably nothing." He took the pad away, tossed it on the table.

Max reached out and Swift moved into the curve of his arm. He put his head back, staring up at the open ceiling beams. He was smiling.

"Happy?" Max asked softly.

Swift assented.

There was a smile in Max's voice as he asked, "What do you say to working on another of those new Christmas traditions?"

BACON WRAPPED SCALLOPS

INGREDIENTS

12 slices of bacon, cut in half lengthwise

24 medium-sized scallops

10 tablespoons butter

6 cloves garlic, pressed

Dash of cayenne pepper (optional)

Salt

Pepper

Toothpicks

DIRECTIONS

Preheat oven to 375°F.

Grease a 9x13 baking dish. If you want to make clean-up easier, line the baking dish with foil (shiny side down) and grease the foil.

Cut the bacon slices in half lengthwise so you have 24 pieces.

Pre-fry the bacon just until it gets some color and it's still limp and soft (it needs to be flexible enough to wrap around the scallops).

Melt the butter in a small bowl.

Add garlic, salt, pepper and cayenne pepper (if using) and stir well.

Set half of this butter / garlic mixture aside for later.

Dip each scallop in melted butter / garlic sauce.

Wrap a strip of bacon around each scallop; secure with toothpick (all the way through the scallop).

Arrange the wrapped scallops on the greased baking dish.

Bake on the middle rack for around 15 minutes (or until the scallops are done and the bacon is crisp).

Place scallops in large bowl and pour remaining butter / garlic sauce from earlier over the scallops and toss gently to coat.

FENNEL, ORANGE, SPINACH, AND OLIVE SALAD

INGREDIENTS

1 fennel bulb, trimmed, reserving 1 to 2 tablespoons fronds

2 cups baby spinach

2 tablespoons fresh lemon juice

2 oranges

¼ cup small olives, such as Niçoise

2 tablespoons extra-virgin olive oil

Coarse salt and ground pepper

Red pepper flakes

DIRECTIONS

Halve, core, and thinly slice bulb (preferably on a mandoline slicer).

In a bowl, toss fennel with 2 tablespoons fresh lemon juice.

Slice away peel and pith of oranges and cut flesh into segments.

 Add to bowl with fennel and stir in spinach, small olives such as Niçoise, reserved fennel fronds, and extra-virgin olive oil.

Season with coarse salt, ground pepper, and red pepper flakes.

SEAN AND DAN FROM THE DARK HORSE SERIES

THE WHITE KNIGHT

"Oysters Rockefeller," I said.

"*Gesundheit,*" Dan said, from behind a copy of *Esquire*.

I leaned on the granite counter separating the kitchen from the den where Dan lay ensconced on the sofa. "But what do you think about them?"

He lowered the magazine and said cautiously, "I don't think a *lot* about them. I don't think I've ever had them."

"I was considering cooking them for Saturday."

For the past month I'd been appearing in a small theater production of *The Long Christmas Dinner* by Thornton Wilder. Our last performance was this evening, and on Saturday we were hosting a cast party. It was the first party I'd ever hosted, or even co-hosted, in a long…well…ever.

I wanted everything to be exactly right.

"Well," Dan said thoughtfully — and the fact that he did give it his serious consideration was one of the reasons I loved him so much, "oysters are kind of an acquired taste. They're expensive too."

"I don't care about that. The expense, I mean."

"Okay, but I'm guessing they don't make great leftovers."

"True." I frowned. Neither of us ate leftovers, so what did that matter?

"Chief, you should make whatever you want to make. If you want to make oysters —"

"It doesn't have to be oysters. I just want to make something nice. Something special."

"Anything you make will be nice and special," Dan assured.

"Now you're humoring me."

He laughed, tossed the magazine aside, and joined me in the kitchen. He looped a casual arm around my shoulders as he stood next to me studying the recipe. "They do look good."

The wind shook the beach house. I glanced out the picture window at the ocean gray and choppy with whitecaps. The white Christmas lights looped over the deck railing twinkled determinedly in the face of the winter gale.

I said, "I wanted to cook them because they're the same era as the play. I thought that would be fun."

"I like that idea."

I liked the smell of his aftershave, grown-up and masculine, like Dan. I liked the fact he hadn't shaved yet because it was just us home together, relaxing. I liked how he looked in well-worn jeans, a white Henley, and white socks. I never knew how sexy socks could be until I saw Dan walking around my house in his white athletic socks. And I liked the fact that, even if he thought I was being a goof, he pretended to take me seriously.

Because he did take me seriously, even when I *was* a goof. Because he loved me and cared about what mattered to me. It had taken me a while to catch on to this, to really trust it, but I'd finally figured it out. Love meant never having to be sorry you were a goof.

I said, "You're going to be here, right?" This was the third time I'd asked. Being a police lieutenant meant Dan's schedule could be unpredictable. Not that I couldn't handle this single dinner party on my own, but it would be so much better with Dan. Everything was so much better with Dan.

He turned his head and met my eyes. I was smiling, but he didn't smile. Or at least his mouth curved into something that wasn't quite a smile, could just as easily turn into a kiss. He said softly, as usual understanding me better than I did myself, "I'll always be here, Sean."

BARBECUED SCALLOPS

INGREDIENTS

2 tablespoons butter

1 small onion chopped

1 clove garlic minced

¼ cup white wine

½ teaspoon chicken stock powder

¼ cup Pernod

Shrimps (shell or tail on) or scallops or both

Freshly ground pepper (to taste)

Olive oil

DIRECTIONS

Melt butter in pan.

Sauté chopped onion till translucent.

Add minced garlic and continue to cook over medium heat until almost brown.

Add white wine and chicken stock powder and reduce to about half — mixture should be at gently smiling boil.

Add 2 tablespoons of Pernod and reduce again.

Add remaining Pernod and turn down heat enough just to keep sauce warm.

Rinse scallops and shrimps, brush with oil and season with pepper.

Grill on heated barbecue, but pay attention — they only take a minute or two!

Toss barbecued shrimps and/or scallops in Pernod sauce, add more pepper and serve over rice.

RIDGE AND TUG

JUST DESSERTS

It was a good thing Ridge was mighty fond of Tug or he'd probably have killed him by now.

As it was, it had been touch and go for a little while that morning. But killing your lover on Christmas morning was so…so…heterosexual. Ridge had exerted superhuman strength and managed to refrain from conking Tug over the head with the nearest Yule log.

Well hell.

Ridge knew he was behaving like an ass. An all-expense-paid holiday trip to Montreal? A four-course meal and performance by burlesque icon (if you paid attention to such things — which Ridge did not) Scarlett James at Old Montreal's Hotel Nelligan on New Year's Eve? And they'd be staying at the Hotel Nelligan as well, so no hassling with snow and crowds and transportation for Ridge.

Tug had every right to expect his wonderful gift would be appreciated.

The Hotel Nelligan was just the kind of place Ridge loved. Used to love. The perfect mix of Old World and modern convenience. Tug had burbled about the comfy beds and spa tubs big enough for two and rooftop dining on French cuisine.

He didn't mention disabled access, but that went without saying.

Tug had talked and Ridge had gotten quieter and quieter until Tug had finally stopped talking and said uncertainly, "You don't —?"

"No, I don't," Ridge had snapped out and rolled his chair away from all the candy cane and tinsel Christmas cheer of the front room, down the hall — newly renovated to accommodate his wheelchair — and out onto the deck that overlooked the ocean.

There he had sat, freezing his ass off while the wind churned the water into white caps and blew a wet salty spray into his face.

Tug did not come after him, which meant even Tug knew how much Ridge was in the wrong this time.

Well, it surely couldn't be that much of a shock to Tug, who had been dealing patiently with Ridge's moods and outbursts all through the autumn and now through the winter. Even Tug with his unfailing good nature and powerful sense of humor had to know by now what an ungrateful, selfish shit Ridge was.

But why did Tug have to keep pushing him? Why couldn't he just accept that Ridge didn't — couldn't —

The French doors opened and Tug came out onto the deck. "You still mad at me?"

Ridge glanced at him, struggled inwardly, and admitted, "Mad at myself."

"I shouldn't have sprung it on you like that." Tug leaned against the railing so that he was facing Ridge. The cold wind ruffled his fair hair and turned his nose pink.

He looked awfully cute and awfully repentant, which should have been a relief — it gave Ridge the upper hand in any negotiations that might follow — but mostly what Ridge felt was guilt. Because Tug wasn't wrong. Ridge was.

Ridge said impatiently, "Why shouldn't you have tried to surprise me? It was a nice gift. A lovely gift. I never had such a nice gift."

Tug's eyes brightened, his cheeks flushed with pleasure — or maybe that was the cold again.

Tug's relief encouraged Ridge, though he was afraid to examine why, to go even further. "I used to love that kind of thing."

"I know. You will again, honey," Tug promised.

Ridge shook his head. "I don't want to travel like this."

"In a wheelchair."

Ridge looked away and nodded. It wasn't just his pride. It was a long trip and he would be exhausted and in pain by the end of it. Even so…

He expected Tug to give him the usual pep talk, but this time Tug didn't say anything. When Ridge looked back at him, Tug said with uncharacteristic gravity, "All right then, honey. We won't go to Montreal. We won't go anywhere. We don't have to travel to have fun together. We don't have to do anything that makes you uncomfortable."

Complete capitulation.

Victory.

Funny how much victory tasted like defeat.

Ridge stared at Tug and Tug gazed right back at him with those big guileless blue eyes.

Not do anything that made Ridge uncomfortable? Well hell. This whole relationship made him uncomfortable. Loving somebody as much as he was starting to love Tug was an uncomfortable business. Living was an uncomfortable business, when you got right down to it.

He couldn't seem to look away from Tug. As if Tug had locked some kind of tractor beams on him, like in one of those stupid video games he was so fond of — and was now getting Ridge hooked on too.

"We'll always do just exactly what you want," Tug assured him.

Ridge opened his mouth to object. Of course he didn't want — or expect — *that* much capitulation.

Tug persisted, "But can I tell you what I want most for Christmas?"

A tiny doubt took root in Ridge's mind. It bloomed into suspicion as Tug's boyish face creased into a lopsided but mischievous smile. The funny thing was, Ridge didn't mind.

He didn't mind at all.

LEMON DROP MARTINIS

INGREDIENTS

½ ounce Jose Cuervo Especial Gold Tequila

1 ½ ounces vodka

½ ounce Triple Sec (may sub Grand Marnier for extra kick)

1 teaspoon superfine sugar (to rim martini glass)

¾ ounce fresh lemon juice

4-5 ice cubes

Twist of lemon

DIRECTIONS

Chill martini glasses in freezer for at least 10 minutes prior to serving.

Place tequila, vodka, Triple Sec, lemon juice and sugar into a cocktail shaker with 4-5 ice cubes and shake vigorously for 30 seconds.

Run the lemon twist around the edge of the chilled martini glass and dunk in a small amount of sugar for a coated rim.

Pour the strained martini into the chilled glasses and serve.

OYSTERS ROCKEFELLER

INGREDIENTS

12 oysters

1 tablespoon butter

1 tablespoon olive oil

2 tablespoons minced shallots

2 cloves minced garlic

4 tablespoons finely chopped fennel root

2 ounces Absinthe (or Pernod)

Sprinkle of salt and pepper

2 cups baby spinach

Small wedge of St. André cheese

DIRECTIONS

Open oysters*, discard top shell and arrange on cookie sheet.

Heat butter and olive oil in sauté pan. Add shallots, garlic and fennel root and sauté over medium low heat until tender, but not browned, about 5 minutes.

Add Absinthe, salt and pepper and stir to combine.

Place spinach in pan and cook just until wilted, 1 to 2 minutes.

Divide spinach mixture evenly (about a kitchen teaspoon each) among the 12 oysters.

Top each with 1 teaspoon St. André cheese. Bake at 375°F for 5 minutes or until cheese is melted.

Serves 2.

*John Lowell, owner of the East Dennis Oyster Farm, offers the following instructions on how to open an oyster. First, always wear a pair of sturdy gloves and use a good quality oyster knife. Lowell says true Cape Codders go in from the side, but it's easier to go in at the hinge and twist the knife to pop it open. Cut the adductor muscle that holds the shell closed. Discard the top shell and separate the adductor from the bottom shell. For the best presentation, take your knife and flip over the oyster meat.

JULIAN AND DAVID

THE DARK FAREWELL

A child was crying disconsolately from down the dark hall.

A woman began to sob, her voice blending in melancholy harmony with that of the child. David, rooted in place at the other end of the hall, shook off his inertia and forced himself forward. But when he reached the closed door of Mrs. Sweet's parlor in the Greenwich Village brownstone where he and Julian roomed, he stopped.

The woman was still sobbing. But now he could hear Julian's voice, husky with weariness and emotion, speaking to her, comforting her. David could not make out the words.

He took off his homburg, turning it uneasily in his gloved hands.

Behind the heavy door, another woman's voice joined in. She sounded shaken. As well she might.

The first woman's voice raised in supplication. Julian spoke reassuringly.

Why? Why did Julian persist in this? Knowing how David felt?

David became aware that he was standing in a puddle of water. Snow melted from his boots and the shoulders of his ulster, dripping to the parquet floor in soft plops.

From the other side of the door came a sudden change in voices, the scrape of chairs, and he moved away from the door, walking a few steps down the hall, going to the window that overlooked the snowy terrace of the brownstone next door.

The snow formed tall, white pyramids on the round finials of the stone balustrade. No sign of their neighbor. Maybe today was too cold even for young Mr. Flipkey and his violin. That was not his real name, of course. His real name was Feldleit. David called him Flipkey, which meant nothing, but sounded suitably dismissive. Dismissive because David did not like Mr. Flipkey. Or, more exactly, did not like the fact that Julian did. Liked Mr. Flipkey's fiddle playing, anyway. Didn't mind that Flipkey fiddled at all hours of the day and night. No, Julian would walk out onto their own terrace and listen, enrapt, for as long as Flipkey chose to play. As though Flipkey were exercising some enchantment over him.

David smiled sourly. At least he didn't kid himself he was anything but what he was. Jealous.

Part of the problem was the way he and Julian had met…

The door down the hall opened. David glanced around as two women exited the parlor. They were both young, both fashionably dressed, though the taller was dressed in mourning. The smaller woman supported her sister down the hall and out the door. There was a flash of gray day, a gust of winter's breath. The evergreen and holly garland knocked against the wainscoting like a ghostly hand.

Julian did not appear.

David waited, trying to decide.

Three days ago he would have gone in at once, intending to soothe and solace, but in truth he would have snapped and scolded. He couldn't seem to help it. They had been so happy together. For a year — a little more than a year, in fact. David had been happier than he could ever remember. He had nursed Julian through his long illness following the terrible shock of the events of last summer, and they had grown even closer during that quiet, closeted time. Julian had regained his health and, mercifully, the troubling visions seemed to leave him entirely. His fits grew less frequent, less violent. There was no sign the troubling predictions of idiocy, feeble-mindedness, or madness that medical books and physicians alike warned of would materialize.

Julian settled into David's world with every appearance of contentment. He was happy, healthy. He charmed David's friends with his boyish enthusiasm and exotic beauty. David had fallen ever more deeply, helplessly in love. He had begun to believe that despite the many obstacles, they might really manage some kind of future together.

But then, two months ago, the visions had returned. And worse, much worse, Julian had begun to hold séances. He didn't call them séances. Mrs. Sweet would never have stood for that, but that's what they amounted to, these private meetings with the grief-stricken.

And, as David feared, Julian's health had begun to suffer. He started having seizures again. Didn't this prove David's point? Didn't Julian understand what he was risking?

So David had done what any loving husband would do. He had forbidden Julian to hold any more séances.

And Julian — sweet, affectionate, always amenable Julian — had amiably, even a little amusedly, pointed out that David was neither his husband nor his father. And he had gone right ahead and continued to do as he wished.

Flabbergasted, furious, three days ago David had finally given Julian an ultimatum. Stop or their connection was at an end.

That very evening Julian moved to an empty room on Mrs. Sweet's top floor.

David couldn't believe it.

Of course, Julian had not really moved out. All his belongings were still right where he'd left them, carelessly scattered around their shared rooms. They both knew that was simply a beat, the light strike of one fencing blade against another. No blood drawn, no harm done. Not a real fight. Not then.

David had drawn first blood. He had only intended to force a quick and painless surrender for both their sakes. Even one night without Julian in his bed was unbearable. So he had informed Julian he would be spending the holidays in Maine with his family. He wished Julian a Merry Christmas and a Happy New Year.

Julian had gone white. He had looked shocked and hurt and then angry. Very angry. He had retired to his room — his new room — and had not spoken to David since.

David had caught his train, of course. He could not afford to back down. He must not set that precedent. That was what he had told himself as the train drew slowly out of the crowded station and picked up speed. *If I back down now…*

But with every white and snowy mile he grew colder and colder, as though he was setting out for uncharted arctic wastelands and not his family's estate for a pleasant holiday visit. He had left the train at the very first stop, abandoning his luggage and parcels, fleeing home to find exactly what drove him away in the first place.

Now he was truly terrified. He had played his trump card and he had lost.

He watched the door to Mrs. Sweet's parlor but still Julian did not appear.

What would Julian say when he did appear? Perhaps nothing. Perhaps he was still not speaking to David. Perhaps he would just give him that long, dark, unfathomable look and turn away again. Which was ridiculous because he was completely dependent on David. His grandfather's estate was still tied up in probate, and probably would be for the foreseeable future.

Was that the trouble? Had David inadvertently made Julian feel beholden? Was that why Julian felt he had to defy David, to flout David's wishes, to risk his own health and sanity? Because the fact of the matter was Julian brought so much more to David than David could ever begin to return…

From outside came the sweet spiral of notes as Mr. Flipkey wandered out onto his terrace, violin tucked under his chin. You might think the cold and damp would throw the instrument instantly out of tune, but then again, Mr. Flipkey's melodies were so foreign and mysterious, who would know if he was playing out of key or not?

Sweet though. Sweet and sad, those delicate brushes of bow to strings. Like the beating wings of small birds.

A lump formed in David's throat.

What if all Julian really felt for him was gratitude? And now gratitude had turned to resentment?

He considered this while Mr. Flipkey continued to play his mournful melody, indifferent to the snowflakes languidly floating down, as though they were white rose petals.

What was Julian doing in there? David listened.

Silence.

Having a fit was not a silent business, so he knew Julian was all right.

He could go to his own rooms and then arrange to casually run into Julian at the Christmas Eve gathering Mrs. Sweet would hold tonight. That way he would not look desperate.

But he *was* desperate. He couldn't help thinking that every minute he let pass was taking Julian further and further from him.

The chair scraped in the parlor. David drew his shoulders back, waiting. But Julian still did not appear.

Finally David couldn't stand it another moment, he walked down the hall and waited in the open doorway. It took him a moment to find Julian in the gloom of the room. Julian stood at the window, gazing down at Mr. Flipkey who was still playing his sorrowful music.

David felt an instant stab of jealousy.

But as he stood there he saw that Julian's eyes were closed. He was not aware of David, that was clear. The line of his body was weary, his face unguarded and sad.

David couldn't bear the sadness, even though he had wanted Julian to regret his actions. This was grief, not regret, and it made his heart twist in his chest. He dropped his gloves and hat on the parlor table, and approached Julian.

The floorboard squeaked. Julian's eyes flew open. In a matter of seconds his expression changed from disbelief to joy to wary suspicion.

For hours David had tried to think of what to say, how he could negotiate a truce that would allow him to save face but still win back Julian. But all his carefully prepared speeches fled.

"I'm sorry," he whispered. "Please forgive me."

Tears filled Julian's dark eyes. "Why did you say it? Why did you end it between us?"

"I didn't mean to. It's the last thing I want. I'm afraid for you. I'm afraid for us both."

Julian shook his head. "I don't understand you, David. I've tried to do exactly as you wished. Always. Except this one thing. And I can't help this. It's who I am."

"But what about all the things we talked about? When you were getting well, we talked about traveling and you maybe one day opening a café or —"

Julian put his hands over his eyes. *"David."* He lowered his hands, his expression older than David had ever seen it. All at once Julian seemed older than him. "One day. Maybe. It's just a dream now. We have no way to make that happen. And in the meantime…"

"In the meantime you're having these visions again." David tried to say it without bitterness, but he was not successful.

"Yes." Julian's eyes looked black and Harlequin-like. "I don't want them, but I can't stop them."

David took Julian's hands in his, and although David was the one who had walked through the snow, Julian's skin felt ice cold. "All right. I suppose I have to accept that. But what about the séances? You don't have to meet these people, you don't have to listen to their stories, and you sure as hell don't have to contact their dead relatives. That's your choice."

Julian shuddered and his hands gripped David's tighter. "I don't want to, but how can I refuse? Especially this time of year when so many are remembering and longing for those who have gone before? I can help them. How can I refuse?"

"You refuse. That's all. You simply *do it.*"

Julian shook his head.

"Yes," David insisted. "It's making you ill. It'll destroy you. You *have* to refuse."

Julian pulled his hands free. "I can't. You're just making it more difficult for me."

"I'm trying to help you!" David spared a quick look over his shoulder, but Mrs. Sweet would be out in the kitchen preparing the evening meal.

Julian said quietly, "If you want to help, don't ask this of me. *Help* me. Help me do what I must. Be my strength and my comfort."

In the silence that followed Julian's words, David realized that Mr. Flipkey had disappeared inside his brownstone once more. The only sound between them was the almost soundless brush of snow against the window.

"I don't know if I can," David said finally. It was painful to say the words, but it was true.

Julian turned from him.

Neither spoke as they watched the wall of white grow higher and higher on the window sill.

Either way he was going to lose what mattered most to him in the world. At least Julian's way would make Julian happy, and somehow that seemed the most important thing as David stared into his own bleak vision of the future. He could not bear to picture himself standing here years from now remembering the slump of Julian's shoulders, the hurt, closed look on Julian's face before he had turned away.

Better to give than receive. Wasn't that the motto of the season?

"But I can try," David said. "I will try for you."

WHITE LADY

INGREDIENTS

2 ounces London dry gin

½ ounce Cointreau

½ ounce lemon juice

1 egg white

DIRECTIONS

Shake well with cracked ice, then strain into a chilled cocktail glass.

(Those were the days, eh?)

SOUTHERN CREAM CAKE

CAKE INGREDIENTS

2 cups sugar (we like to use extra-fine sugar for making cakes)

3 cups cake flour

1 cup milk

¾ cup butter, slightly softened

3 teaspoons baking powder

Pinch salt

1 teaspoon vanilla or 1 tablespoon coconut liqueur

4 eggs

DIRECTIONS

Combine flour, baking powder, salt and set aside. Beat butter with sugar until light and fluffy; add eggs, one at a time, beating after each addition. Gradually add flour mixture alternatively with milk/vanilla. (Begin with ⅓ flour mixture, ½ of the milk, etc., until all ingredients are used). Spread batter evenly in two 6, 8 or 9-inch round cake pans and bake in a preheated 350°F oven till a toothpick inserted in center of cake comes out clean.

CUSTARD INGREDIENTS

2 cups milk

2 eggs

½ cup sugar

4 teaspoons cornstarch

1 teaspoon vanilla (or coconut)

DIRECTIONS

Combine ingredients for custard in a double boiler and cook until mixture coats the back of a spoon. Use as a filling between cooled cake layers.

A layer of currant jelly may be spread directly on the cake layers before filling to help keep the crumbs in place.

Fill between the layers with the custard filling, then sprinkle each with coconut. Top the entire cake with the remaining boiled icing.

JAMES AND SEDGWICK

THE DICKENS WITH LOVE

"Your mother hates me." I said when Sedgwick joined me on the terrace.

"No." He brushed away the powder of snow and joined me, leaning against the blue stone wall and gazing out at the moonlit shingle beach. His broad shoulder felt solidly comforting against my own.

I smiled, though I don't suppose Sedgwick could see it in the dark. "Oh yes. Every time she looks at me she sees a line of unborn grand-children. Your father can't look at me without wincing."

I didn't bother to go into the cool and courteous disbelief of the younger brother, the two older sisters and even the nieces and nephews. All right, perhaps not the nieces and nephews. Perhaps I was reading too much into their clear, curious gazes.

"They don't know you, James." Sedge put his arm around me. "Once they know you, they'll realize that I'm the lucky one. They'll love you. As I love you."

My throat tightened. To answer was impossible.

I had been to church that morning, the first time in my adult life I had gone to church with a purpose beyond attending a wedding or a funeral. I had stood next to Sedgwick in the family pew and refused to let myself think beyond the words on the page of the book Sedge held for both of us. I was taking it one word at a time.

The breeze carried the scent of ocean and marshland and curry, the latter thanks to the spice grinding facility in the Rye Harbour industrial estate. It smelled foreign. Alien. Which made sense as I was half a world away from home.

No. England, East Sussex to be exact, was my home now. These politely stricken strangers were my family.

Into my pained silence Sedge qualified, "Well, not exactly as I love you, but in their own restrained and familial way."

That got a snort out of me. Sedge's arm tightened, hard and reassuring. He bent his head and, breath warm against my ear, whispered, "Don't let them spoil things, Jamie. I love you so much. We've waited so long."

I shivered.

A year. That's how long we'd waited, what with one thing or another. A whole year of waiting, dreaming, planning. I'd given up everything, my entire life, to be with Sedgwick Crisparkle.

And I'd do it all again in a heartbeat.

"They're horrified about what I did with your book."

"*Your* book," Sedge said firmly. "And there you're most definitely wrong. They all think you're bloody brilliant. As do I. You've kept *The Christmas Cake* in the family, yet still managed to get the money I needed to open the school."

I smiled. I was rather proud of my solution to what had initially seemed like a Gift-of-the-Magi dilemma. Rather than selling the lost Dickens Christmas book that had brought Sedgwick and me together almost a year to the day, I'd had the book copied and republished as a pricy, exclusive and very limited edition just in time for Christmas. Sedge would have all the money he needed for his school.

But again, Sedgwick didn't see the smile and he misread my silence. He burst out with uncharacteristic fury, "Goddamn them."

"Sedge —" I was genuinely startled. He swore so rarely, lost his temper so rarely.

"How fucking dare they hurt you? They know what you mean to me." He turned as though to go back and do battle with them, my own personal and highly incensed archangel. I grabbed him back, laughing — at least in part I was laughing.

"Don't do it. Don't say a word to them. They're doing the best they can. I'll win them over. I can be very charming when I try."

He let me hold him, but I could feel his heart banging with righteous wrath against my own. "I know you can," he said seriously, as though I might need reassurance on this score too.

I really was laughing then. "Sedge, it's okay. It really is. So long as it doesn't matter to you, do you think I care what any of them think?"

His spectacles glinted in the moonlight. "Is that true, James? I wanted you to have a real fa —"

I interrupted, "I know. And maybe we'll get there yet." I drew his head to mine. "In the meantime…Happy Christmas, Professor Crisparkle."

STARDUST MARTINI

INGREDIENTS

Vodka

Crème de Cacao

Goldschläger

Headache tablets (optional)

DIRECTIONS

Combine four parts vodka with one part of Crème de Cacao in a cocktail shaker cup.

Shake it baby, shake it all you can tonight.

Pour mixture into martini glass.

Slowly and gently add the sparkling Goldschläger.

(The gold flakes should slowly descend through the drink like stardust).

BREAD PUDDING

INGREDIENTS

1 loaf stale French bread

1 quart milk

10 tablespoons (1 ¼ sticks) sweet butter, softened to room temperature

4 eggs

1 ½ cups granulated sugar

2 tablespoons vanilla

1 cup raisins

1 cup confectioners' sugar

4 tablespoons whiskey

DIRECTIONS

Crumble the bread into a bowl. Pour the milk over it and let stand for one hour.

Preheat the oven to 325°F. Grease a 9-by-13-by-2-inch baking dish with 1 to 2 tablespoons of the butter.

In another bowl, beat together 3 eggs, the granulated sugar and the vanilla. Stir this mixture into the bread mixture. Stir in the raisins.

Pour into the prepared baking dish, place on the middle rack of the oven, and bake until browned and set, about 1 hour 10 minutes. Cool to room temperature.

To make sauce, stir 8 tablespoons butter and confectioners' sugar together in the top of a double boiler over simmering water until sugar is dissolved and mixture is very hot. Remove from the heat. Beat the remaining egg well and whisk it into the sugar mixture. Remove pan from base and continue beating until sauce has cooled to room temperature. Add whiskey to taste.

To serve, preheat broiler. Cut pudding into squares and transfer each square to a heatproof serving dish. Spoon whiskey sauce over pudding and run under broiler until bubbling.

Serves 8-10.

TIM AND LUKE FROM THE "IN A DARK WOOD" SERIES

THE PARTING GLASS

"Mirror, mirror on the wall," Luke said, enunciating around his toothbrush. He wore a large yellow bath towel slung fetchingly around his lean hips, and a dab of shaving cream under his right ear.

I drew back from the long mirror over the bathroom counter and the double sinks. "I was trying to think if I should shave or not."

"Why would you want to shave?"

"I don't know." I frowned at my reflection. "I look okay, right?"

"You're asking for an objective opinion? I'm kind of partial to your looks."

"Okay. Good."

He grinned at me and toothpaste spilled out of his mouth. I laughed. Luke laughed too, rinsed, spat, patted his face with a plushy yellow towel. He straightened, still smiling but serious when he said, "You know, we don't have to go to this thing tonight."

"Yeah, we do. It's New Year's. Karen will be disappointed if we don't show up."

"She's going to have a houseful of people. She won't notice if we're not there."

"Hey. I'd like to think that's not true."

"You know what I mean."

I did, yeah. And I appreciated that he was, as usual, looking out for me. We'd been together since May. Well, not immediately *together* together because it had taken Luke a month to leave his job and put his place on the market, but even when we were apart I felt like we were together. It was a first to feel so secure. To know that whatever came at us, we'd be facing it together. I still found that sort of amazing.

"You know what?"

His reflection slanted hazel eyes my way in inquiry.

"I'm looking forward to tonight."

"Are you?" He looked surprised, and no wonder. For the first two years of my sobriety I'd been afraid to go anywhere, do anything that might put me in proximity with alcohol. Hell, coffee with friends had seemed perilous. Not that I'd had so many friends back then.

"I am. I'm not even sure why exactly. I'm looking forward to the new year. And I like the idea of celebrating with friends. I know for sure I'm not going to drink. Plus I'll have someone to talk to all night. The best looking guy there."

"That's funny," Luke said. "I was thinking the same thing."

"That you're going to be the best looking guy there tonight?" I teased, squeezing past him on my way to the bedroom.

He reached back and caught my arm, pulling me back against him. He was smiling as he pressed a Crest-flavored kiss against my mouth. I smiled a kiss back, reached down and unfastened the towel at his waist.

"But I guess no one would notice if we were a little *late…*"

FINN AND CON

LOVERS AND OTHER STRANGERS

Christmas morning.

Finn knew he had to make an effort.

It was difficult though. Everything was difficult now. Ever since the autumn. Ever since Fitch...

He had been okay at first. Shocked and horrified, but he had been dealing with it. He had to deal with it because he knew Con would never put up with anything else.

But then the sand had started to slip out from under his feet. And suddenly he wasn't okay. He couldn't stop thinking about it.

Couldn't stop imagining...

Couldn't stop remembering...

Con had started watching him, frowning, starting to wonder what was the matter with him, starting to question why they were together.

Con denied it, of course. But it was right there in his eyes.

Finn was denying it too, but of course he was thinking the same thing. The only reason they were together was because of Fitch. And that wasn't a good enough reason. In fact, it was a really bad reason.

He missed Fitch desperately. Which was bizarre because he hadn't let himself think of Fitch for three years. Now he couldn't stop thinking about him.

He couldn't work. He couldn't eat. He couldn't sleep.

His brain wouldn't turn off. His thoughts were stuck on a loop. A terrible, terrible loop.

"I need some time on my own," he had finally told Con.

"I don't understand," Con had answered. His face had been guarded, giving nothing away.

"I don't understand myself," Finn had said. "But I need to be alone." What he meant was, *I need to be away from you.*

Maybe Con had read between the lines. "Why don't you go back to The Birches," he had said finally. "Maybe you can work there. I've got this book due anyway."

So it was just exactly what Finn had thought. Con was only too glad to be let off the hook.

He went back to The Birches and he did try to work. He tried to pretend everything was normal. But Martha and Uncle Thomas had seen something that Con didn't or wouldn't.

Clinical depression. That was the official diagnosis, and the recommendation was a brief hospital stay "just to get stabilized." Finn had panicked. Rescue had come from an unexpected quarter. Con.

When Uncle Thomas had phoned to let Con know the situation, Con had shown up within the hour with an alternate plan. He would move into The Birches and lend a hand around the place until Finn was feeling more like his old self. It was a casual, low key offer, more neighborly than loverly, it seemed to Finn. But it had stopped him panicking. He even agreed that maybe he did need a little help.

Con and Martha and Uncle Thomas — and the little pink tablets — had seen him through the worst of it. And now Finn was…trying.

Better.

He was better. A lot better. They could all see that. Though it was still difficult.

And today, this morning, was Christmas and he needed to make an effort. Needed to show everyone that he appreciated everything that had been done for him. That they did not have to keep putting him first, did not have to put their own lives on hold.

Finn had finally shaken off his preoccupation last night to ask Con about his new book, and Con had said the book was on hold. Said it absently, indifferently.

That was when Finn had finally, belatedly realized just how much trouble everyone was going to in order to keep him glued together. He had been so dismayed, so ashamed he had nearly gone into another tailspin. But this morning, he'd woken to the determination to stop monopolizing everyone's time and energy.

This morning, when Con had kissed him as he did every morning and said, "Merry Christmas, Huckleberry," Finn had really looked at him. Con's was not a kind or friendly face. In fact, he looked like one of those impious Renaissance priests. He had high, elegant cheekbones and a mocking mouth. His eyes were pirate eyes, dark and enigmatic. He wore his pale hair longer these days, and he did not bother with anything but jeans and baggy wool sweaters. He had always looked so tailored and fashionable, even working at home. Something had changed inside Con too. That morning his smile had been reassuring and the expression in his eyes was attentive, grave and...

"Why are you doing this?" Finn had asked dully several times over the past weeks. "Why are you bothering?"

And each time Con had said simply, "I love you."

This morning Finn had realized that it was perfectly true. The expression in Con's eyes was love. That wasn't complicated at all. That really didn't have anything to do with Fitch. Or with anyone other than themselves.

Finn had smiled back at Con.

Con's expression had changed. He had lifted his hand and brushed Finn's stubbly jaw. And they had simply laid there for a few moments looking at each other. Not speaking. Finn's brain had felt quiet, almost peaceful, as he considered the cool blue shadows in the corners of the white room. The patterned adumbration through white lace. The shaded dips in the snowy duvet and the bisque flannel sheets.

"What are you thinking about?" Con had asked softly.

Shadows and light. But he wasn't going to talk about shadows anymore. He'd thrown enough gloom on his loved ones. Finn said, "Light. White."

And Con had smiled, a very white smile, as though this was exactly the right answer.

He would be back in a minute or two with Finn's breakfast which they would eat in the privacy of this room, as they had eaten breakfast for the last month. And then they would go downstairs and Finn would make a serious effort to be normal.

It was a good day to start because Christmas was always the same at The Birches. Lots of little traditions and routines to carry him through. Last night they had opened presents in front of the giant, flocked spruce tree in the front room. This morning there would be an endless stream of neighbors and visitors in for coffee and pastries, and this evening they would have Christmas dinner. It was a good day in its own right. The memories were happy. Almost entirely happy.

Finn's stomach growled. Where was Con? It was taking him a long time to get breakfast together.

The door opened and Con was back with the breakfast tray. He was smiling as he set it down on the bed.

"You look the cat that got the cream," Finn said. The fact that he was noticing Con's expression was probably another good sign.

Con did look satisfied with himself. He nodded at the tray and Finn looked down. White china. Oatmeal, milk, sugar. A white rose in a little glass of snow, a piece of driftwood, three smooth white and speckled stones, a glittery piece of white quartz, a white feather, and a wide, creamy silk ribbon. It was as though Con had been on a scavenger hunt.

Finn picked up one of the egg-shaped stones. It felt cool and grainy to the touch.

"Not quite fifty shades, but...white," Con said.

Finn made a little face, put down the stone and picked up one of the tiny white berries rolling around the tray like waxy pearls.

"You can't eat those," Con told him quickly.

Finn rolled the bead-sized berry between his fingers. "No. What are they?"

"Mistletoe."

Finn looked up. Con was smiling with uncharacteristic tentativeness. Finn began to smile too. He reached out his hand.

SAM AND RHYS

GHOST OF A CHANCE

"All you have to do is say yes," Roger said.

We were the only two people sitting in the waiting room. There were chairs draped in dust covers and some back issues of Haunted Times and TAPS. I looked at the front desk. The receptionist smiled at me and went back to her filing.

"You're curious, right?" Roger pressed. "This is the truth you've spent your life pursuing. You wouldn't pass up this opportunity."

"No," I said slowly. He was right. Sort of. I was a history teacher by trade. The paranormal studies were mostly a hobby. A hobby I was passionate about, but not exactly my life's work.

"So say yes."

"That's it? I don't have to sign any paperwork? No…waivers?"

Roger laughed. "No. You just have to want it."

"I see." I didn't though. Not completely. In fact…this was so weird. I couldn't quite remember why I was there. It must have been Roger's idea. But then that was sort of strange too because —

"You've been thinking about it a lot since Sam died."

My heart seemed to stop. "Wait." I could hardly form the word. I felt frozen, stiff. "Sam's dead?"

Roger stared at me as though I were insane. "Rhys, Sam has been dead a year."

"No. That can't be." My heart began to bang in slow, heavy beats. Cold sweat broke out over my body. "No. I would know."

"You do know."

I shook my head.

"Rhys. What's the matter with you? Sam died Christmas Eve. He was driving down from San Francisco. You were going to spend the holiday together. There was an accident. He never regained consciousness."

"No." I jumped up. "No. That's wrong. I know that's wrong."

"Not this again," Roger groaned. "You're in denial because you never told him how you felt. You were too afraid to take a chance after C.K. You feel guilty about it and so you've blocked it out."

I began to pace around the laboratory as though I could walk away from what he was telling me. "I was going to tell him. I was going to tell him that weekend."

Roger rose too. He held up a test tube. Green liquid bubbled up. "Exactly! But don't you see? You can tell him. You can tell him now."

"But he must know. He has to know. It was just the words. I tried to let him kn —" I had to stop. I was going to be crying in front of Roger and his lab assistant in a minute. I pressed the heels of my hands to my eyes.

"No. He doesn't know. You have to say the words," Roger said. "Like now. You have to say the words."

I lowered my hands and stared at Roger's kindly face. His watery, near-sighted blue eyes gazed earnestly back at me. He smiled. I had never noticed how yellow his teeth were — or that he had such sharp incisors. In fact…

I asked slowly, "Wait. Do I know you?"

* * * * *

"Wake up. Wake up, Rhys. You have to wake up now." Sam's voice was raspy with weariness. "Rhys, I'm talking to you. You need to listen. Wake up." That insistent tone was starting to hurt my head. He could be such an asshole sometimes.

"Please, Rhys. Come on. This isn't fair."

Yeah, but life wasn't fair. It wasn't fair when he used that soft coaxing voice either. That voice that made me want to give him whatever he was asking for even when I knew it was probably a bad idea.

"Rhys, I'm telling you to WAKE THE FUCK UP."

My eyes snapped open.

Instantly, there was a confusion of bright light and noise. Chaos. What was happening? Something was really wrong. I couldn't swallow. No. Worse. I couldn't seem to breathe. There was a tube in my mouth, a tube filling up my throat and pushing air into my lungs while I was trying to exhale. When I tried to free my head, it hurt like hell.

"No, Rhys." Sam kept me from clawing out the obstruction choking me. "Don't fight it. Lie still. You're okay. They're going to take it out."

More noise, lights, commotion…

* * * * *

Someone was holding my hand. A warm, hard grip. I squeezed back reassuringly. Took an experimental breath.

That was better. That was the way it was supposed to work.

"Rhys?"

I opened my eyes.

Better here too.

Quiet.

A soothing lack of light. Like twilight, only…

Sam was leaning over me. I could make out that big, familiar blur. I was lying flat on my back in a room that was not my own. Not Sam's either. A hospital room. What the hell?

"Rhys?"

A rusty voice answered for me. "My…glasses."

An electric silence followed this request, and then Sam said in a shaky voice unlike his own, "Your —? Yeah. Of course. They're here somewhere. How the hell you didn't break 'em…"

My head hurt. My ribs hurt. My back hurt. I was taking slow, painful inventory as my glasses settled on my nose and Sam's face and the room behind him drew into sharp focus.

Yes. A hospital. I was in a hospital bed. Hooked up to a bunch of machines. There was fake garland around the window and a miniature Christmas tree in a pot on top of a cabinet in the corner. And there was Sam, grim and craggy and so important to me that I couldn't seem to hold all that feeling in my heart.

"I thought you…were dead," I got out in that creaky voice.

"Me?" Sam's face was so gaunt. His eyes glittered. He looked ill. No wonder I'd thought…but no. That didn't make sense. Sam was okay.

"What…happened?"

"You're going to be fine now."

Now.

"What happened?" It was tiring to talk. "An accident?"

He nodded. "You were driving up Friday night so we could spend the weekend together."

I remembered. "I was staying. Through Christmas." Our first Christmas together. Important. A turning point. When you started spending holidays together, that meant something.

"Right." Sam's voice was funny. So husky. So gentle. But Sam was gentle. People didn't see that. He wasn't in a gentle line of work. Being a cop didn't call for gentleness, and Sam was so big and so rough looking…but he was very gentle. When he trusted you.

Had we reached the point of trusting each other?

Sam was still talking slowly, still watching my face. "A trucker fell asleep on the Grapevine. You were caught in a five-car pileup."

I swallowed. My throat felt scraped and raw. My mouth tasted horrible. My ribs hurt. My right leg… Maybe I'd better save the inventory for later. I was starting to scare myself.

"Everyone…okay?"

I could see by Sam's face, and the way he made the decision not to tell me whatever it was that made him look like that, that everyone was not okay.

"You're okay," Sam said. "That's all I care about."

"Did I…miss it?"

He stroked my hair. "Did you miss what?"

"Christmas?"

His smile was so broad, so bright, it made my tired eyes blink. "No. No, this is Christmas Eve. You got back in plenty of time."

I couldn't match that smile, but I did my best. "Good." My eyes were closing whether I wanted it or not. "I have to…tell you about my dream."

"Okay," Sam said softly. His mouth brushed mine. "And then I'll tell you about mine."

KEIR AND RICK

In Sunshine
or in Shadow

It rained Christmas day.

Rick originally had the day off. So had Keir, but the resigning and then unresigning had cost him his place on the holiday roster, so Rick gave up his spot too. At least that way they could share the misery.

And it *was* miserable.

It started out mildly miserable, dragging their weary asses out of bed and into the station. The final day of four twelve-hour shifts. But things cheered up a little there. Some of the guys and gals had brought in cookies and cakes and fudge. There was decent coffee for once. And Santa gag gifts. Rick got a mug that said Good Cop. Keir winked at Rick and whispered, "Does that mean I can be Bad Cop tonight?"

Keir got a T-shirt that read Undercover Cop. Rick had murmured, "Under covers duty, huh?"

It was all talk anyway. They knew they were both going to be too tired to do more than fall into bed and kiss each other goodnight.

So much for the good times. The day turned seriously miserable with a domestic dispute that deteriorated into a homicide. Deke Johnson, 45, violated his restraining order and shot his ex-wife Harriet, 40, before their three kids and the family dog — right in front of the Christmas tree, no less.

The sad truth was, in addition to a rise in traffic accidents, family disputes and child custody battles, violent crime spiked around the holidays. Not just robberies and home invasions, but good old-fashioned homicide. Add a little melancholy and a lot of booze to the seasonal punch, and you had a recipe for one hellish witch's brew. And the City of Angels had a bad habit of getting drunk off her ass every Christmas.

Johnson didn't deny murdering his wife, and he didn't seem to care about being arrested. He did try twice to break free so he could explain to his hysterical kids why he'd had to shoot Mommy. The second time, Rick, who was royally pissed off at the idea of some self-centered asshole killing his ex in front of his own kids, knocked him down, and Keir leaped to intervene. The uniforms pretended not to see anything, and Keir hustled Rick outside.

The night was cold and smelled of smog and rain and eucalyptus. They walked past the crowd of neighbors and sightseers and crime scene technicians, around the side of the house, stepping over the dog bowls and tricycles.

Rick leaned back against the dripping siding and drew a couple of deep breaths.

Keir kept one eye on Rick and one eye on the wet, shining walkway, to make sure they were not disturbed. He didn't say anything. He didn't need to. Rick knew exactly what he was thinking, and he knew exactly how Rick felt.

"Sorry," Rick said finally.

Keir shrugged. "It's a fucked up night. Even if it is Christmas."

"Sometimes it feels like we're just garbage men. We're just here to clean up the mess."

It was startling to hear that from Rick. Keir was usually the one the job got to. He said firmly, "No way. We're the guardians at the gate. We're keeping the wild things out tonight." Not all the wild things, but they were only human. They did what they could. He hooked his arm around Rick's neck and brought their heads close together. Their warm breath mingled. Keir said softly, "And tomorrow we start three days off."

Rick nodded.

The rest of their shift was mostly uneventful. It was ten o'clock by the time they stopped off to eat on their way home. A Chinese Restaurant in Van Nuys. The place was dimly lit — emergency and Christmas lights only — and nearly deserted. Christmas music was playing. They got a booth way in the back. They ordered their dinner and then quietly, circumspectly, held hands across the table until the waitress started down the aisle with their meals. When she left, they went back to holding hands.

Every time Keir looked across the table, Rick's gaze met his, and they smiled tiredly at each other. Not the best Christmas ever. But they were together and somehow that went a long way toward keeping it from being the worst Christmas ever.

Rick broke open his fortune cookie, read the little piece of paper, and laughed. He nudged Keir's foot under the table.

Not the best Christmas ever. But looking good for the best day *after* Christmas ever.

NOEL AND ROBERT

ICECAPADE

Coffee.

Noel's nose twitched. He pried open his eyes, tried to focus.

Robert stood beside the bed, cradling a yellow mug of coffee in his big hands.

"What day?" Noel croaked.

"Tuesday. Merry Christmas," Robert replied. "How do you feel?"

Noel sat up very cautiously, prepared for that dismaying, sickening swoop of giddiness that had defined the last feverish week.

Thank God. Thank you Baby Jesus. And Father Christmas and Grandfather Frost and the Snow Maiden and anyone else who might have had a hand in this Christmas morning miracle. He was okay again. The vertigo had passed. He could sit up without falling over. He could smile reassuringly at Robbie and reach for his coffee without spilling a drop.

"Happy Anniversary," he said in a flu-raspy voice. He cleared his throat, took a mouthful of coffee.

Robert sat down on the edge of the bed. He wore his wool plaid bathrobe and he was already shaved, his dark hair neatly combed despite the fact that it was six o'clock in the morning. Noel liked to tease him about sleeping in a suit and tie, but it wasn't quite that bad. Although maybe it had been back when Robert was Special Agent Cuffe.

"I thought our anniversary was New Year's Eve?"

Noel shook his head. Barely a twinge of dizziness. He really was on the mend. He smiled widely at Robert. "No. Last Christmas Eve was when we really got together." He took another sip of his coffee, tasting the bite of whisky and the sweetness of Bailey's. Déjà vu. A year to the day.

Robert watched him and observed, "True." He added, "You look a lot better. You certainly sound a hell of a lot better."

Noel made a noncommittal noise and hid his face in the over-sized mug. Flu for the holidays was bad enough, but he'd developed an inner ear infection that had literally knocked him on his ass. He hadn't been able to sit up without help or take three steps without hanging on to Robert for support. It had been up to Robert to take care of everything, including running the stables. Something he knew nothing about and cared for even less. Noel had been as helpless as a baby perched precariously on a spinning ball, and that feeling of powerlessness had culminated yesterday afternoon in something that had probably looked all too much to Robert like a bout of hysterics. Robert had dealt with the tears — which had been embarrassingly more like sobs — as coolly as he'd dealt with everything else that week. He'd held Noel, told him he was okay, he was going to be fine, that it was just the fever making him feel like he'd reached the end of his rope.

Noel wouldn't have blamed Robert for packing his bags and high-tailing it after that. But no. Here he was, shaved and combed and calm as ever.

The ironic thing was the flood of tears had seemed to open Noel's sinuses or maybe the antibiotics were finally working their magic. Whatever it was, by last night he'd been able to turn over in bed without feeling that the bed was rolling over on him. And today... Noel felt almost back to normal.

But poor Robbie. What a shitty holiday season for him. Noel risked a look.

Robert, as grave as ever, said, "Want to see what Santa brought you?"

Noel stepped into his slippers. Robert brought his robe and Noel shrugged into it. He didn't need help to walk anymore, but he was still surprised and grateful for the warm hug that went with the robe. He hugged Robert back so fiercely he nearly knocked him off balance.

Noel muttered, "Sorry for this. I didn't even have a chance to pick up your Christmas present."

"I don't care about presents."

"I do."

"I know you do." Robert sounded amused. "Don't worry. Someone obviously thought you were a good boy this year."

No lie. There was a landslide of gaily wrapped parcels beneath the ten foot tall silver spruce tree dominating the front parlor. The fireplace was ablaze and crackling. A tray with more coffee and pastries sat on the table before the sofa. Noel could smell the wonderful aroma of roasting turkey from the kitchen.

"You did all this?" Noel sat down heavily on the sofa. He couldn't believe it. He couldn't have done a nicer job of preparation himself. It was all the more touching because he knew Robert didn't give a damn about the trappings of Christmas.

Robert had done all of this for Noel.

Noel swallowed hard.

"You okay?" Robert frowned. "Maybe you shouldn't be up yet."

Noel shook his head, found a napkin on the breakfast tray, and gave his nose a good hard blow.

"You want some more coffee?"

Noel shook his head. "I got you a pony," he said.

"Finally."

"Really."

"I know. The owner of White Rock Farm called when you didn't show to pick up the horse."

"I thought we could..." Robert didn't ride. It wasn't that he was afraid of horses; he just wasn't interested in them one way or the other. Whereas Noel's life revolved around the stables, the horses, riding. He wanted to share that with Robert. In fact, he was more and more conscious of wanting to share everything with Robert.

Robert said with seeming sincerity, "I would like that."

It closed Noel's throat up again. He met Robert's dark eyes, said huskily, "You know, I thought last year was the best Christmas of my life, but this year is better."

Robert made a sound that was somewhere between a snort and a splutter. "Maybe you are still feverish."

Noel laughed too. "I think so." But then honesty compelled him to say, "No. I know it sounds…it's just…I've never had anyone. To depend on. Like this."

"Yeah." Robert poured himself a cup of coffee. "I know."

"I never wanted to depend on anyone."

"I know. Safer that way."

That wasn't how Robert Cuffe had grown up, though. He was the product of a loving family and a responsible job. He had lost both those things, but somehow losing them hadn't changed him from the kind of person you could rely on, count on, lean on.

Noel had loved Robert Cuffe from practically the first time they'd met, but he wondered if he had ever really truly and completely understood him — or even trusted him — until last night.

He looked at the avalanche of presents beneath the tree and said, "I wish I had something to give you right now."

Robert answered, sounding genuinely amused. "You do. You have. You gave me the last year and you gave me today and you're giving me all the days and nights ahead. You don't really think a pair of cufflinks or even a new car would make me any happier than I am right now, do you?"

"For richer, for poorer, in sickness and in health?"

"Well? That's the truth, isn't it?"

"Yes. It is for me."

"It is for me too." Robert was smiling, but he was serious.

Forever and Ever. Till Death Do You Part… A light went on in Noel's brain. "Robbie," he said slowly. "How do you feel about diamonds?"

BRIE CHEESE OMELETTE

INGREDIENTS

½ cup grated cheese (use Brie cheese for a creamy filling)

1 cup chopped fresh vegetables such as tomato, cilantro, green onions, and mushrooms to fill

Olive oil

3 eggs

Fresh-ground pepper

Salt

Bacon crumbles (optional)

Sour cream (optional; dollop or to taste)

Truffle oil

DIRECTIONS

Grate cheese.

Cut fresh vegetables, leaving separate any that need pre-frying (any that would be too strong nearly raw, like onions or garlic, or wouldn't taste good raw, like potatoes or asparagus).

Pre-fry or pre-blanch any vegetables that need it.

Warm your skillet with a light coating of olive oil over medium heat (medium-low for a gas range).

Beat the eggs and season with salt and pepper. (The longer you beat the eggs, the smoother your omelettes will be.)

Pour the eggs into the skillet when it is hot, and watch as they bubble and cook. When the base becomes somewhat firm, lift an edge of the base and tilt the pan so that the excess uncooked egg on top runs under, and quickly drop the cooked portion back. Do this on a few different edges until there isn't any excess runny uncooked egg on top. Do not flip, or the egg will become too dry.

Add filling when the top of the egg no longer slides or moves when the pan is tilted.

Coat one half of the egg with half of the cheese, spread the vegetables evenly over the cheese, and then top them with the rest of the cheese.

Fold the other half of the egg over the vegetables and press lightly with the spatula. Let cook until the cheese is melted and vegetables are steaming.

Serve. Top with fresh herbs and sour cream, sprinkle with truffle oil if desired.

(This omelette is featured in *The White Knight*, but I'm pretty sure Robert will want Noel to have a proper Christmas breakfast.)

BAILEY'S IRISH COFFEE

INGREDIENTS

1 (12-ounce) wine glass, preheated

10 ounces brewed coffee

1 shot glass of Bushmills Irish whiskey

1 ½ jiggers Bailey's Original Irish Cream

¼ cup heavy cream, whipped until stiff peaks form

Ground cinnamon or chocolate shavings (optional)

DIRECTIONS

Pour whiskey into heated glass.

Add hot coffee.

Add the Bailey's and stir well to blend.

Top with a mound of whipped cream.

Sprinkle with cinnamon or shaved chocolate.

Serve responsibly.

GRIFF AND HAMAR

OTHER PEOPLE'S WEDDINGS

It was like a bad dream.

Or a bad movie.

One of those straight-to-DVD horror flicks where the normally intelligent protagonist has a brain cloud and forgets to bring his phone charger — coincidentally on the very same *exact* night his car breaks down in the middle of nowhere.

Were Griff sitting in the front row of a theater — or his own living room couch — he'd have been scoffing and making jokes. But instead he was sitting in his car on the loneliest stretch of highway in all of North Dakota. Or so it felt sitting there in the dark as the wind shook the car. Nothing to joke about, that was for sure.

There was not a house, not a light, not a sign of life for as far as he could see. In the far distance he could just make out the silver framework of a couple of power towers. A tumbleweed rolled past his stationary car.

This was his own fault. He should never have attended the Armstrong-Conrad wedding this evening. Who the hell got married on Christmas Eve? He had tried to no avail to get Christie (short for Christmas) to rethink her plans. She already shared a birthday with Baby Jesus, did she really want her wedding tied up with the holiday as well? But yes, it appeared she did. Was adamant on the subject. Originally she'd tried for Christmas day itself.

Griff should have stipulated he couldn't attend the wedding if she insisted on this particular date. He should have settled with looking in, making sure everything was running smoothly, and ducking out again. But no. Control freak that he was, he'd stayed all the way until the reception was underway. And now here he was stuck by the side of the road on Christmas Eve.

Which would have been bad enough. Getting stuck on any night would have been bad enough. But Christmas Eve? Especially this Christmas Eve which would have been the first he and Hamar Sorenson had spent together since junior high. He could have cried with frustration and disappointment.

Another gust shook the car. If the wind blew any harder it would knock the stars right out of the sky.

Worst of all, Griff couldn't even explain to Hamar where he was, why he wasn't answering the door when Hamar finally managed to get off work and come over to Griff's, which would be… Griff flicked on the cab light and checked his watch. Hamar should be getting off work right about now.

What would he think when Griff didn't answer the door? Would he think Griff forgot they were getting together? Or that Griff lost track of the time? Would he think Griff was playing some weird, mean trick? Or maybe Hamar would be delayed. He often was on their date nights. The pitfall of being Sheriff in a small town like Binbell.

Griff groaned. The sound was startling in the vast surrounding silence.

Okay. Get a grip. It wasn't the end of the world. Yes, it was disappointing. He'd gone to such pains to make sure everything would be perfect tonight, the first of what he hoped might be a lifetime of Christmases together. He'd bought new sheets, warm, super soft, flannel sheets, and he'd prepared — okay, bought — a very special Christmas Eve supper for them, starting off with smoked oysters. A bottle of Dom Perignon was chilling in the fridge.

True, Hamar would probably be just as happy with hot sandwiches, a shot of whiskey, and a roll in the hay. But Griff wanted everything to be special, perfect, as perfect as Griff could make it because…because he had realized a couple of weeks ago that he loved Hamar. Not the love for someone he'd grown up with, known like a brother, even had a crush on for a brief time, but real love, grown-up love, the kind of love that made the good times so much better and the bad times bearable. The kind of love that could see you all the way through your old age.

And he hoped that Hamar felt the same. They had been seeing each other since the previous February. Hamar seemed happy to spend most of his — admittedly rare — free time with Griff. He was an enthusiastic and attentive lover. But there had been no words of love spoken between them, no indication that Hamar wished their arrangement to become permanent. Anyway, gay marriage was so far still banned in North Dakota, so it was sort of moot. Hamar was nothing if not practical. He would not be wasting time thinking about things that couldn't happen anyway. That was Griff's department.

Anyway, Griff had planned — considered planning — or planned to consider — asking Hamar if he maybe wanted to move in together.

If things had gone according to plan.

If the moment had seemed right.

Because if the moment wasn't right on Christmas Eve, when would it be?

Damn Christie Armstrong. Well, now Christie Conrad. Would she eventually try to schedule the birth of her first child for this date as well? Probably. That at least would not be Griff's problem.

He sighed, leaning forward to stare out the windshield at the black sky blazing with stars. He should be grateful there was no snow in the immediate forecast — although there was still plenty of it along the side of the road. It was okay. He wasn't going to freeze to death. He had a wool blanket in the back seat and, Christmas or not, someone would be along this road early tomorrow morning. He'd be fine. He'd explain everything to Hamar when he saw him at Christmas dinner. Griff had been invited to Hamar's mother's house tomorrow, so that was something to look forward to.

He tried to comfort himself with the thought. It was a long, long time since he'd spent a Christmas with the Sorensons. The house would be full of candles and red tulips and there would be dark beer and glögg — mulled spiced wine — with the Scandinavian cheeses, crackers and liverwurst enjoyed before the fireplace. At dinner there would be pickled herring and tart beet salad and the most delicious mustard-crusted ham. Lots to eat and drink and very good company to share it with.

Griff had bought Hamar a hand carved chess set. They had played chess and checkers a lot as boys and they had recently gotten back to playing board games in the evenings. Was that a good sign or was it a sign they didn't have enough to talk about?

Griff shivered. He turned around and felt for the wool blanket in the back seat. It was below zero tonight, that was for sure. He hoped he could wait till morning to pee. The idea of getting out in that freezing, wind-scoured, pitch-black night was not a happy one.

He bundled himself in his coat, wrapped the blanket around himself, and put back the car seat. He determinedly shut his eyes.

He dreamed he was flying through the bitterly cold night on Santa's sleigh. Griff grabbed the toys and parcels from Santa's packs and handed them over to an elf who dropped them down into the chimneys below them. Sometimes the elf's aim was good, but sometimes he missed, and Griff could hear the toys and packages hitting the rooftops. He handed over a chess set, and the elf simply threw it out of the sleigh, and Griff could hear all the pieces knocking on the rooftops as they sailed over.

Knock. Knock. Knock.

Griff pried opened his eyes.

KNOCK. KNOCK. "Griff?" Hamar called from outside the car. He tried the door handle. "Griffin, can you hear me?"

Griff sat up and fumbled for the door. The blast of frigid air that blew in made him gasp. But the next moment, Hamar's warm arms were around him.

"What happened?" Hamar's voice sounded muffled, he was holding Griff so tight it was hard to breathe. He was smothered in the surprisingly pleasant scent of leather and Hamar's stale aftershave. "I've been searching for you for hours."

"I think the alternator went out."

"Why the hell didn't you call?"

Griffin grimaced, though Hamar couldn't see it as Griff's face was still pressed into the rough front of his sheepskin-lined coat. "The battery is dead on my cell phone."

"For God's sake," Hamar exclaimed. "I was afraid you were in an accident!"

"I'm really sorry."

For the length of time it took to hustle Griffin over to his SUV, Hamar treated him to an accurate and gruesome recounting of the catastrophes that had befallen others on Christmas Eves past, present and probably future. Then they were inside the SUV which was blessedly warm thanks to the blast of a very efficient heater.

"I really am s-sorry. Th-thank you for coming to get me," Griffin managed between chattering teeth.

Hamar directed all the heater vents his way. "Why aren't you on the main highway?"

"I was in a hurry to get home, so I, er, took a shortcut."

Hamar's face in the wan overhead light said it all. He looked haggard and weary, which was sort of gratifying, though mostly Griff just felt guilty. Guilty and grateful. Hamar must have searched every back road from Binbell to Minot.

"Next time you decide to take a shortcut, call me first."

"Okay." Griff smiled. *Next time* sounded very good, even though Griff planned to make sure there were no repeats of this adventure.

Hamar left him defrosting and went to lock up his car. He returned with Griff's day planner and cell phone. Griff took them gratefully. That was something he really appreciated about Hamar. Hamar never made him feel like his job wasn't equally important or useful in the greater scheme of things.

It was just getting light when they stopped at a gas station and convenience store. Griff used the restroom, afterwards splashing tepid water on his face. He blearily examined his reflection. His shirt was wrinkled, he needed a shave, and his hair was sticking up in tufts. The thought of a real sleep and a hot shower was like heaven.

He found Hamar in the little café, watching the spectacular sunrise gilding the harsh landscape in delicate shades of pink and peach and gold.

Christmas morning. Definitely not what he had been hoping — and planning — for.

He drank the two cups of terrible but boiling hot coffee Hamar bought him, and ate a hot pretzel, after which he felt much better, even if he looked like he'd spent the night on the prairie, which, granted, he had.

"I had such nice plans for last night," he told Hamar sadly.

Hamar just shook his head. He too looked better after a couple of cups of coffee. Unshaven, red-eyed, but back to his usual imperturbable self.

"I can't believe you came looking for me last night," Griff admitted.

Hamar's blond brows drew together. "Of course I came looking for you."

Maybe that had been the most practical thing to do. It still felt good.

Griff was smiling as they walked back out to Hamar's vehicle and climbed inside, and he wasn't even exactly sure why.

"Something funny?" Hamar asked.

"Just...happy," Griff admitted.

They looked at each other for a moment. Hamar adjusted the rear-view mirror, which did not need adjusting, and said, "What *did* you have planned last night?"

"Oh." Griff shrugged, self-deprecatingly. "You know me." Hamar would probably think he had gone to way too much fuss. Maybe it was a good thing he had been saved from making a fool of himself.

"Yes," Hamar said. He gave a grim smile. "Champagne?"

Griff shifted uncomfortably. "Yeah."

Hamar gave an under his breath laugh and shook his head. He adjusted the heating vents some more and then said suddenly, "I figured. Listen, I was going to talk to you last night, but that didn't work out, so I don't think I'll wait. I'm just going to say it."

"Okay," Griff said a little uneasily. Hamar sounded brisk and businesslike.

"My annual vacation is next April."

"Right. I remember." Last year Hamar had gone backpacking with college friends. Griff figured it would be something like that again this year. At least it was only two weeks.

Hamar cleared his throat and said gruffly, "I think we should go to California and get married."

Griff's jaw dropped.

"You…"

"I do, yeah."

"But…"

Hamar smiled self-consciously. "You're a wedding planner. Didn't you ever want to get married yourself?"

"Well, yes. Of course. I just didn't think it would be — I didn't think you would want that."

Hamar shrugged. "I never really thought about it until you."

"Me being a wedding planner and all."

Hamar said dryly, "I can't deny I never expected to know the difference between chocolate ganache and devil's food. Let alone the cost effectiveness of Chantilly lace over Schiffli. But if you think I want to marry you because of repeated exposure to *Brides* magazine, think again."

As Griff stared, he realized there was a funny little twinkle in Hamar's eyes.

"Oh. You mean..." Griff could feel his face getting warm.

Hamar said, "I guess you were probably picturing something pretty different. But I love you. Will you marry me?"

Hamar was right. Being a wedding planner Griff had imagined every possible romantic variation on this theme. Moonlight, roses, and Prince Charming in a matching tux. Hamar had not been part of those fantasies. Never. Griff's feelings for Hamar ran too deep. Dreaming of what could never be with Hamar would simply be too painful.

Nor had a proposal in front of a gas station after a freezing night in his car been part of the fantasy.

But here he was with Hamar, who looked as confident and assured as ever — except for that little trace of uncertainty in his blue eyes — and it looked very much like none of his fantasies were coming true.

Reality was better.

SWEDISH GLÖGG

INGREDIENTS

4 ounces dried apples

3 ounces seedless raisins

3 ounces prunes

1 ounce dried orange peel (pommerance)

2 ounces almonds

1 ounce cardamom

1 ounce cloves

1 ounce cinnamon sticks

1 cup granulated sugar

2 bottles port

1 bottle claret or dry red wine

Brandy

Almonds, raisins and cloves (optional garnishes)

DIRECTIONS

The day before, tie fruits, almonds and spices in cheesecloth; put in large pot. Add sugar, port and claret or dry red wine. Bring to boil; then simmer over medium heat until reduced to about 2 ½ bottles. Pour into glass jar; cover; cool for 24 hours.

Next day, remove spice bag from wine.

Heat 1 part wine with 1 part brandy; do not boil.

Serve in punch glasses. If desired, garnish each serving with a couple of almonds, raisins and cloves.

You will be unsurprised to learn servings vary.

SWEDISH MUSTARD-GLAZED CHRISTMAS HAM

INGREDIENTS

9 lb. corned ham

2 carrots, peeled

2 celery ribs

2 bay leaves

5 white peppercorns

2 yellow onions, peeled

18 cloves

½ cup mild Swedish mustard

2 egg yolks

6 tablespoons honey

3 tablespoons fine bread crumbs

DIRECTIONS

Place a ham in a large pot. Add carrots, celery ribs, bay leaves, peppercorns, and onions, each studded with 6 cloves. Cover with water, cover pot, and simmer over low heat, skimming occasionally, for 3 hours.

Remove ham from broth (reserve broth for dip-in-pot) and place on a cutting board. Cut away and discard rind. Preheat oven to 325°F.

Combine mustard, egg yolks, and honey in a bowl and mix well. Place ham, fat side up, on a rack set in a roasting pan. Glaze top of ham and bake for 25 minutes. Increase heat to 400°F and cook, basting with glaze, for 15 minutes. Sprinkle with bread crumbs and bake until golden, 15 minutes. Cool, then slice. Serve with coarse mustard.

Serves 12.

TIM AND JACK

CARDS ON THE TABLE

"Where the hell have you been?" Jack yelled before I even closed the front door.

"Sorry," I apologized, shrugging out of my jacket. "Sorry I'm late. I swear to God it couldn't be helped. I'm mostly packed. We can be on the road in half an hour. Promise."

He caught my arm as I was brushing past, heading for the bedroom. He sucked in a sharp breath. "Jesus, Tim. What happened?"

I said quickly, though I should have known by then there was no heading off the inevitable lecture, "It looks a lot worse than it is."

"Really? Because it looks like a split lip and a black eye." He followed me into the bedroom, watching, angry and at a loss, as I grabbed my suitcase and threw it on the neatly made bed. The bed sloshed in warning.

"Sorry," I said again, automatically. That would be all we needed. A leak in that fucking waterbed as we were about to take off on our trip up north. We were heading to San Francisco to spend Christmas Eve with Sam, one of Jack's best friends from his police academy days, then on to Mendocino to spend Christmas with my family, then back to Los Angeles so Jack could be back at work on Thursday. I was just grateful Jack's parents had moved to Florida so we didn't have to try and include them in the holiday endurance run.

"What happened?" he asked in an ominously quiet voice. "Did you have a seizure? Were you driving?"

"Hell no, I didn't have a seizure!" I'm not sure why that incensed me so much because though I'd been seizure free for six months, I'd only been driving for one, and it still felt pretty new to me. I knew Jack was still worried about the thought of me behind the wheel if I did have another seizure.

"Well, you didn't walk into a wall!" He was yelling at me again. It was so unlike him. I couldn't understand it. I wasn't that late and he was mostly used to my unpredictable schedule — as a cop, his own wasn't much better.

"Look, the interview didn't go smoothly. Mayer punched me. And I, er, punched him back."

Jack's jaw dropped. Which I guess was better than having him flap it at me.

Reminded of my injuries, I noticed how much my mouth and eye were smarting. A lot. I abandoned the suitcase and went to the bathroom. The sight in the mirror was not reassuring. The fact that I was wearing a suit and tie almost made it worse.

I turned the cold water tap on.

Jack appeared in the mirror behind me. His face was stern. His gray eyes looked dark and there was no evidence of dimples. "I can't take this," he said. "We can't go on like this."

It felt like being punched all over again. I gripped the side of the sink. "What does that mean? What are you talking about?"

"You're so goddamned reckless!"

"You haven't even heard my side of what happened."

"You're a reporter and you punched your interviewee. Is there another side to that?"

"He punched me first!"

"Great. That's your side of it? We've had this conversation, Tim. How many times?"

"What are you talking about? When have we had this conversation?"

Jack shouted, "You take stupid, reckless chances. And I can't deal with this anymore."

He walked out of the bathroom, leaving me to gape at my battered reflection. After a dazed second or two, I bent and splashed cold water on my face, trying to think.

Once, and not that long ago, I'd have charged back in there and we'd have had an argument that probably would have ended with one of us — me — walking out the door. But I'd learned a few things in the past months. Learned them from Jack, as a matter of fact.

I turned off the faucet, dried my face, and went into the bedroom. No Jack. I went into the living room and he was sitting on the couch, leaning forward, massaging his forehead.

I sat down beside him. He didn't look at me. I said, "I'm not sure what's going on here, but I don't take stupid, reckless chances. Not anymore. Because of you. Because I don't have to prove anything anymore. Mayer is a thug and the interview fell apart, but I'm telling you, I did not provoke him. I was protecting myself, that's all."

"You shouldn't be talking to guys like Mayer. He's scum. He's a killer."

"It's for the courts to decide if he's a killer. And interviewing him is my job, Jack. I don't give you a hard time when you come home with a few bruises."

He burst out, "Why do you have to — why can't you —?"

I stared at him. "What? Write a society column? What are you talking about?"

He massaged his head some more.

I tried to joke, "You wouldn't be saying this to me if I was a girl."

He raised his head. "What?"

"Jack, come on. Who gives anybody this kind of bullshit hard time over their job nowadays?"

"You know your situation."

"Yeah, better than anyone. And you know that I am taking care of myself and being responsible about my health. You know I haven't had a seizure in half a year. And when was the last time I came home with a black eye?"

He didn't look at me.

"What's really going on here?" I asked. Something had happened. Somehow I had managed to really screw things up. But when? Everything had been going great between us as far as I could tell.

Nothing from Jack.

I didn't know what his expression meant. I said slowly, "Should I finish packing for Sam's or should I grab a cardboard box?"

He shook his head.

I put my arm around him, pressed my forehead to his. "Please don't be mad at me. It's Christmas Eve."

To my relief, Jack turned to me, kissed me. He put his arm around me and pulled me closer. "Sorry," he whispered. "Sorry. Just don't take dumb chances."

"I don't. I promise."

He nodded.

We sat there for a couple of minutes. I looked past his head at the clock and said, "We've got to get moving or we won't be there until late."

"We're not going."

"What? Why not?"

Not that I minded. I'd have killed for an early night in my own bed with Jack. I wasn't all that crazy about Sam, a big, dour bruiser of a cop, although I liked Rhys, his boyfriend, a lot. Even if he was a little obsessive on the topic of the afterlife.

"Rhys is in the hospital. He got into a car accident driving up Friday."

"My God. Is he okay?"

Jack nodded. "Sam says he will be, but I guess it was touch and go. He was in a coma for a couple of days. He's out of it now. Sam says he keeps talking about some guy named Roger."

I laughed. "Good for Rhys."

Jack gave me a sour look, but I could see the dimple trying to make an appearance. He was holding my hand, or more exactly my wrist where I wore the snazzy sterling Medic Alert bracelet he'd given me. His fingers absently stroked the sturdy silver links.

"So…it's just you and me tonight?"

He nodded. His gray eyes were still a little moody, but he was finally smiling again. "That okay with you?"

I pumped my fist. "Yes, Virginia, there is a Santa Claus!"

"Merry Christmas." Jack's mouth found mine. "And don't call me Virginia."

HEROIN WINGS

INGREDIENTS

4 pounds chicken wings

1 cup Parmesan cheese

2 tablespoons dried parsley

1 tablespoon dried oregano

2 teaspoons paprika

1 teaspoon cayenne pepper or crushed red pepper (optional)

1 teaspoon salt

½ teaspoon pepper

½ cup butter

DIRECTIONS

Preheat oven to 350°F.

Cut the wings into drumsticks (save the tips for soup, so the recipe says or you could just buy drummettes).

Combine Parmesan, parsley, oregano, paprika, salt, and pepper in a bowl.

Line a shallow baking pan with foil (or you'll be spending the next month cleaning the pan).

Melt the butter in a shallow bowl or pan.

Dip each drumstick in butter, roll in the cheese and seasoning mixture, and arrange in the foil-lined pan.

Bake for 1 hour or until they get as crispy as you like.

WYATT AND GRAHAM

PERFECT DAY

It started to fall apart right before Christmas.

Everything had been fine up until then. Better than fine. Graham and I were seeing each other a few times a week, talking almost every day — talking about moving in together, in fact. It was relaxed and easy and I started to believe in it, trust in it, count on it.

And I know Graham did too.

Ten months. Almost a year. But then along came Christmas.

Not an easy time of the year to be alone. Not an easy time of the year to be in a relationship either, at least not a new relationship. Not with all that potential for disappointment and comparisons and miscommunication.

But I really did think —

Part of learning to be a couple is figuring out the way through all those different, sometimes conflicting, holiday traditions.

"Do you go home for Christmas?" I asked Graham.

It was a Sunday morning and we were having brunch at Metropol Bakery.

"I haven't seen my parents in eighteen years," Graham replied, calmly picking the cranberries out of his smoked turkey breast sandwich. "Not since I told them I was gay and they told me to get out."

I was shocked and I don't think I hid it very well. Graham had mentioned his parents a few times and I'd never had any hint that he wasn't on polite if distant terms with them. It underscored how much we still didn't know about each other.

"Did you want to go to your parents for Christmas?" he asked.

"If you do."

"If Bill and Dana don't mind, sure. I'd like that."

"Mind? They'll be thrilled." My parents loved Graham. They absolutely believed he was my Mr. Right. He talked sports and gardening with my dad and cooking and politics with my mom. He was clean, polite, and employed. You bet they loved him.

Graham grinned and that was that.

"What did you want for Christmas?" he asked a couple of evenings later.

"Me?"

He laughed. "Yeah you. Can you give me a few ideas of something you might like?"

"You mean a list?"

That was apparently even more amusing. "If you want to make a list."

I didn't want to make a list. I wanted him to surprise me with something he'd chosen particularly. Having to come up with ideas seemed too much like handing over a grocery list and asking him to remember to pick up a bottle of milk. I didn't want him to give me a list either — and, in fairness, he didn't offer one.

"I don't mind surprises," I told him, hoping he'd see what I was getting at.

"I don't want to get you something you already have."

A reminder that for all the time we spent together and the discussions about moving in together, we didn't live together, didn't really share a life.

"What did you do these last couple of Christmases?" I asked later that night. "Did you spend the day on your own?"

We were at Graham's, in bed. We'd finished making love and we were lying there, quietly. Not talking, just holding hands. Looking at the stars through the skylight.

I can't say that Graham tensed, but I could feel something changed. He said, "I spend Christmas with friends."

"Oh." I knew a lot of his friends by now. He knew a lot of mine. I was wondering which friends he'd spent the holiday with.

He said abruptly, "I usually spend Christmas with Jase's parents."

"Oh."

Until that moment, I had never given a thought to Jase's parents, or to the fact that Graham might still be close to them, that they might — probably did — regard him as another son. That Graham probably loved them too. That he might prefer to spend Christmas with Jase's family over mine.

And even if he didn't prefer Jase's parents to mine, I couldn't help feeling guilty — awful, in fact — that I was taking Graham away from these people who had already endured the worst thing that could happen to parents.

Graham turned his head my way. I knew it was too dark for him to read my expression, just as it was too dark for me to read his.

I said hesitantly, "Did you want to —?"

"No." He said it with finality. So much so that I didn't feel I could question it. But I did question it, and although he probably meant to reassure me, I didn't feel reassured.

It all came to a head over the Christmas tree.

I usually got my tree the first weekend in December. That's what we did when I was growing up and I continued the tradition when I had a place of my own. I like Christmas. I like it all. The music, the decorations, the presents, the special feeling in the air — the fact that most people are a little nicer, a little kinder, a little more generous during the holidays.

This year, I kept putting off getting the tree until the weekend before Christmas. Graham went with me to the tree farm. We were tying the tree onto the roof rack of my car when he said, "You're going to a lot of trouble when you spend most of the time at my place anyway."

"Maybe we should set it up at your place?" I was partly kidding. Partly not.

Graham barely hesitated. "Okay. Sure."

"Do you have a tree stand? Decorations?"

"I've got everything."

That turned out to be the truth. He had everything from tree skirt to tree stand to boxes of ornaments — all neatly organized and labeled. Labeled in handwriting that wasn't Graham's.

When I saw that square, legible writing I knew I had made a mistake. But it was too late by then. So we dragged out the boxes and set up the tree. We strung the lights through the fragrant needles. And then we began taking the ornaments out, one by one. There were a lot of very old bulbs and beautiful handmade ornaments. Someone had taken their tree trimming as seriously as I did. Graham, who had said very little from the time we set up the tree, stopped talking altogether.

After hearing my too cheerful, too loud voice break the silence a couple of times, I had nothing to say either.

Graham finally, mercifully, went to turn the stereo on. When he came back, I was holding two clay ornaments, one red, one green. They were imprints of small hands, a child's hands. I turned them over and read JASON KANE, age 5.

I looked up, saw Graham's face, and looked down again.

He said in a muffled voice, "Why don't I get take-out for dinner?"

I nodded.

A second later the front door shut.

Graham didn't come back. He didn't phone. It got later and later. I decorated the tree, put the boxes away, and went home.

He didn't call the next day either. Or the next.

I could have called him, I guess.

I didn't.

I drove up alone to my parents on Christmas Eve.

"Where's Graham?" Mom and Dad asked.

"Not coming." I couldn't leave it like that though. "I don't think things are going to work out with Graham."

"Oh no!" my mom exclaimed. "What happened?"

My dad came to the rescue. "Wyatt'll tell us when he's ready."

But no. I didn't think I'd be able to talk about it. Not that trip anyway. I lay awake that night wondering what Graham was doing. Wondering if he was lying there in that big empty bed staring up at the stars and grieving for Jase.

My heart felt like a lump of coal.

It was still a good Christmas though, and if I did occasionally think about Graham, who was probably once again spending the day with Jase's parents, I didn't let my preoccupation spoil the day for my own folks.

We had reached the hot turkey sandwiches and coffee part of the evening when the doorbell rang.

"It can't be the mailman today," my mother said cheerfully as I went to answer it.

Graham stood on the doorstep, hands shoved in the pockets of his navy parka, snowflakes in his dark hair.

"Hi!" I know I looked and sounded dumfounded. I was.

"Wyatt." Graham's gray eyes were somber, his expression a mix of pain and embarrassment. He was wondering what the hell he was doing there. Which made two of us.

"You're…" I didn't finish because yes, he was obviously there, and yes, he obviously hadn't come for dinner. "Come in."

"No. I don't — that is, I wanted to see you. To talk to you."

And whatever he had to say wasn't going to work in front of an audience. That I understood perfectly. "Hold on." I half closed the door, grabbed my coat off the hook on the wall rack, and yelled, "I'll be right back."

I closed the door on the inquiries of where I was going. Graham turned and we walked by silent agreement away from the house toward where his jeep was parked. The sound of our boots crunching in the snow was immediately swallowed by the vast white stillness.

"I don't know what to say to you," he said. "I only know I couldn't let another day go by, this day go by, without trying to talk to you."

I said gruffly, "You could have called. You didn't have to drive all this way." Especially if this was going to be the conversation I guessed it was.

He didn't answer.

I stopped walking. "Graham."

He stopped walking too. "Why did you leave that night?"

"Why did I —? Huh? So you could come home!"

"What are you talking about?" He seemed honestly bewildered.

I was already sorry for that flash of bitterness. "Look, we both know you didn't want me there."

His brows drew together. "You're wrong, Wyatt."

I laughed shortly. "No. I don't think so. The last person you wanted or needed to deal with that night was me."

He put his hands on my shoulders, gazed intently into my eyes. "Wyatt, you're wrong. I did want you there. I always want you there."

Why did he have to say that? I pulled away and wiped my eyes on my coat sleeve. "I know you care about me." Exasperatingly, my voice shook. I steadied it. Took a deep breath. "But the fact is, you still love Jase. You were right. You're not ready to move on. I've been pushing you the whole way."

"You're wrong."

I shook my head. "No. I'm not. I saw your face that day. Not just that day either. It's exactly what you said at the start. You miss him all the time."

"Yes, I miss Jase. But that doesn't change the fact that I love *you* and want to spend my life with *you*." Graham's hand was a warm weight on my shoulder. He turned me to face him once more. "I wanted you there that night. When you left like that, without a word…I figured you were angry or hurt or both. I thought maybe I should give you some time. And I was…embarrassed, I guess."

"Embarrassed?"

His face twisted. "I feel like I'm always breaking down in front of you. It's not fair to keep putting you through that. It's a strain on our relationship. I know that. But sometimes…something will get to me. That night was tough. You're right. But having you there helped."

"You didn't come back. You didn't call. It didn't feel like I was helping." I was still trying to wrap my head around the idea that Graham believed he was always breaking down in front of me. He was one of the least demonstrative guys I'd ever known. Not cold, but not effusive. Not by a long stretch.

"All I can tell you is when I got home and saw you were gone…" The pain in his eyes surprised me. "I thought I'd better give you a little space. I hoped you'd call. I thought you would." He glanced automatically toward the house.

Seeing the situation from Graham's standpoint, I felt a stab of remorse. It had never occurred to me he would feel anything but relief at being let out of spending Christmas day with my family.

"I was waiting for you to call. I felt like it was your move."

"Why would it be my move? Aren't we in this together?" He was frowning.

I wanted to believe him. I did believe him up to a point. But if he was wrong? If he was only saying what he wanted and hoped was true? I wasn't sure I could take it. Either way, I wasn't sure I could take it. Something inside me seemed to snap. I blurted, "I feel like I can't live up to Jase, to what you had with Jase."

Graham looked stunned. I rushed on, afraid if I didn't get it out now I never would. "I feel like I can't compare. Like you've already had the best there is and anything I can offer is just going to be second best."

"Sweetheart. Wyatt. Stop."

I stopped. That had been way more than I had ever meant to say. And Graham thought *he* was always falling apart?

Graham pulled his gloves off and rested a warm hand against my face. "Listen to me." His gray eyes held mine. "Everything is completely different with you, completely new. And I'm glad. I don't compare you to Jase. You're nothing like him. That doesn't take anything away from either of you. I loved Jase but he's gone. You're here now and I love you with all my heart."

There was a lump in my throat. "Is that true?"

"You must know."

I looked into Graham's face, into his unguarded gaze, and I did know. I could see the depth of his emotion, the emotion he kept so firmly in check, regardless of what he thought.

"When I see you, I see the future," he said. "I don't know what that future holds. I just know I want it."

It was still snowing, but all at once it felt like the sun was shining. I began to smile. "I'm pretty sure one thing that future holds is a turkey sandwich and a cup of coffee."

PERFECT TURKEY SANDWICH

INGREDIENTS

6 slices applewood-smoked bacon

¼ cup mayonnaise

¼ cup crumbled Maytag blue cheese or other mild blue cheese

4 ½-inch-thick slices country-style white bread (about 5x3 inches)

4 leaves radicchio

6 ounces thinly sliced cooked turkey

4 teaspoons butter, room temperature, divided

DIRECTIONS

Cook bacon in large skillet over medium heat until crisp. Transfer to paper towels. Pour off fat from skillet; reserve skillet.

Mash mayonnaise and blue cheese in bowl to coarse puree; season with pepper. Place bread on work surface.

Divide cheese mixture among bread slices, spreading evenly. Divide bacon, radicchio, and turkey between 2 bread slices.

Top with remaining bread, cheese side down.

Melt 2 teaspoons butter in reserved skillet over medium heat. Place sandwiches in skillet.

Spread 2 teaspoons butter on top pieces of bread.

Cover with lid that is slightly smaller than skillet. Cook sandwiches until lightly browned, about 4 minutes per side.

CHRISTMAS COFFEE

INGREDIENTS

Stir together in a small saucepan:

½ cup granulated sugar

¼ cup unsweetened cocoa

¼ teaspoon cinnamon (or cardamom)

⅓ cup water

Whipped cream, for garnish

Milk, for serving

Sugar, for serving

DIRECTIONS

Over medium heat, boil sugar, cocoa, cinnamon and water for 1 minute, stirring frequently.

Add to coffee, stir and serve immediately. Stir again if served later.

Serve with whipped topping, milk and sugar.

Good with a splash of brandy, Frangelico, Kahlua or Bailey's, if desired.

MARK AND STEPHEN FROM THE I SPY SERIES

I SPY SOMETHING
CHRISTMAS

I closed my eyes, dozed.

Music was playing downstairs. Bing Crosby. Very traditional. I smiled. The floorboard squeaked and I opened my eyes to soft light and wonderful smells. Irish coffee and warm gingerbread.

Stephen set the tray on the bed and crawled in beside me once more.

"You're spoiling me."

"Lena is spoiling us both." He broke off a piece of gingerbread and held it out to me as though he were feeding me wedding cake. I raised my head, nibbled the gingerbread, licked his fingers when I'd taken the last bite. He closed his eyes and gave a twitchy smile. I kissed his fingertips and let my head fall back in the pillows.

"Favorite Christmas carol?" I asked.

"Modern or traditional?"

"Both."

"'Silent Night.' 'Please Come Home for Christmas.' You?" He offered another bite of gingerbread.

I took a bite. Swallowed. "This year? 'I'll be Home for Christmas.'"

He smiled, understanding. "Traditional?"

"Not really a carol. The Christmas section of Handel's Messiah."

"I should have guessed that. My turn. Favorite Christmas movie?"

"Mister Magoo's Christmas Carol."

Stephen laughed.

"Quite serious. It's one of your classics, yes? I loved that razzle-berry dressing and woofle jelly cake."

"You do enjoy your food. I'm not sure where you put it." He stroked my ribcage.

I sucked in my stomach. "Yours?"

"It's a Wonderful Life."

I said, "You've made a difference in a lot of people's lives. A good difference."

His green gaze was grave. Sometimes he saw too much. "Best Christmas memory?" he asked.

"This," I said. "Tonight."

GINGERBREAD CAKE

INGREDIENTS

½ cup white sugar

½ cup butter

1 egg

1 cup molasses

2 ½ cups all-purpose flour

1 ½ teaspoons baking soda

1 teaspoon ground cinnamon

1 teaspoon ground ginger

½ teaspoon ground cloves

½ teaspoon salt

1 cup hot water

DIRECTIONS

Preheat oven to 350°F (175°C). Grease and flour a 9-inch square pan.

In a large bowl, cream together the sugar and butter. Beat in the egg, and mix in the molasses.

In a bowl, sift together the flour, baking soda, salt, cinnamon, ginger, and cloves. Blend into the creamed mixture. Stir in the hot water. Pour into the prepared pan.

Bake 1 hour in the preheated oven, until a knife inserted in the center comes out clean. Allow to cool in pan before serving. Serve with a dollop of whipped cream.

NATHAN AND MATTHEW

SNOWBALL IN HELL

New Year's Eve in the City of Angels.

Not so many angels out and about that night, and Matthew and his squad were kept busy with a knifing, two shootings, and an attempted kidnapping. By the time Matt finally got away it was about twenty minutes till the Witching Hour. He made for the Biltmore Hotel, knowing Nathan would be there.

It was standing room only at the Biltmore, dames and gents alike in silly hats and tinsel tiaras, blowing plastic horns and paper fizoos in each other's faces. Everybody was talking and nobody was listening. The floor was littered with soggy confetti. Champagne glasses were overflowing, and seeing that this was the Biltmore, maybe it really was champagne spilling down the fronts of party frocks and dress uniforms.

Matthew worked his way through the crush of people in the elegant lobby with its parquet floors and rich jewel-toned carpets and carved ceilings. He made it to the bar but couldn't find Nathan anywhere. He knew what that meant, and his heart sank.

Well, what had he expected? Sure, things were different now, but maybe not different in all things. Nathan had been honest about what he needed, and Matt would somehow have to learn to accept it.

And if he couldn't accept it… Then he would be equally honest.

But he wasn't there yet. Not by a long shot. Yes, he was disappointed and, yeah, it hurt like hell that Nathan couldn't do without for a single night, but Matthew had entered into this knowing he was going to have to take Nathan as he was. So he resisted the urge to search any further. Finding Nathan rolling around in the undergrowth at Pershing Square wasn't going to do either of them any good.

So Matt left the party as midnight was chiming and drove home through the eerily silent streets. He tried not to think about Nathan or his own disappointment. He thought he was mostly successful, but when he reached his own street and saw Nathan's Chrysler Highlander parked in front of his house, happiness and relief hit him in a warm rush.

And with it a little stab of shame that he had wronged Nathan. It was frightening to care so much for someone he knew so little.

He parked beneath the trellised carport and walked back to the street. Nathan was sleeping in his car, head tipped back, his hat over his face. When Matt tapped on his window, he jumped and then grinned sheepishly, tiredly.

Matthew opened the door and Nathan unfolded wearily.

"How long were you waiting?" Matthew asked.

Nathan raised a shoulder. "Not so long."

"Come inside," Matthew told him.

Nathan threw an instinctive look at the dark windows of Mathew's neighbors. "No. It's all right. I just wanted — needed — to wish you…

Auld Lang Syne. It wouldn't have seemed right to start the new year off without seeing you." He offered his hand.

Matthew took his hand, but didn't release it. "Come inside," he said again.

He could see Nathan wavering, recognized the longing because he felt just the same. Nathan said reluctantly, "Your neighbors are going to notice if I spend another night here."

He was right, but Matthew just couldn't bring himself to care enough to give up the pleasure of being together, even for a few hours. He placed his other hand on Nathan's shoulder, guiding him toward the house. "Then we'll have to think of some reason for you to visit. Don't we share a Great Aunt Gertrude? How's she doing these days anyway? How's her lumbago?"

Nathan shook his head, but Matthew caught the whisper of his laugh. Then he was unlocking the side door and letting them into the silent and dark house. The door closed behind them. Matthew felt for the chain, slid it into place, and took Nathan into his arms. Nathan hugged him back fiercely.

"Happy New Year, Nathan," Matthew said softly, and kissed him.

ARISTOCRATIC SPARKLING PUNCH

1942 RECIPE FROM *GOURMET MAGAZINE*

INGREDIENTS

Sparkling water

1 bottle Burgundy

4 ounces Brandy

2 bottles Champagne

Raspberries or strawberries

2 oranges

DIRECTIONS

Dissolve 1 cup cube sugar in 1 cup — from a quart — of sparkling water, and pour into a punch bowl.

Add 1 bottle Burgundy and 4 ounces brandy, stirring well. Place a block of ice in the bowl, and pour in 2 bottles Champagne and the rest of the sparkling water.

Garnish the top of the ice block with strawberries or raspberries, or other fruit in season, and float thin slices of 2 oranges on the punch.

SPAM HASH

INGREDIENTS

2 largish potatoes

½ onion

¼ can of spam

Pat butter/margarine

Tomato chopped (optional)

DIRECTIONS

Wash potatoes.

Cut into quarters and boil until firmly cooked, remove from water and cool.

Chop onion.

Chop up ¼ can spam into chunks.

Take large frying pan, add in large blob of butter and heat.

Add in onions and cook gently until nice and translucent.

Take potatoes and chop them into smaller chunks.

Add these and the spam chunks into the pan with the onions and continue to fry and stir.

Turn down frying pan and cover if possible and continue to cook for another 5-10 minutes. At this stage you can add in some chopped tomato if you like. If the mixture is sticking too much, add in a little bit of water and stir.

Once cooked, serve with your favorite veggies!

Serves 2 guys used to wartime rations.

SOMEBODY KILLED HIS EDITOR

It rained Christmas day.

It had rained every day since I arrived in San Francisco. It's not that I particularly minded the rain, but the wet, gray weather didn't do a lot for my mood — or for the headache I'd had ever since the plane had touched down on the tarmac at San Francisco International Airport.

"It's the shift in barometric pressure," I told J.X. "It's giving me a migraine."

He looked sympathetic — he had been looking sympathetic for three days, so he was probably starting to run low on milk of human kindness, though you'd never guess from the soft look in his dark eyes. "Maybe you should call your doctor? Ask for a prescription for your migraine medicine."

This holiday scene takes place between *Somebody Killed His Editor* and *All She Wrote*.

I waved that idea off. "No, no. I'll be fine."

"We could stop and fill the prescription on the way."

"It'll be impossible to get hold of anyone today."

"You should try at least. You don't want to have the day spoiled by a migraine."

"Ha. No fear of that!"

I felt a little guilty at the wide, relieved smile that greeted my words. Of course, what I was thinking was that nothing, not even a raging migraine, could make this disaster of a day worse than it was. Or would be.

It was my own fault. I'd wanted to see J.X. We'd only had one chance to get together since the murderous events at Blue Heron Lodge, but picking Christmas weekend was a bad move. Our relationship — could you even call something this new, this tentative, a relationship? — was not ready for the weight of all those expectations and comparisons that inevitably came with the holiday season.

Not that our budding romance — could you call something this new, this tentative, a romance? — would necessarily fare badly by comparison to what holidays had been like with David, my ex.

If it had just been me and J.X., it might have worked out all right. But no. We were spending the day with his family. His parents and his nephew and his ex-wife. J.X.'s ex-wife, not the nephew's. The nephew was just a kid. Six or seven or something. And the ex-wife was because J.X. had felt duty-bound to marry his dead brother's pregnant girl-friend in order to give the kid a name. It just didn't get more soap opera-ish than that.

He was a real idealist, J.X.

That's what worried me. I'd already disappointed him once. You only got so many chances with idealists.

* * * * *

"At least let me drive you back," J.X. said in an undervoice.

"That would make me feel even worse!" I looked past him to where his four-year-old nephew was peeking around the hall corner. The kid looked like a miniature J.X., minus the Van Dyke beard. Gage stuck his tongue out at me. I took the high road and ignored him, saying to J.X., "I don't want to take you away from your family."

The family that hated me on sight.

"Yeah, but the idea is for you and me to spend the weekend together."

"We did. We have."

J.X.'s brows drew together. He opened his mouth.

"Julian? Oh." J.X.'s mother — "call me Mrs. Moriarity" — stopped at the end of the hall. "We were just about to serve pie."

Laura Dolores Moriarity was of Castilian Spanish descent, an icy, blue-eyed blond. In looks, J.X. took after his father who was what they used to call "black Irish." Mr. Moriarity was pleasantly distant. Then there was Nina, who was both pretty and pained. Maybe J.X. thought that marriage had all been platonic on her side, but he was the only one who did.

The only comfort was that they probably would have hated me just as much if I'd been female. But I don't think being the gay boyfriend helped.

"Be right there," J.X. said over his shoulder.

Laura raised an eyebrow and departed.

"Kit, are you going to be there when I get home?" J.X. asked bluntly.

"The thing is," I hedged apologetically, "I'm afraid I'm coming down with the flu. I think maybe the best thing I could do is grab a red-eye flight and go home."

"Kit." I felt that dark, hurt look right in my solar plexus.

"Julian? Gage is hoping you'll help him put his train se — oh." Nina hastily backed up and disappeared around the hall corner.

The doorbell rang. "That's my taxi," I said, and I don't think I could quite hide my relief.

"To hell with the taxi," J.X. said. "Don't go like this, Kit. Let me drive you back to my place. Maybe you'll feel better if you lie down. At least we can talk."

Oh God. Not that. Not The Talk.

"I wouldn't think of it!" I said honestly. I dragged on my coat and fumbled with the door handle, almost shaking it to get it open. "I'll call you!"

"Kit!" I closed the door on his protest and ran down the rain-slicked steps to the waiting taxi.

COLIN AND SEPTIMUS

THE DARKLING THRUSH

Septimus invited me to his home for the Yule Feast. I thought perhaps there would be a party, and I told myself I wouldn't mind that. This would be my first and only Yule spent across the Great Big Sea and I might as well see how a traditional feast was properly done.

But I can't deny I was pleased to discover that Septimus and I were spending the afternoon alone. I was tired of being looked at and whispered about by my colleagues at Leslie's Lexicons. There was no need to pretend with Septimus.

Besides. Septimus was…Septimus. I was happy to spend every moment I could with him.

"I brought you this," I told him, handing over a bottle of mulled wine.

Septimus smiled and kissed me — right there in front of his butler. "We'll have it after our dinner."

I smiled too because I knew that meant we would be spending the night together.

The meal was indeed a feast. We started with raw oysters, supped right out of the shell. Then bouillon that tasted of wild herbs and venison. Champagne was next, served cold and dry, and pâtés made from veal and goose livers.

I knew roasted boar was the most traditional of Yule suppers, but I was relieved when the brownies carried in a large platter with roasted goose. The goose was golden-brown and tender, stuffed with sage and onion and pine nuts. There were small potatoes in a white sauce, exotic roots and vegetables, and cranberry and orange sauce.

"I can't eat another bite," I told Septimus, pushing my plate away at last.

He laughed as though this were nonsense, and I suppose it was since after that I consumed my fair share of plum pudding, chocolate truffles, cheese and nuts and biscuits.

When we finally pushed away from the table, I was convinced I wouldn't need to eat for a week.

"I expect you'll be hungry enough by breakfast," Septimus said slyly, and I felt my face warm.

He led the way to his library. I had been in that wonderful room several times, but that afternoon, he reached behind one of the old, rich tapestries, and one of the towering shelves slid soundlessly away to reveal the entrance to another, smaller room. I followed Septimus through that low doorway. There were two brocade chairs, a small inlaid table, an old-fashioned lamp, and all four walls were lined with books. Very old, very valuable books.

Septimus chose several volumes while I gazed around myself in awe.

"I've never heard of half these books!"

"No." He smiled faintly.

"Do you keep them for the texts or for Perusing their previous owners?"

"It depends. On the text and on the owner." He handed me a gilt-edged volume. "Go ahead and Peruse to your heart's content."

"Truly? You don't mind?"

Septimus nodded. "We'll spend all day here if you like."

There followed one of the happiest afternoons I can ever recall. The books in that secret library were a treasure chest of fabulous sights and sounds and smells… Sometimes the jewel was the text. Sometimes the rush came from the imprint of a powerful previous personality.

> *Necile gathered the softest moss in all the forest for Claus to lie upon, and she made his bed in her own bower. Of food the infant had no lack. The nymphs searched the forest for bell-udders, which grow upon the goa-tree and when opened are found to be filled with sweet milk. And the soft-eyed does willingly gave a share of their milk to support the little stranger, while Shiegra, the lioness, often crept stealthily into Necile's bower and purred softly as she lay beside the babe and fed it.*

"That's sweet," I murmured, turning the browned page. I could feel many small ghostly hands turning the pages with me. Their smiles and laughter were like sunlight.

"Try this one," Septimus said.

It was like being hand-fed chocolates. I closed my eyes and rested my hand on the cover. This one had lain forgotten many years in a dusty attic. The imprint of previous readers was very faint. Twin sisters…an elderly collector…

> *The young man came swinging along, debonairly; he was whistling under his breath. He was a dapper figure in a long coat and a silk hat, under which the candles lighted a rather silly face. When he reached the spot on the sidewalk where the Flanton Dog lay, he paused a moment looking down. Then he poked the object with his stick. On the other side of the street a mother and her little boy were passing at the time. The child's eyes caught sight of the dog on the sidewalk, and he hung back, watching to see what the young man would do to it. But his mother drew him after her. Just then an automobile came panting through the snow. With a quick movement Cooper picked up the dog on the end of his stick and tossed it into the street, under the wheels of the machine.*

I shook my head. It was growing late and I was tired from Perusing so many books. I looked across at Septimus and he was watching me, smiling.

"Overwhelming after a time, isn't it?"

"A little. They're nearly unspoiled they've been so little touched since their last reading."

"One more then." He handed over the final book. The cover was of faded blue-and-amethyst silk, patterned with lotus and lilies. When I took the book in my hands, I felt a faint and funny tingling. I looked at Septimus in surprise.

His smile was almost rueful.

I turned the pages gently, but the book fell open to the place where it had been most read.

Juventius, if I could play at kissing
your honeyed eyes as often as I wished to,
300,000 games would not exhaust me;
never could I be satisfied or sated,
although the total of our osculations
were greater than the ears of grain at harvest.

I looked at Septimus and he cleared his throat a little self-consciously. "I knew you would have no difficulty Perusing that one."

I smiled and turned out the lamp.

VICTORIAN ROAST GOOSE RECIPE

INGREDIENTS

FOR THE STUFFING:

3 medium onions, peeled

4 large apples, peeled, cored and chopped (Bramleys for preference)

2 tablespoons crumbled dried sage leaves

½ teaspoon freshly-ground black pepper

1 tablespoon butter, finely cubed

FOR THE GRAVY:

Giblets and wing-tips of the goose, finely chopped

1 onion

1 carrot, sliced

2 tablespoons goose fat or cooking oil

600ml stock

1 bay leaf

3 sprigs parsley

1 sprig thyme

Salt and black pepper, to taste

4–5 kg goose

2 teaspoons coarse sea salt

DIRECTIONS

Prepare the goose by thoroughly rubbing the body cavity with the salt. If you don't want your stuffing to be overly oniony (I love the flavour, personally) parboil the onions in lightly-salted water for 10 minutes. Remove and allow to cool.

Chop the onion very finely then combine with the chopped apples, sage, pepper and butter. Use this to stuff both the neck and body cavities of the goose. Sew or skewer the openings close and truss the bird.

Place the bird in a roasting dish (preferably on top of a trivet or wire rack) and roast in an oven pre-heated to 230°C for 20 minutes.

Reduce the heat to 180°C and turn the goose onto its side and roast for a further hour. At this point turn the goose onto the other side and drain any excess fat from the roasting tin.

After an hour turn the goose onto its back and roast for a further 30 minutes. To ensure that the goose remains moist baste every 30 minutes. As a rule of thumb a goose should be cooked for 45 minutes per kg.

Whilst the goose is roasting prepare the gravy. Add the goose fat to a large pan and when sizzling add the goose parts, onion and carrot.

Cook until well browned then add the stock and seasonings. Allow to simmer, partially covered for an hour, skimming occasionally to remove any fat.

When ready strain and place in a warmed sauce boat to serve.

Serve with roast potatoes and all the trimmings.

VIC AND SEAN

UNTIL WE MEET ONCE MORE

"How'd it go?" Sean asked, opening the door to Vic's knock. He kept his voice down, so the old lady, Sean's Aunt Miriam, must be in bed. That was a relief. Vic had just about had his fill of female relations that night, though Aunt Miriam was practically another species from his own mother.

"It went the way you thought it would." Vic removed his scarf, shrugged out of his wool coat. Sean took them, limping over to the coat closet and hanging them neatly. Aunt Miriam was as fussy as a Fleet Admiral about keeping things shipshape.

"You okay?" he asked over his shoulder.

Vic nodded. "I could use a drink."

Sean nodded toward the sitting room, and they moved silently down the hallway.

There was a fire going in the hearth and a decanter of whisky on the table next to the arrangement of holly and candles. Vic flung himself down on the horsehair sofa while Sean poured out a pair of stiff drinks.

Sean watched Vic toss his back and said, "So we're right where we were before you went to see her. No harm, no foul."

Vic threw him a dour look. "She asked me what I thought I was doing by throwing away my brilliant career in politics."

Sean laughed. They both looked guiltily up at the ceiling with its broken ceiling medallion. But not a creature stirred. Not even a mouse. Though the old house probably had plenty of them.

Sean remarked, "I didn't realize you had a brilliant career in politics."

"Neither did I. Apparently I could have if I wanted it."

Sean snorted. Vic looked up out of his gloomy preoccupation long enough to be glad that Sean wasn't taking this personally. It wasn't personal, that was the weirdest thing about it. It should have been personal. The question of who her only child intended to spend the rest of his life with should have been of personal interest and importance to Abigail Stone.

"She informed me that as far as she was concerned there was no purpose to my military service if I wasn't going to use it as a springboard for the future."

Sean's brows rose. He took a thoughtful mouthful of whisky. "Sort of missing the point, isn't she?" he asked mildly. He had a right to ask, having nearly given his life, not to mention a lot of the use of his leg, in the service of his country.

Vic shook his head and finished his drink. Sean leaned forward and refilled his glass.

"Look, Stoney," he said crisply, "I know you're angry and disappointed, but the fact is, we're no worse off than we were."

"That money is mine. She has no right to block me from my inheritance."

Sean shook his head. "You'll get it eventually. In the meantime, I've got my savings and my disability. We're not going to starve."

Vic winced inwardly. His own retirement pay was negligible as he'd chosen to retire after a measly twelve years. At the time he'd made the decision he'd had plenty of options, though politics had not been one he'd seriously considered. "That money could make a big difference to us."

"Yeah? Well I, for one, am relieved I won't have the Manchurian Candidate's mom for my mother-in-law."

Their gazes met and after a long instant, Vic grinned. "True, right? Why the hell are you sitting over on the other side of the room?"

Sean rose and came around the low table to join Vic on the lumpy sofa. Vic put his arm around Sean's broad shoulders and pulled him closer still. "Ah hell. I know we'll be okay. I just wanted to…"

"Keep me in the style to which I've never been accustomed?" Sean was laughing at him now.

Vic grimaced. "Something like that."

The clock on the bookshelf began to chime. Twelve lazy, silvery chimes. Midnight.

"Merry Christmas," Sean said. He touched his glass to Vic's.

"Cheers. Anyway, Mother made a point of saying she had nothing against you personally. She always thought you were a nice boy."

"I am a nice boy."

"And if we wanted to see each other on a regular basis, she couldn't see why anyone would — could you stop laughing?" But Vic was laughing too now, reluctantly. His arm tightened around Sean. Maybe Sean was right. It was only money after all, and he'd gladly have given every cent he ever earned to have what he had at this very moment: Sean alive and well and in his arms.

Sean stopped laughing and said, "Hey, if it makes things easier for you, we don't have to move in together right away. We could —"

"Shut up, you," Vic growled.

"Make me." Sean smiled, eyes glinting in invitation.

And Vic did.

CLASSIC CHRISTMAS SUGAR COOKIES

INGREDIENTS

1 cup butter or margarine, softened

1 package (3 ounces) cream cheese, softened

¾ cup sugar

1 teaspoon vanilla

1 egg

3 cups all-purpose flour

⅛ teaspoon salt

DIRECTIONS

Preheat oven to 375°F.

Beat butter, cream cheese, sugar, vanilla and egg in large bowl with electric mixer on medium speed until light and fluffy. Stir in flour and salt until blended.

Cover and refrigerate dough at least 2 hours but no longer than 24 hours.

Roll one-fourth of dough at a time, ⅛-inch thick on lightly floured cloth-covered board. (Keep remaining dough refrigerated until ready to roll.)

Cut dough with assorted cookie cutters. Place about 1-inch apart on ungreased cookie sheet.

Bake 7 to 10 minutes or until light brown. Immediately remove from cookie sheet to wire rack. Cool completely. Decorate as desired.

RUGELACH (FILLED CREAM CHEESE COOKIES)

INGREDIENTS

DOUGH:

2 cups all purpose flour

2 tablespoons sugar

¼ teaspoon salt

1 cup (2 sticks) chilled unsalted butter, cut into ½-inch pieces

6 ounces chilled cream cheese, cut into ½-inch pieces

FILLING:

½ cup sugar

1 teaspoon ground cinnamon

12 tablespoons cherry preserves

8 tablespoons dried tart cherries

8 tablespoons miniature semisweet chocolate chips

8 tablespoons finely chopped walnuts

⅓ cup (about) whipping cream

DIRECTIONS

PREPARATION FOR DOUGH:

Blend first 3 ingredients in processor.

Add butter and cream cheese and cut in using on/off turns until dough begins to clump together.

Gather dough into ball. Divide dough into 4 equal pieces; flatten into disks.

Wrap each in plastic and refrigerate 2 hours. (Can be prepared 2 days ahead. Keep refrigerated. Let soften slightly at room temperature before rolling out.)

FOR FILLING:

Line large baking sheet with parchment paper.

Mix sugar and cinnamon in small bowl.

Roll out 1 dough disk on floured surface to 9-inch round.

Spread 3 tablespoons cherry preserves over dough, leaving 1-inch border.

Sprinkle with 2 tablespoons dried cherries, then 2 tablespoons chocolate chips, 2 tablespoons cinnamon sugar and 2 tablespoons walnuts.

Press filling firmly to adhere to dough.

Cut dough round into 8 equal wedges.

Starting at wide end of each wedge, roll up tightly. Arrange cookies, tip side down, on prepared baking sheet, spacing 1 ½ inches apart and bending slightly to form crescents.

Repeat 3 more times with remaining dough disks, preserves, dried cherries, chocolate chips, cinnamon sugar and walnuts.

Place baking sheet in freezer 30 minutes.

Position rack in center of oven and preheat to 375°F. Brush cookies lightly with whipping cream.

Bake frozen cookies until golden brown, about 40 minutes.

Transfer cookies to racks and cool completely. (Can be made ahead. Store in airtight container at room temperature up to 1 week or freeze up to 1 month.)

Makes about 32 cookies.

Helpful hint: Freezing the rugelach before baking helps the cookies maintain their shape.

WILL AND TAYLOR
FROM THE DANGEROUS GROUND SERIES

KICK START

The walkie-talkie crackled and Taylor said, "Romeo to Base."

Romeo? Will, who had been blowing on his hands to warm them, spluttered a laugh, and picked up his walkie-talkie. "Base."

"Refresh my memory. Whose idea was this again? Over."

Will grimaced, looked up at the stars burning bright and cold in the black night sky of the Mojave Desert. Not another light for miles out here. Nothing but Joshua trees and sand and the sharp cutout ridge of distant mountains. "Not sure now."

"Yeah, that's what I thought. Yours."

"Thanks for not saying I told you so."

Taylor's wicked laugh rustled across the six chilly miles of empty airwaves and Will's lips twitched in instinctive response. "That is one nasty laugh, buddy boy. I could get a search warrant based on that laugh."

"Base, standby," Taylor said, suddenly all business.

Will waited, his eyes scanning the darkness. Nothing moved in the sky or on the ground. He caught motion out of the corner of his eye. A shooting star. He smiled faintly. Taylor was not much for the great outdoors.

At the same time Taylor, sounding relaxed again, said, "Go ahead, Base."

"You were saying?" Will replied. It was only the two of them out here, after all.

"I was saying, this is one hell of a way to spend Christmas Eve."

Will was terse because he wasn't enjoying freezing his ass off any more than Taylor was, "We need the money."

The following silence stretched long enough to start sweat prickling on Will's hairline. They had left the DSS in October to start their own security consulting business. It was not a great time to start a business, even when you had the experience and qualifications. Taylor had gone along with Will's plan, but Will had the uneasy feeling his partner was still…withholding judgment.

"Copy that," Taylor said at last. "Doesn't change the fact that we're currently one step up from snipers."

Will started breathing again. "Not if we don't shoot anybody."

Taylor said darkly, "That depends on how much longer we're stuck out here."

Will peered at the luminous dial of his watch. "I make it half an hour."

He could feel Taylor's sigh though the walkie-talkie remained silent. Taylor hated this op for a dozen reasons, starting with the fact that it was Christmas Eve and ending with the fact that any half-awake civilian with a radio and a pair of binoculars could have handled this. They were simply providing backup for the backup.

"I'll make it up to you, Romeo," Will said suddenly, surprising himself.

"Roger so far." There was a smile in Taylor's voice. "Should we switch to a secure channel?"

Will was reminded of all those crazy phone calls Taylor had made to him while Will was posted in Paris. In fact, the memory of those calls warmed him now. Well, what the hell. Why not? It was just them and the coyotes, and any smart coyote was safely curled in his den, dreaming of rabbits and the spring. "Affirmative," he said.

"Yeah?" Taylor sounded alert and interested.

Will realized with blinding clarity that there was no going wrong with this, anything he said would, at the least, make Taylor laugh. But Taylor wouldn't laugh. Will realized that too. Realized that however awkward he was at verbalizing…stuff, the very attempt would mean something to Taylor. Taylor, who spent more than his fair share of time putting it all on the line. Phone lines included.

"Yeah," Will said boldly. "That's right, Romeo. They don't call me Roger Wilco for nothing."

ONE YEAR LATER

"Roger Wilco." Taylor started to laugh.

"I don't recall hearing any objections," Will said mildly. "Then or later."

"No and you won't." Taylor lounged back in his chair and grinned at him.

Will leaned across the table and topped up Taylor's glass again.

"You trying to get me drunk, William?"

"I shorely am," Will drawled. Not drunk enough to ruin Christmas morning for either of them, just drunk enough to put Taylor in that agreeably pliable and affectionate mood his rare boozing triggered.

Taylor laughed again and reached for his glass.

ADRIEN AND JAKE
FROM THE ADRIEN ENGLISH MYSTERIES

THE DARK TIDE

A touch so light, so delicate, it was hardly more than a breath, a sigh tracing the length of my throat…bisecting my chest…and then, to my relief, diverging from the roadmap of scars, off-roading to flick the tip of my right nipple.

I arched off the bed. Not far, since my hands were tied to the headboard — tied loosely and with something soft. Silk scarves? I could free myself in an instant, but it wasn't about freedom, was it?

The teasing touch moved to the tip of my other nipple.

I gasped. "That tickles!"

"It's a feather." I could hear the smile in Jake's voice.

"Ah."

The feather ghosted its way over my ribcage…down to my abdomen. I sucked in a breath as the feather dusted and danced still lower…

"How's that feel?"

I nodded. Everything felt lovely, from the cool, crisp linen sheets to Jake's warm breath against my face. The feather teased and thrilled as it brushed across my thigh…groin…thigh…

I wriggled one of my hands free and pulled off the blindfold.

The hotel room was nearly dark in the fading afternoon light. Jake gazed down at me, his mouth quirking. "I wondered how long that would last."

"I like to look at you," I said. "I like to touch you."

He nodded, pulled the other scarf off, freeing my wrist. He lowered himself beside me on the wide four-poster bed, touched the tip of a drooping white peacock feather to my nose. I laughed and blew at the bobbing green-blue eye of the feather.

"How long before your mother's knocking on the door again, do you think?"

"I've got the Do Not Disturb sign out."

"Baby, you're an optimist."

"Maybe." I smiled at him, looped my arm around his neck, pulling him down to me. He kissed me. I kissed him back. "Next year we're staying home for Christmas. I don't care who comes up with what plan."

"Uh huh."

He rested his head on my chest. For a time we lay there, breathing in soft unison, the muted sounds of London traffic providing a soundtrack to our thoughts.

"Regrets?" I asked at last.

Jake raised his head, studying me. He leaned back on his elbow. "No regrets."

I smiled faintly.

He reached out, brushed the hair out of my eyes. "That's not right. I have regrets. I regret the gutless, asinine things I did, the people I hurt. I regret hurting you. I regret the time I wasted. But if all those gutless, asinine things were somehow part of how I got to this moment, then no. I don't regret anything."

Considering what a painful journey he'd had to get to this moment, I thought that was a brave statement.

"You?" Jake asked. "Regrets?"

"Just the time we wasted."

"We're not wasting any more time." He reached around, found the feather.

I could feel my smile turning wry. "Is this going to be enough for you?"

He looked puzzled for an instant. Then his expression grew grave. "This? No. The feather and blindfold routine in an overpriced hotel? No. I need more. I admit it. I need entire nights and entire days. Hundreds of them. Thousands of them. I need breakfast and lunch and dinner and every dessert we can squeeze in. I need every minute we can get."

"For as long as we both shall live?"

"Yeah. That's pretty much it."

I closed my eyes, smiling. "I guess that'll work."

His laugh was quiet. I felt him bend over me, felt his mouth graze mine... My eyes shot open at the soft tap-tap-tapping on our room door.

PIMM'S CUP

INGREDIENTS

Ice cubes

4 lemon slices

4 cucumber slices

1 cup seltzer or lemon-lime or ginger ale soda

1 cup lemonade

3 cups Pimm's No. 1 Cup, available at liquor stores

DIRECTIONS

Fill 4 (8 to 10-ounce) highball glasses with ice cubes. Divide the lemon and cucumber slices among the glasses.

In a large pitcher, pour in the seltzer, lemonade and Pimm's. Stir to combine. Pour mixture into prepared glasses.

Cheers!

TRADITIONAL BRITISH SHERRY TRIFLE

INGREDIENTS

6 ounces Madeira, sponge or pound cake, halved and cut into thick slices
(OR 1x160g packet trifle sponges if you actually live in Britain)

3 tablespoons sweet sherry

1x135g block jelly made up to one pint (Oh dear!)

10 ounces fresh strawberries or raspberries, or defrosted frozen ones plus
a few extra for decoration

1 to 2 cups thick home made custard following this recipe or,

1x500ml packet ready made custard

2 cups double or whipping cream, softly whipped

Handful flaked almonds, toasted (optional)

DIRECTIONS

The trifle can be made in one large glass dish or into individual
glasses. Line the bottom of the dish or glasses with the cake slices
or trifle sponges. Sprinkle with the sherry and leave to soak for 5
minutes.

If using fresh strawberries, slice thickly (reserve a few for decoration); if using frozen leave whole. Otherwise, lay the fruit evenly
over the cake. Press lightly with a fork to release the juices.

Pour over the liquid jelly making sure it covers the sponge. Place
the dish into the refrigerator and leave until the jelly is set.

Once set, spoon over the custard, again in a thick layer.

Finally, finish with a thick layer of whipped cream either spooned
over or piped using a piping bag.

Decorate with strawberry slices or raspberries, and toasted, flaked
almonds if using.

Serves 6. (Jake will probably eat Adrien's serving)

CHRISTMAS
WALTZ

HOLIDAY CODAS 2

JOSH LANYON

GRIFF AND PIERCE

STRANGER
ON THE SHORE

Kind.

That was the word. People were kind. Very kind. And curious. Because…what a story. Long-lost heir returns after twenty years. Mystery solved. Happy endings all around. Well…mostly.

It was going to make a hell of a book, though Griff was no longer sure he was the right person to write it. It was definitely different being one of the principal players in a case. It gave you a whole new perspective.

But anyway, no need to make a decision on that. Not right away. In the meantime…Christmas.

Jarrett had gone full out. Making up for lost time. And, more dismaying, looking ahead to a future where he wouldn't be around to celebrate holidays.

"After all, I'm not getting any younger, my boy," he had said when Griff had tried to talk him out of arranging fireworks on Christmas Eve.

A private fireworks show? That was just...

But Griff didn't have the heart to squash Jarrett's enthusiasm. Jarrett's heart attack had scared him. Scared Jarrett too, which was why he kept chirping ominous things about not being around forever.

"Don't say that," Griff would say to Jarrett, and Jarrett would pat him fondly on the shoulder or the back. At least he didn't pat Griff on the top of the head and tell him to go play, so that was something to be grateful for.

The Christmas Eve Ball—yes, *ball*, not a cocktail party; formal dress was required—was enormous. In fact, the word "enormous" really didn't seem to do this lavish extravaganza justice. It seemed like everybody on Long Island showed up, certainly everyone in Syosset was there. There was a dance band playing big band numbers, which gave an idea of the type of event it was. There were ice sculptures and caterers (sometimes it was hard to tell the difference). The towering Christmas tree was decked in generations' worth of glittering and hand-painted antique ornaments. Miles of pine garland—the real thing—wreathed the staircases and hallways. Everybody in attendance got presents, including the waitstaff. Griff received a ridiculously expensive watch, which merely seemed to emphasize that time was fleeting and it would be best to pick his battles.

He drank a lot of champagne. Not his beverage of choice, but he was nervous and tense and self-conscious. It was all that kindness. People trying very hard to show that he was accepted and welcomed. Which he appreciated. He did. But he didn't enjoy feeling like a charity case. Life had not been a picnic for him growing up, but he also had never felt like some sad, pathetic victim. Until all that kindness was directed his way.

So he smiled and drank more champagne and wondered if Pierce was going to make it or not. Pierce had been delayed over a juvenile-court matter, and Griff very much loved the fact that Pierce was willing to give up his Christmas Eve for some kid caught in the rigid machinery of the legal system, but... It would have been easier if Pierce had been with him this evening.

And tomorrow would be just as tiring. Christmas dinner here with Jarrett and Marcus and Muriel. Chloe had opted to spend the holidays in San Francisco with Michaela, who was unable to forgive Griff for turning out to be Brian. Well, it really wasn't about that, but either way Griff understood. He was surprised to find how much he missed Chloe, though. Her unguarded and occasionally outrageous comments came as a relief sometimes.

Later that same day there would be a second Christmas dinner with Pierce's parents. They still didn't know what to make of Griff and Pierce's relationship, but treated Griff with unfailing kindness.

More kindness. From every direction. Sometimes he wasn't sure he could hold up under the weight of it.

He was standing on the fringe of the crowd gazing out the window at the red, green, and silver fireworks, when warm lips nuzzled the back of his neck. Griff jumped and turned, swallowing a laugh, already registering Pierce's aftershave and cologne—or maybe it was something more fundamental. The almost electric energy of Pierce's presence.

Pierce, unsurprisingly, looked fantastic in a tux. He probably owned a couple of them. White and black? This one was black and severe and suited Pierce's classic handsomeness. He was smiling, but as his amber gaze studied Griff, his own smile faded. His expression grew attentive and, yes, kind.

"Feeling overwhelmed?" he asked softly.

"It's beautiful," Griff replied, conscious of the crowd around them, conscious that people were trying not to look like they were listening.

"Which doesn't answer my question." Pierce drew Griff away from the crowd at the window. "Come and buy me a drink."

Yeah, like it wasn't a hosted bar. But Griff obligingly went along to the bar with Pierce. Pierce ordered Black Velvet. Griff declined another champagne cocktail.

"Ah." Pierce took a long, grateful sip.

"Everything go okay?" Griff asked.

Pierce nodded noncommittally. Then he smiled. "Glad I made it home before Santa arrived."

"Yeah, well, we're not home yet." Not true. Technically Griff was home, but these days home was really Pierce's house in Syosset.

"We can leave right now," Pierce said. He was perfectly serious. "Say the word."

Griff shook his head. "I can't do that to Jarrett."

Pierce considered him, then sipped his drink. *Your Honor, I refuse to answer on the grounds I might incriminate myself.*

Griff watched him. To look at Pierce, you'd never believe he'd ever experienced even a moment of self-doubt. But Griff knew him better now.

"I have to ask you something," he said finally.

"Yes," Pierce answered promptly.

Griff laughed. "You don't know what I'm going to ask."

Pierce winked at him. Man, that effortless, assured charm. It was effective, no doubt about it.

"But it's kind of private," Griff said.

"Then the answer is definitely yes." But Pierce put a hand beneath Griff's elbow, guiding him away to a little alcove where they could only be overheard by the Fontanini angels.

"You can be honest with me," Griff said. "I want you to be honest, even if you think it's going to hurt me."

Pierce stopped smiling. He said quietly, "I'm always honest with you."

"You are, but this is something you may not be honest with yourself about."

Now Pierce was frowning. He said, "Go on."

Unexpectedly, it was hard to say the words.

Griff struggled for a moment and then said, "Are we together because you feel bad about the past?"

"I don't think you should drink champagne," Pierce said.

"It's a serious question."

Pierce didn't answer for so long that Griff began to wish he hadn't asked. Don't pose any question you couldn't bear to hear answered truthfully. Rules for Happy Living. He wanted, maybe even needed, to believe what he and Pierce had was real, but it was that damned newshound instinct. He just couldn't help pushing to find out the truth. If it killed him.

And for a couple of seconds, it felt like it might.

Pierce said slowly, carefully, like the lawyer he was, "Are you asking me if I feel sorry for you?"

"No. I know you don't feel sorry for me. But I know you feel guilty about the past. And I wonder if—"

"No." Pierce spoke with utter conviction. "I wish I'd done some things differently, yes. But you should know me well enough by now to know however sorry I feel about what's past, I wouldn't cheat both of us out of a chance at future happiness because of misplaced guilt."

"Because this really matters to me."

"It really matters to me too," Pierce said.

"Everybody is trying so hard to make up for what happened, and I just don't want that between us."

"That's not what is happening here. That is not what is between us."

"I don't want that. Not for us." Maybe he was a bit insistent, but it seemed very important that Pierce understand this point, but also that he understood what Griff was not saying aloud.

And maybe Pierce did because his lean cheek creased in a reluctant smile. "I swear to tell the truth and only the truth. Now you tell me something. How much of that champagne did you drink?"

"I may have lost count."

"You may have. Not that glassy-eyed doesn't look good on you."

"'Coz I'm not going to ask again."

"No, we've talked it out, and it's settled," Pierce agreed. He was relaxed and confident again. Also amused. A little.

But that was okay. That was what you wanted with someone you were hoping to spend the rest of your…Christmas with.

"What are you smiling about?" Pierce asked softly, leaning closer.

"Hm? Not sure," Griff evaded.

"Well, let me give you a good reason." Pierce kissed him, then kissed him again. On the third kiss, the Fontanini angels blushed.

BLACK VELVET COCKTAIL

What I like about Pierce's taste for Black Velvet cocktails is that they reflect his appetite for both earthy and elegant. These cocktails are a heady mix of champagne and Guinness.

INGREDIENTS

Your favorite champagne (or sparkling wine)
Guinness

DIRECTIONS

Pour the champagne into a tall glass or a champagne flute. Slowly pour the stout on top. Keep an eye on the balance. (It should be about half and half.)

CON AND WES

EVERYTHING I KNOW

"What did you want for Christmas?" Wes asked.

It was asked absently, almost in afterthought as they ate a late dinner at Wes's house. It was the week before Christmas vacation began. Wes was working more overtime than usual, trying to finish up a couple of construction projects before the year's end—and since he always worked a lot of overtime, Con felt like they'd barely seen each other in weeks.

Of course that was as much due to Con's schedule as Wes's. Between school and the regular drives up north to visit his mother...

"I want to spend Christmas together," Con said.

Wes smiled, his brown eyes warm. "We're definitely spending Christmas together."

But they already knew that. They were having Christmas dinner at Wes's mom. Lizzy would be back East, spending the holiday with her mom and Grammy Angie, so it was just Con and Wes—and Wes's mom and Wes's job.

Con understood. They both lived busy lives. He just wished sometimes it could be him and Wes. Just the two of them. But even when it was just the two of them, like right now, Wes was often distracted, preoccupied with work. He was a workaholic.

Which Con respected. Even admired. But…

Wes leaned over—Con craned to meet his kiss—and Wes's affectionate expression changed. "Hey," he growled. "What are you doing up?"

Con sighed inwardly.

"I want a drink of water," Lizzy said from behind him.

Con and Wes drew apart again. Lizzy padded across the kitchen floor in her pink nightie and fluffy pink robe, heading straight for Con.

"Do you think Connor is a drinking fountain?" Wes was still trying to hang on to the forbidding Papa Bear voice, but Lizzy just giggled and reached out for Con to pull her onto his lap, which of course he did. She smelled like bubble bath and little girl.

"You're supposed to be in bed," Con told her as Lizzy made herself comfortable.

She gave him a look of sweet understanding. She had both of them wrapped around her littlest little finger. And well she knew it.

"How about a tune-up for that death trap you drive?" Wes suggested.

It took Con a second to remember they had been discussing Christmas presents.

"You don't have to do that," he said uncomfortably, picking his fork up again. They were having casserole. Wes was a master of casseroles. He had a casserole for every occasion—and occasions no one other than the Campbell Soup people ever conceived of. This one had ground beef and noodles. Actually, they almost all had ground beef and noodles. Con chewed and considered.

He didn't want to reject a potential gift if that's what Wes wanted to give him. And it wasn't really about the money because they had had several talks about money, and Wes had done his best to reassure Con on that score. It did continue to bug Con that he was always in the position of "taking." But in their last conversation, Wes had asked him to please stop talking about "taking," and Wes had been serious.

"You don't talk about giving and taking in a relationship. Not like that," Wes had said, as though he had experience at relationships.

But then again, remembering some of the problems with Eric, maybe Wes was right. Maybe his instincts were the truer.

"I know I don't have to," Wes said now. "But I worry about you driving back at night and breaking down on the road somewhere."

This was delicate ground. Once before, Wes had offered to loan Con the money for car repairs and he had declined. When Wes had pressed him, Con had gotten snappish. That was before the big talk about giving and taking.

"That would be a thoughtful gift," Con said, making an effort.

Wes's mouth firmed like he was trying very hard not to make any sound or expression that would lead Con to think he was being laughed at. "Okay, we'll see what Santa thinks," he said briskly. He looked at Lizzy. "Speaking of Santa, I think he's checking his list right about now."

"Ha ha ha!" Lizzy chortled.

Or maybe it was "Ho ho ho!"

* * * * *

"Well, what are you getting Wes?" Pip asked.

They were on the playground, gazes trained on the two-legged whirlwinds kicking up sand and filling the air with shrieks. The kids were always wild in the days before the winter break.

"Not sure. He's not easy to buy for." If Wes needed something, he bought it. And he bought the best he could afford. But he didn't go in for a lot of toys and gadgets. Unless the toys and gadgets were for Lizzy. Lizzy was Wes's weakness. And Miss Lizzy was the original material girl.

"Surprise him," Pip advised. "Go for something totally romantic."

Con assented noncommittally. He'd feel silly trying to buy Wes a romantic gift. Like what? Wes was so…pragmatic. Plus, Wes didn't like surprises. No, Con would be getting Wes some kind of gift certificate—if he could think of something both inexpensive and personal enough. His own finances were severely limited. Of course you didn't have to have money to give someone a wonderful Christmas gift, but you did need time, and he had as little of that as he did cold cash. It was frustrating because it was their first Christmas together. He'd have liked it to be special.

Just the fact that it was their first Christmas made it special. And hopefully there would be other Christmases even more special.

"Robin, stop throwing sand," Pip shouted. In normal tones she said, "Do you think he's going to ask you to move in?"

"I don't know." Con doubted it. Not in the short term, anyway. Not that Wes was rigid exactly, but he had everything just the way he liked it in his life. He was not particularly adventurous, and he was definitely not experimental.

"You're spending a lot of time together."

"Yeah, but he said early on he didn't want to send any confusing messages to Lizzy."

"That was in the beginning. You guys have been together for a couple of months now."

"I don't sleep over there on the nights Liz is home. Which is still most nights."

As though choreographed, they turned their backs as a gust of wind sent a small dust devil skipping and hopping toward them. Or maybe that was just a very sandy kid wishing to lodge a complaint.

When they turned to face the yard again, Pip said, "If he asked you to move in, would you?"

"Yeah."

Pip threw him a curious look. "You're that sure?"

Con nodded. He was. Yes. He loved Wes. But he knew what Pip was really saying. Wes was older; he had a kid and a job that took up most of his time and attention. He was a passionate and attentive lover, but he was not Prince Charming. Pip thought Con deserved Prince Charming. She thought he deserved moonlight and roses and champagne. Wes was fine for now, but Con would be settling for less if he moved in with Wes. That was Pip's view.

But as much as Con would have liked moonlight and roses and champagne, he understood Wes. He was like Wes in a lot of ways. He liked security and stability, and he understood all about responsibility and commitment.

He didn't think moving in with Wes would be "settling." He also didn't think that would be happening anytime soon.

* * * * *

"Con," Wes said abruptly.

Con looked up. It was Thursday night, and they were having another late dinner at Wes's. He'd be heading home after dinner because Lizzy was not staying over at her mom's after all. It was disappointing, but it couldn't be helped. Tomorrow night wouldn't work because Con would be driving north to visit his mother. In fact, that's what he'd mostly been thinking about, that he should have let Wes take his car in for a tune-up because the engine was making that weird ticking sound again.

At the grim expression on Wes's face, the tuna casserole he'd just swallowed seemed to lodge in his throat. "What's wrong?" he got out around the lump of tuna and noodle.

"I think I made a mistake," Wes said.

"About what?" Con tried to sound neutral, but given the precarious start to their relationship, maybe his instant anxiety wasn't unreasonable. Or maybe it was just that tuna casserole didn't agree with him. One casserole too many?

Wes was still gazing at him with that uncharacteristic mix of unease and worry. "I wanted to surprise you, but I just realized maybe…"

"You made a mistake?"

"Maybe." Color rose in Wes's face. "The thing is, we haven't had a lot of time to ourselves, and you've been working so hard, I just thought maybe you'd like something…different. Something more…"

Wes seemed to be waiting for Con to fill in the blank. Con said cautiously, "More…different?"

Wes gave a tiny shake of his head. "Romantic," he said in a pained tone.

"Romantic?" Con echoed in astonishment.

Wes went redder. "Yeah. I thought over what you said about spending Christmas together, and I thought if we went away somewhere for a few days where we wouldn't have any interruptions—"

"We're going away for Christmas?"

"If you want to," Wes said. "I probably should have asked. I *know* I should have asked. I know you're not crazy about surprises."

"I'm not?" Con felt like laughing—and he felt like crying—and he wasn't even sure why. "Where are we going for Christmas?"

"Hawaii," Wes said. "Blue water, white sand."

"Moonlight and roses?" Con suggested. "Champagne?"

"Er, sure. If that's what you want," Wes said, but he was starting to smile too, looking more like his usual assured and capable self. "I want our first Christmas together to be..."

Con missed the rest of that. *Our first Christmas together.* Those were the words he needed to hear. Everything else was fine by him.

He glanced over his shoulder at the empty hallway and then leaned forward. "It already is," he said.

WORLD'S BEST TUNA NOODLE CASSEROLE

INGREDIENTS

10½ ounces cream of chicken soup

½ cup mayonnaise

¼ cup milk

½ cup diced yellow onion

½ cup diced celery

6 ounces albacore tuna

6 ounces cooked egg noodles

¼ cup shredded Cheddar cheese

Salt and pepper to taste

DIRECTIONS

Mix the cream of chicken, mayonnaise, and milk together in a large bowl. Add the diced celery and onion.

Fold in the tuna, followed by the cooked egg noodles and shredded Cheddar cheese. Season with salt and pepper.

Place in a casserole dish.

Cook at 375°F for about 40-45 minutes, just until the top starts to brown. Feeds 4-6.

CAREY AND WALTER

Slings and Arrows

"Everything is not a joke," Walter said.

Which was a clue to how tense he was about the upcoming Christmas dinner with his father and his father's new wife. Walter usually liked Carey's sense of humor.

"I don't think everything is a joke," Carey said, surprised.

"Of course you do." That was so unfair it almost seemed like Walter was trying to pick a fight. Which really was out of character.

Carey didn't enjoy confrontation, and he sure as hell didn't want to fight with Walter, so he was quiet. Walter turned away and walked to the frost-edged window of the apartment, staring bleakly out at the night. In the raw silence, Carey could hear the departing wail of a distant train.

"Maybe you shouldn't go," Walter said finally.

"Go?"

"Come. To Christmas," Walter said tersely. He turned to face Carey, his gold-rimmed spectacles glinting blankly, his expression withdrawn.

It was unexpected and painful. So painful that it took Carey a moment to say, "Look, Walt. I…know how to act in public. I'm not going to chew with my mouth open or talk about what we do in bed."

Walter's expression went tighter, closed like a fist.

"I don't…understand," Carey said at last.

"I've changed my mind," Walter said with the same cold preciseness he'd used back when he'd been Dr. Bing's teaching assistant rebuffing all slackers and goof-offs. "I don't think it would be a good idea for you to come with me. You can go to your parents', correct? They'll be happy to have you stay for a few days. We both know you'll have a better time there."

Carey swallowed. He was afraid the sound was audible. But Walter's expression did not change. He was not going to relent. He did not want Carey to go with him. It was that simple. Simple as an arrow through the heart.

Carey said stiffly, "In that case, maybe I should just leave tonight." He couldn't imagine lying next to Walter in that perfectly appointed bedroom with all this between them. Hurt. Anger. Bewilderment.

"I think that's a good idea," Walter said.

* * * * *

Was it over?

Carey wasn't sure.

They had been together for just under a year. Walter loved him. He loved Walter. There was no question of that. There was no question that they were happy together. But Walter could be odd. Odd and hurtful. And Carey wasn't sure that love was enough.

Four months ago Walter's father had abruptly remarried. Walter had attended the small, private civil service without Carey. It had sort of bothered Carey, but he had understood. There was no love lost between Walter and his father.

"Believe me, you don't want to go," Walter had told him at the time.

"I want to go if you want me there."

"I don't want you there," Walter had said.

That was Walter at his most bluntly honest, but Carey had forborne to take offense. The little Walter had shared about his childhood had been alarming to someone who had grown up in a big, noisy, affectionate clan like Carey's. No wonder Walter had a few, well, intimacy issues.

When Walter had returned, he had said the wedding went smoothly and that he thought his new stepmother would suit his father. Carey had not pressed for more information. He was not sure he wanted to know.

But this was Christmas. Their first Christmas together. This mattered to Carey. Not least because they had both been invited to spend it at Walter's family estate. And they had accepted. Together. As a couple.

Otherwise they could have spent it at Carey's family—where they would always be welcome with or without formal invitation—together and as a couple.

Instead they would be celebrating Christmas apart. And Carey wasn't completely sure if they still were a couple or not. Was Walter ashamed of him? Did Walter really think Carey would make inappropriate jokes or use the wrong fork or…

Or was it something else?

Something even worse?

Who knew with Walter…

This time Carey didn't feel like being understanding or patient. It took him less than fifteen minutes to pack his suitcase (later he discovered he'd forgotten his toothbrush) and headed straight for the front door.

Walter was still staring out the window at the black and starless night. He didn't turn around, and he didn't say anything to stop Carey.

"Have yourself a merry little Christmas," Carey said bitterly. He regretted that crack later, but at least he refrained from slamming the door.

* * * * *

Christmas Day passed without a word from Walter.

Carey had told himself he wasn't expecting to hear from him, but the letdown was something akin to discovering Santa had skipped your zip code. His family showed unusual discretion and tactfully didn't ask.

It was a nice Christmas. It was a Christmas like all the Christmases that had come before it. And probably all the Christmases that would come after. The thing that would have made it different, remarkable, memorable was Walter.

"Maybe next year," his sister Susan said, and Carey smiled noncommittally.

He stayed over the weekend. Walter wasn't flying back until Monday anyway, so there was no reason to hurry home.

On Monday Carey debated staying another night, but it was starting to feel like he was hiding out. If he didn't go home, he needed a reason, and that reason would have to be there was something seriously wrong between him and Walter.

If he went home now, they could pretend it had just been an ordinary, run-of-the-mill argument. Carey wasn't sure he was ready to face it being more than that. Once he'd stopped being so angry, he'd started missing Walter. He still loved Walter. Doubts about the future didn't change that.

But sooner or later they were going to have to face it. Whatever *it* was.

* * * * *

The minute Carey unlocked the front door, he knew Walt was home.

The apartment was silent, but the silence had a living, breathing quality. Relieved, Carey pushed open the door and walked inside.

There was a neat tower of expensively wrapped red and green parcels on the chrome and glass coffee table. His own gift to Walt, a plum-colored cashmere pullover, hung over the arm of the sofa. All other signs of Christmas had been cleared away. Walt was in the kitchen, making a grilled-cheese sandwich.

He looked up at Carey's entrance. "How was your family?" he asked.

"Fine," Carey said. "How was yours?"

"Fine." Walter was unsmiling and serious. But that was usual for Walt.

"Did you have a nice Christmas?" Carey asked.

"It was all right," Walter said politely. "How was yours?"

Carey opened his mouth. But he couldn't do it. Couldn't play the game, couldn't be a part of this. He wasn't built like Walter. His former relief that everything could go back to normal vanished—because this was not normal.

"I missed you," he said. "But I guess I better get used to that."

Walter's pale, bony face reddened. "Carey—"

Carey waited, but Walter didn't go on.

Carey let out a long weary sigh. He hadn't realized how tired he was. It was the effort of holding back all that sadness and worry. But there was no holding it back now. "That's what I thought," he said.

"What did you think?" Walter turned off the stove and came across the kitchen to Carey, but Carey put a hand up to stop him. Walter did stop. He looked stricken.

"Carey," he said in a very different voice.

"I don't know any way to explain it that I'm not going to sound childish or petty," Carey said. "But this isn't about where we spend the holiday. Or how we celebrate, except that holidays are for spending with the people we love."

"Next year we'll spend it with your family," Walter said quickly.

"No. I don't think we will because…" Carey swallowed but made himself go on. "I'm not sure we'll be together next year. I don't think we will be."

Walter put a hand out to grip the back of one of the kitchen table chairs—as if Carey had punched him. No, more like Carey had delivered some mortal blow. "Of course we're going to be together," Walter said. He sounded almost frightened. "I love you, and I know you love me."

"I do," Carey admitted. "But I just spent the most unhappy five days of my entire life. And I don't even know why."

"Why what?"

"Why it had to be that way. You shut me out—and not the first time—and there's no debate, no discussion. It's just the way it is. And then when you decide to open the door again, everything goes back to the way it was. Except now I'll be waiting for the next time the door slams."

"It's not like that," Walter said. "If I'm…if I'm closing doors, it's to protect you."

"Give me a break, Walt," Carey said, surprised to find himself getting angry.

"It's true."

Carey shook his head and turned away. Walter caught his arm. "Wait."

Carey stared at Walter, seeing the jump of his Adam's apple, the little nerve pulsing in his cheek. He seemed unaware his fingers were digging into Carey's forearm. Walter kept himself in tight check all the time. Only with Carey did he ever let his guard down.

"I love you, and I don't want to lose you," Walter whispered.

It killed him to hurt Walter. "I love you too, but we're already losing each other if we can't be honest."

"Wait. Listen to me," Walter said. "Just…listen."

Walter didn't go on, but Carey listened anyway. And he did feel like there was some kind of plea in Walter's struggling silence.

"Walt," he said helplessly. "*Talk to me.*"

"I don't want you to see me like they do," Walter burst out. "I don't want you to see me through their eyes."

"I don't. I wouldn't. What does that even mean?"

Walter flushed red and then went very pale. His voice was almost inaudible as he said, "I don't know why you love me, but you do. And I don't want you to stop. I know it's not logical. It's not rational. But I don't want you to change toward me."

Relief washed through Carey. This was one explanation that had not occurred. Maybe it should have, knowing even the little he did about Walter's childhood. He was shocked too. Shocked by how much damage Walter's parents had casually inflicted on their only child… shocked because it was clear to him that Walter had come to terms with it, accepted it. Accepted the warped views of those shallow, selfish, *stupid* people.

He was still angry, but now it was on Walter's behalf. "I'm not going to change."

"You don't know that."

"Yes. I do."

Walter shook his head. "Sometimes, even now, it's a struggle for me not to see myself like they do."

"They don't see you at all. If they did, they'd know you're strong and smart and kind and a *great* person. A great man."

Walter's smile was strange. He didn't bother to argue. Like he thought Carey was delusional, but that he found his madness charming.

"You have to have some faith in me."

"I do. This is about not having faith in myself."

Carey said carefully, "But it's also about not having faith in me and what I feel for you. If you think my feelings can be changed by someone else's bad opinion, you must not know I love you."

"I know you love me." There was a touch of the old, arrogant Walter. It was kind of a relief to see it.

"That's right. I do. And I don't want a stack of expensive presents. I want you. All of you. The good and the bad. The real you. Isn't that how you want me?"

Walter said instantly, "Of course."

"Buying a bunch of presents is like something your dad would do."

Walter looked startled and then dismayed. "It wasn't like that. I just want you to feel appreciated."

Carey started to smile. It was going to be okay after all. This was something they could work on. Together. Happiness filled the hollow ache he'd carried inside for the past five days.

Watching him, Walter smiled tentatively in response. He drew Carey toward him, and this time Carey yielded.

He said softly, "Okay, well, as far as making me feel appreciated, I've got a couple of ideas…"

PILLSBURY BACON CHEESE PULL-APARTS

The SO and I have this for breakfast A LOT during the holidays. It's obviously not a very healthy choice, but it is delicious and very quick to prepare.

INGREDIENTS

2 eggs

¼ cup of milk

1 can (16.3 ounces) Pillsbury Grands! Flaky Layers refrigerated biscuits

1 (2.1 ounces) pkg. precooked bacon, cut into ½-inch pieces

1 cup shredded Cheddar cheese (I use a Cheddar-Jack mix)

¼ cup finely chopped green onions (4 medium-size onions)

DIRECTIONS

Heat oven to 350°F. Spray 11x7 or 12x8-inch (2-quart) glass baking dish with cooking spray or smear with butter. Beat egg and milk with wire whisk until smooth. Salt and pepper to taste. Separate dough into 8 biscuits and cut each into quarters. Gently stir biscuit pieces into egg mixture to coat evenly. Fold in bacon, cheese, and onions. Spoon mixture into sprayed dish; arrange biscuit pieces in single layer.

Bake at 350°F for 28 minutes or until golden-brown. Cut into squares. Feeds 3-4 hungry people on Christmas morning.

RYO AND KAI

BLOOD RED BUTTERFLY

Ryo had probably had worse Christmases. He couldn't remember one, though.

First, he had to work. That was a drag, but he was the new man on the totem pole at Barton and Ross Investigations, so fair enough. He was the guy pulling stakeout duty on Christmas morning. Somebody had to be. Too bad, because it was his and Kai's first holiday as a couple, but he could wait a few hours to see what goodies Santa brought him. Except what Santa had brought seemed to be strife and unhappiness.

Ryo shifted position behind the wheel of the sedan. His butt ached from sitting for hours. Though not as much as his heart ached.

You were supposed to be honest with the people you loved, right? You didn't tell them lies to keep the peace or make life easier on yourself. So when Kai had started in about how Laurel and *Ojiisan* were forcing Kenji to spend Christmas with them, Ryo had intervened.

"Dude, you have to think about what's best for Kenji," he had said.

"I *am* thinking of that!" Kai had snarled. He was pacing up and down the living room floor, past the towering Christmas tree piled with gifts and toys for his little son. "It's our first Christmas together."

"Yeah, so you've said about a dozen times now. But if Kenji wants to be with his mother and Oji—"

"Laurel's lying!"

"Dude."

"It doesn't matter. It's *my* turn. I've waited and waited for this." Kai's fox-brown eyes glittered dangerously in his pale, furious face.

No wonder the kid was scared of him.

But Ryo did not say that. There were some truths you could not ever share. Instead he said, "Look, what do a few hours matter? He'll be here the day after Christmas, right? He'll love it. He gets two Christmases for the price of one."

"It's not the same! This was our first Christmas. You're not going to be here. Now Kenji's not going to be here." Kai whirled away again and started another lap of the festively decorated room.

He'd gone all out. It looked—and smelled—like Santa's Village in there. Garland and candles and a couple of life-size reindeer statues. Whatever. If it made him happy, it made Ryo happy.

But then disaster. Laurel had called to say Kenji now wanted to spend Christmas Day at home. He was worried that Santa might not find him at his father's or some such excuse. The thing was, Kenji didn't really need an excuse. Not in Ryo's opinion. If he was happier waking up Christmas morning in his own bed, well, *he* was the little kid, after all. Kai was just going to have to swallow his disappointment.

But he had not swallowed his disappointment. He had been ranting and raving for nearly an hour when Ryo had made the mistake of trying to reason with him.

To Ryo's way of thinking, not only was it unfair to blame Laurel and *Ojiisan* for this change in plans, it wasn't healthy. Yes, it was Kai's turn to have Kenji spend Christmas—more than his turn—and yes, Kenji would have had a great time. He usually ended up having a great time, even if he always arrived on their doorstep shy and uncertain and sort of reluctant. But that was beside the point. The kid didn't want to be there. And that wasn't anyone's fault.

Or even if it *was* partly the fault of Laurel and *Ojiisan* for those years of keeping Kai from his son and creating this unnatural tension...there wasn't any point dwelling on what couldn't be changed. Right?

"It seems to me like you're more concerned with what you want than what Kenji wants," Ryo said.

Kai had gone perfectly silent and perfectly still. When he turned, his face was bone white and his eyes were red and glowing. Okay, not literally red and glowing, but if Kai had been drawing himself for a manga—*Blood Red Christmas*—his eyes would surely have been red and glowing.

"What?"

Ryo said, "All I'm hearing is how disappointed *you* are. You're not five years old, Kai. So next year, maybe he'll be ready to spend Christmas Eve over here. And in the meantime you'll have the day aft—"

"*Get out!*" Kai had yelled. "Get the fuck out of my house."

Gee, it was practically like old times.

Except… "It's my house too," Ryo had pointed out. Loudly. "So *you* get out."

"Fine! I'm going."

And he had. Stopping only to grab his car keys, he had flung out of the house and driven away into the rainy gray afternoon. Without so much as a jacket.

"Good!" Ryo had yelled as the front door slammed shut.

Peace and quiet at last.

Ryo got a beer out of the fridge and made himself a sandwich. Maybe after lunch he'd have a nap. He would be working all night, and it would be wise to take advantage of this lull in the storm. But he couldn't sleep. Every time he glanced at that giant Christmas tree sparkling and alight, the embodiment of all Kai's anticipation and hopes over these past weeks, his heart felt heavy.

He hated Kai being so hurt and disappointed, and maybe that was one reason he hadn't been patient enough. He couldn't fix this, and so he wanted it not to matter so much to Kai. He wanted him to be reasonable and wise. But Kai was not reasonable and wise. Well, sometimes. But he was also headstrong and impulsive and emotional.

Kai did not call, and he was not home by the time Ryo had to leave for work.

Ryo didn't think he was in the wrong, but he did think he could have handled things better. Anyway, he hated quarrelling with Kai, and quarrelling during the holidays added a special level of awfulness to it. So he scrawled SORRY *xoxo* on a Post-it note and left it stuck to the fridge door.

Raindrops hit the windshield. A silver Toyota splashed past Ryo and parked half a block up. The taillights went out.

That would be Ellison, Ryo's relief. He checked his watch. Nine thirty. Shift over. And not a peep out of his phone all night. He checked his messages to be sure. But no. Nothing. Not a word from Kai.

He started the engine. He could always drop by his mom's and spend Christmas morning there. If Kai wasn't home…well, that was going to be pretty damned depressing. Or if Kai was there but still wanting to fight, that would be worse.

For a few moments he sat watching the rain bouncing off the hood of his car, car engine idling; then he drove home.

* * * * *

Kai's Tesla was in the garage, so Ryo knew he was back. That was a relief. More of a relief than he wanted to admit, in fact.

The house was so quiet he thought Kai must still be sleeping. And that could either be a good sign or a bad sign. There were no lights on, no music. The Christmas tree was a dark form in the gloom.

Ryo tiptoed through, heading for the bedroom, stopping only to plug in the Christmas tree lights. In the sudden dazzle of blue and red and green and gold, he was startled to spot Kai huddled on the sofa. Kai looked straight at him. His eyes were dark in his haggard face. He said nothing.

"What is it?" Ryo went over to him, sitting down on the sofa, pulling Kai to him. He was thinking death and disaster at the least. Their earlier quarrel was forgotten.

Kai shook his head, but he leaned into Ryo. He was not crying, but there was something so sad, so heartbroken in his silence, that tears would have been a comfort.

"Tell me," Ryo said softly.

Kai moved his head in negation again, but he said into Ryo's chest, "If you're not on my side, then I have no one."

"I'm always on your side. Always. You don't want me to lie to you, do you?"

He felt Kai swallow. Kai said in that same smothered voice, "I don't know. No. Only sometimes."

Ryo smiled faintly.

Kai said, "I do want what's best for Kenji. But if I don't push this— he's my *son*. He doesn't know me. I don't know him."

"I know. But you can't force it." Ryo kissed the top of Kai's head. He smelled like he had been out in the rain for a long time. He felt chilled. His own Ice Princess. But now he knew the ice was a thin and too-fragile shell. "I am *always* on your side. I guess the truth is, I can't stand it when anyone hurts you. I didn't want it to matter so much to you because there isn't anything I can do about this situation."

"I don't need you to do anything except…"

"Except what?"

"Be the one I matter to."

Ryo's heart squeezed. "*Kai-chan*. You do matter. You matter more than anyone or anything."

And that was the truth. Ryo wasn't even asking for it to be true in reverse. Because if that wasn't what love was about—putting someone else first—what was it?

He held Kai quietly, safely, in the soft prism of many-colored lights, and it was enough.

THE CLASSIC JAPANESE COCKTAIL

The funniest thing about this cocktail is it actually is not Japanese. It was invented by Jerry Thomas and appeared in his 1862 bartending guide **How to Mix Drinks, or the Bon-Vivant's Companion**. *The recipe has changed a bit over time. I liked the idea of Kai—who is a hybrid in every way—having a favorite drink that's also not exactly what it appears to be.*

INGREDIENTS

2 ounces Cognac

½ ounce orgeat

½ ounce fresh lime juice

Dash of Angostura bitters

Lime peel or lemon peel for garnish

DIRECTIONS

Pour the ingredients into a cocktail shaker filled with ice. Shake it up. Strain into a chilled cocktail glass. Garnish with lime or lemon peel.

Makes one cocktail.

JAKE RIORDAN
FROM THE ADRIEN ENGLISH MYSTERIES

BROKEN HALLELUJAH

Baby, I've been here before
I know this room, I've walked this floor
I used to live alone before I knew you.

Yeah, once upon a time. Halle-fucking-lujah.

The first time he'd heard that song it had been in that very building. Cloak and Dagger Books. It had been around this time of year. Not quite this late in the season. The song was on a Christmas album that Adrien had played a lot. Rufus Wainwright. Jake had never heard of Rufus Wainwright before then. Never heard the song "Hallelujah." Now it seemed to be on every time he turned on the radio.

What the hell did it even mean?

And remember when I moved in you
The holy dove was moving too
And every breath we drew was Hallelujah

This coda takes place one year after *The Hell You Say.*

Such a weird song. Such a weird time in his life.

It was all over now. Over and done. And he did not believe in wasting time on regrets over the things that could not be changed.

Should not be changed.

But here he sat in his car, watching the dark and silent building across the street.

Sometimes it seemed like a dream, those months. Ten months. Not even a year. How could the most important relationship of his life have been the briefest?

But that's how it felt sometimes. And that's what he would tell Adrien if he had the chance. If Adrien came home alone tonight, Jake would get out of his car, cross the street, and try to tell him…something. It was Christmas Eve after all, and if there was ever a night for holding out an olive branch—for asking forgiveness—this was the night.

That's all he wanted.

That's all he'd ever wanted those other nights he'd parked here. Waiting for the right moment. Trying to get the nerve up.

Maybe there's a God above
But all I've ever learned from love
Was how to shoot at someone who outdrew you

You could refuse to take a phone call, but it was a lot harder to turn away from someone standing in front of you. Too hard for someone as softhearted as Adrien. No, Adrien wouldn't turn him away. Not on Christmas Eve.

But he wasn't coming back tonight.

It was past midnight now. The windows above the bookstore remained dark. The surrounding streets were silent and empty.

Adrien would be at the Dautens'. Or at Snowden's. He'd be with people who loved him. Which was where he belonged. It was where everyone belonged on Christmas Eve.

And Jake…had spent too long sitting here already. He could not afford to arouse suspicion. He did not want to have to lie. Okay, compound the lie. He turned the key in the ignition.

Still, engine idling, exhaust turning red in the taillights, he waited a few minutes longer.

The stars above the city lights twinkled with cheerful indifference, blazing that cold and broken hallelujah.

JAKE AND ADRIEN

THE DARK TIDE

"You were laughing in your sleep last night." Jake's eyes met mine in the mirror over the sink. He was taking his turn shaving in the small hotel bathroom.

"*I* was?"

His cheek creased, and the electric razor accommodated the sudden curves in his still half-bristly face.

"Good to know I'm having a good time," I said.

His brows drew together, and he flicked off the razor. He turned to face me. "*Aren't* you having a good time?"

"Yes!" I don't know who was more surprised at my previous comment. Me or Jake. "Yeah. I'm sure as hell having a better Christmas than the last three years."

"But?" I had his full and thoughtful consideration. Which still caught me off guard sometimes. Jake paid attention to details. No question. Which could occasionally be dismaying when you were used to—and even enjoyed—flying under the radar.

"Are *you* having a good time?" I asked.

"Yes. I am." He said it without hesitation. "We're both here, and we're both healthy. It's our first Christmas together. I've never been happier. That's the truth."

Yes. I could see in his face that it was the truth.

"You don't mind the fact that every minute of this trip is preprogrammed—that our first Christmas is being spent running from one end of London to the next?"

He lifted a negligent shoulder.

"Or that the rare times we're alone, my cell phone rings? Or someone knocks on the door?"

His mouth twitched.

I felt obliged to point out, "We're having our Christmas dinner in a restaurant."

"I've had my Christmas dinner in worse places. I've had years I didn't get a Christmas dinner."

I sighed.

He reached out, unhurriedly pulling me into his arms. He didn't kiss me, though. He studied me, and I studied him. Jake asked, "Are you fretting over the bookstore?"

"No."

"Uh-huh."

I amended, "Well, mostly no. I do hope it's still standing, but I guess we'd have heard if it wasn't. No, mostly I just…wish we were home. I'd have liked our first Christmas to have been a little less busy. Less crowded. We're not even moved in yet. You've got this very small window of free time, and we're using it up here. I guess in a perfect world—"

Jake interrupted quietly, "Let's go home."

"Huh?"

"You've convinced me. Let's leave early. Let's do the Christmas thing with your family this afternoon, and then tomorrow let's see about grabbing an early flight home."

My heart leapt at the idea. But…

I said uncertainly, "I… How can we?"

"Your mother didn't think you'd agree to come at all. She got you here for Christmas. I don't think she's going to kick up too much of a fuss if we check out early."

He was right. Lisa had been as startled as anyone when in a moment of weakness I'd agreed to her plan for a family holiday abroad. I think I'd partly done it because I hoped the change of scenery would help distract Jake from his own family's struggle to accept his coming out. There's nothing like Midnight Mass at St. Paul's to put things into perspective. Provided you don't mind looking at the world through binoculars. Or possibly opera glasses.

Anyway, Christmas in London with all the trimmings had sounded good in theory—and a lot of it had even been good in practice—but the thing I wanted most for Christmas was to…well, it would sound schmaltzy to say it aloud, but through the years there had been a few dreams—no, *dream* was too strong, but there had been some wistful imaginings about spending *this* holiday of all holidays with Jake. Suffice it to say figgy pudding had not played a big role in the proceedings.

But the fact that there even were proceedings…that might explain why I had been laughing in my sleep. *Joy*. It wasn't just for Christmas anymore.

I smiled up at Jake. His heart was thumping steadily against my own. It occurred to me that he was a comfortable place to lean—not that I had ever wanted to lean on anyone, and I didn't plan on making a habit of it, but for these peaceful moments…

"Let's go home," Jake repeated.

I nodded. "Yeah. Okay. Let's go home."

His mouth touched mine. Sweet and warm and tasting a little bit of preshave lotion. I broke the kiss to laugh.

Jake looked surprised.

"Best part of this," I said.

He raised his brows.

"Lisa will totally blame *you*."

ADRIEN AND JAKE

THE ADRIEN ENGLISH MYSTERIES

From: *A Coal Miner's Son: Don and Ricky-Joe – A Backwoods Romance*

Ricky-Joe put down his guitar and made a couple of notes. The new song was coming along. Not easily, because a drop of his heart's blood was in every word, but it was coming. And maybe someday Don would hear that song on the radio—or more likely Spotify—and remember…

> *I'd shorely hold up the ceiling of the darkest mine shaft for you*
> *I'm caving in, you cave in too*
> *'Cuz diamonds come from coal, it's true*
> *I'm caving in, you cave in too*

The meter was a little rough. Don had always said timing was Ricky-Joe's problem. But it was no use thinking of Don now. Their second chance at love had gone up in flames with the fire that had destroyed the bonsai orchard. Don would never forgive him, and Ricky-Joe couldn't blame him. Only a fool would leave his guitar in the bright sunlight where a cruel and random sunbeam might glance off those steel strings and spark a raging inferno. You only got so many chances in this bottomless mine pit of a world, and Ricky-Joe had wound up with the shaft.

Again.

He wiped a tear away and made another notation on the chord chart.

The door to his motel room burst open, and Don charged in. Ricky-Joe flew to his feet.

"Don!"

Don looked exhausted beneath the grime and coal dust. Actually, it was smudges from the smoke, because it had been a long time since Don had worked the mines. Thank Jiminy Cricket for that, but was it really an improvement if he had to go back to being a butcher's apprentice and killing baby cows? Beneath the weariness in his sapphire eyes was a twinkle.

"Ricky-Joe." Don held up something in his big, strong, workmanlike hand.

Ricky-Joe's eyes popped at the vision of the small and twisted plant. "Donnie, is that what I think it is?"

Don nodded solemnly. "Yonder little fellow survived that conflagration that took out all his leafy kinfolk."

"A baby bonsai," breathed Ricky-Joe.

"Babe, I know you feel to blame for what occurred in the orchard yesterday. I know you must be planning to run away to Nashville again. But this wee limb of greenery is the symbol of our love. A love that can withstand—"

"Something funny?" Jake asked.

"Hm? Oh." I showed him the cover of the paperback. "I found it in the drawer of the bedside table."

His dark brows rose. "*A Coal Miner's Son*? I guess it makes a change from Bibles and phone books."

"You ain't just a-kidding." I smiled at the green plaid flannel pajama bottoms he wore. We hadn't had much time for jammies and such in our previous acquaintanceship. I kind of liked the, well, touch of domesticity official sleepwear brought to the festivities.

However brief their appearance would be.

Jake crawled into bed beside me. His skin looked smooth and supple in the mellow lamplight, his face younger. He smelled of toothpaste and the aftershave he'd worn at dinner.

"I thought that meal would never end," I said. "It felt like we were sitting there for years."

"There did seem like a lot of courses. The food wasn't as bad as I expected, though." Jake glanced at our hotel room clock. "Hey. It's officially Christmas."

"So it is. Happy Christmas."

"Merry Christmas." He nodded at the book I held. "Were you, er, planning to read for much longer?"

I tossed the book to the side. It made a satisfying *thunk* as it hit the wall. "No," I said, and reached for him. "I shorely wasn't."

BABY, IT'S COLD

"God, my head," I moaned.

Rocky, his own head buried beneath his pillow, muttered a laugh.

"How much did I drink?"

Muffled by down and flannel, he replied, "Too much."

At least the bed had stopped spinning. That was an improvement. It had been a good party, though. A *great* party from the bagpiper through the oyster shooters.

Speaking of shooters…

"*Why* did I do that?"

He didn't answer. We both knew why I'd got plastered at the annual Christmas Eve party at Bella Louisa's. The Christmas card from my father. The first word I'd had from him in eight years. Deck the halls, glad tidings, etc. Except… It hadn't felt like that at the time.

And two Italian margaritas, three glasses of wine, an unknown number of shots, and one Italian coffee later, it still didn't feel like it.

I shuddered at the memory, and Rocky heaved around in the bed-clothes and put his arm around me, trying to draw me close.

"Don't move me," I begged. "I have internal injuries."

He started to laugh, the heartless bastard.

"I think my skull is fractured," I persisted.

He ignored my pleas for mercy and hauled me over into his arms. He was not the most comfortable pillow in the world, but he was warm, and the velvety bristle of his jaw and nuzzle of his soft lips against my forehead felt kind of nice.

"I'm probably going to be sick on you," I mumbled into his neck.

"You don't have anything left to be sick with."

I shuddered again. Moaned. Loudly.

Rocky's chest jumped with a silent laugh. He nuzzled my forehead again and said, "You're glad he's okay, though, right? You were worried after the attacks in Paris."

"Of course I'm glad."

My father had moved to France eight years earlier to start a new life—and a new family. It still hurt. I still didn't understand it. Oh, I understood starting a new life. But I didn't understand why there was no room for me in that life. I never would.

I never would—and I had got used to it being that way.

But now he'd sent that card. *Joyeux Noël*. And a note. *If I send you a ticket, will you come to Paris?*

"I'm not going," I said.

"I'll drive. You can sleep on the way. You'll feel better in a couple of hours."

"I don't mean Big Bear. I mean France."

Rocky didn't say anything.

I said with a burst of energy, "I mean, it's too late. *Eight* years? If he cared, he should have said something like…oh, say, six years ago. Six years ago it would have still meant something. *Four* years ago it would have still meant something."

"Jess."

"No, I mean it." I opened my eyes and glowered into the soft gloom of the cocoon shaped by sheets and blankets and Rocky's arms. "I don't even know why he's doing this now."

"Yes, you do. Come on, Jesse."

I shook my head. Closed my eyes.

Rocky's breath was warm against my face. He'd had too much to drink the night before too. But I didn't mind. I was glad we were comfortable with each other now. At home with each other—even when we weren't at home. "He's doing the best he can with the tools he's got."

"He's an asshole."

"He can be. That's for sure. But he does love you. This is proof of that."

"Is it?" I said bitterly. "Even the way he did it. A note on a Christmas card. Not even a phone call."

"He's afraid."

I growled, "He oughta be afraid."

I expected Rocky to laugh. Instead, his arms tightened, and he said, "You're okay, Jesse. I got you. I love you."

I don't know why, but it made my eyes sting, made hot prickle beneath my eyelids. I shook my head, rested my face against the pulse beating at the base of his collarbone. Slow, steady, solid thumps.

Rocky said, "He's afraid you're gonna feel like you feel. He's afraid you're going to turn him down. He *is* an asshole, but he's your old man. And if you want a relationship with him, you got to accept that and go with it. And if you don't want a relationship, then that's okay too. But…"

He didn't continue. I opened my eyes, looked at him. "But?"

His green eyes met mine. "If what you're thinking is you do want a relationship with him, but you're still mad and maybe not ready to forgive him yet…well, you can't predict the future. These last few weeks prove that."

"Yeah, whatever," I muttered because his words struck home, filled me with a vague dread. Nowadays the world seemed like a frightening place a lot of the time. Unsafe. Uncaring. Unknowable.

Rocky was smiling at me, his expression wry with understanding, and I thought *but not here*. Here was safety and caring and acceptance.

"Maybe," I said gruffly. "I'll think about it."

"Good," Rocky said. That time his kiss was brisk and businesslike. "Now I'll make you a nice hot breakfast, and we can get go——"

I moaned.

CLASSIC CANNELLONI

Cannelloni is one of those classic dishes served at Italian holidays. The recipe comes from a site called Cooking with Nonna, and it's WAY out of my league. But I would love to be the taste-tester.

INGREDIENTS

FOR THE RAGOUT:

1 pound of quality chopped meat (should be half veal and half pork)

1 pound peeled tomatoes

1 small carrot

1 small onion

1 stalk of celery

Extra-virgin olive oil

FOR THE STUFFING:

1 pound of chopped meat as above

½ pound fresh ricotta

6 ounces grated parmigiano cheese

1 egg

Nutmeg, salt & pepper

FOR THE BESCIAMELLA:

8 ounces butter

3 tablespoons white flour

1 quart hot milk

Salt, nutmeg

FOR THE PASTA:

1 pound white flour

3 egg yolks and 1 whole egg

Pinch of salt, warm water, if needed (hmm?)

DIRECTIONS

FOR THE RAGOUT:

In a casserole put a few tablespoons of extra-virgin olive oil (enough to cover the bottom).

Finely chop the onion, carrot, and celery. Sauté until the onion is soft but before it changes color.

Add the chopped meat. Salt and pepper as desired, and sauté for a few minutes until the meat turns color.

Add the tomato puree, stir, and bring to a boil.

Add one cup of water, cover, and lower the heat. Cook for about two and a half hours.

SERIOUSLY. Stir occasionally. The sauce will turn brownish and thick.

FOR THE BESCIAMELLA:

In a small saucepan melt the butter at very low heat.

Add the flour while mixing with a whip. Make sure it becomes creamy.

Slowly add the hot milk. Bring to a boil at low flame.

Add salt and nutmeg – the Besciamella should be thick and creamy.

(Like Jesse, this is the part where I give up and go eat dinner at my favorite Italian restaurant.)

FOR THE CANNELLONI STUFFING:

Sauté the chopped meat—note: there are two batches of meat in this recipe—in a frying pan at low flame. Salt and pepper to taste.

Remove from the flame when the color of the meat turns brownish.

Wait until it cools, and put it in a bowl. Add the ricotta, parmigiano, nutmeg, and one egg.

Mix well, and put the bowl in the fridge.

FOR THE PASTA:

On a wooden board make a fountain with flour – in the middle put the eggs and salt.

Mix and work the dough well. Add a touch of warm water if needed. The dough will become smooth and compact.

With a rolling pin or with a pasta maker, make strips about ⅛-inch thick. Then cut them in squares 4x4 inches.

Boil some water and put the pasta squares (6 at the time) into the boiling water.

Boil for one minute, remove the pasta squares from the hot water, put them in cold water, and then on a tablecloth to dry.

Repeat the process for all the pasta squares. You should have about 20 squares.

ASSEMBLING THE CANNELLONI:

(It's going to help if you have all the main components in front of you and ready to go—the pasta squares, the Stuffing, the Ragout, and the Besciamella.)

Cover the bottom of the oven pan with a layer of Besciamella and a layer of Ragout.

Make sausage shapes from the stuffing, about half the length of the pasta squares, and put in the center of the pasta. Roll the dough and fold on both sides. Place all the cannelloni in the pan.

Cover all the cannelloni with the Besciamella and then with the remainder of the Ragout. Sprinkle a generous dose of parmigiano on top.

Now pop 'em in the oven and cook for 20 mins at 400°F.

I have no idea how many this feeds. PROBABLY NOT ENOUGH FOR THE WORK INVOLVED.

COLIN AND THOMAS

THE FRENCH HAVE A WORD FOR IT

Appendicitis for Christmas.

That was even worse than a lump of coal. A lot worse.

"*Ce n'est pas possible*," Colin protested, hand to his right side.

But yes, it was possible. It was probable. According to *Monsieur le Docteur*, it was *certainement*. And if it wasn't appendicitis, what the heck was making him so sick? Because he was sick. He had done his best to talk himself out of it, but he was feverish, nauseous, and the pain that had started out in his belly had moved to his side and was steadily getting worse.

"I'm flying home for Christmas tomorrow," Colin said. "Can you just give me something for the pain, and I'll see a doctor in the States?"

Yeeeah. No. It didn't work that way. In fact, what was going to happen was Colin was going to be prepped for surgery. *Tout de suite.*

"I have to make a phone call," Colin said, trying not to show his mounting panic.

* * * * *

It took two tries to locate Thomas, who was in New York working a protection detail for an actress mostly famous for playing the love interest of dudes whose real costars were the souped-up cars they drove.

"Col, I'll have to phone you back." Thomas was regretful but brisk. He did not like personal calls when he was working, and Colin knew better. And as miserable as Colin felt, his face warmed with embarrassment because it was a point of pride with him that he was the first and only one of Thomas's lovers who *got* it, who understood about Thomas's job. Completely. Totally.

But this was an emergency.

"Thomas, I'm not going to make Christmas. You've got to let my grandfather know."

And Thomas, who rarely raised his voice and never swore, said, "Damn it, Colin. You can't do this. You *cannot* do this to that old man. You can't just change your mind."

"I'm not! I mean, I am, but it's not my choice—"

But Thomas wasn't listening. He said quietly, fiercely, "Do you really not understand what you're doing? You can't make promises and then break them."

"I'm not. I'm—"

"Just because you're not in the mood, or it's inconvenient, or whatever the hell the excuse is going to be."

The hell. Thomas was so angry so fast. It had to be because he had been expecting Colin to back out. And it was true that Colin was nervous and uncertain about going home again. He was homesick, but he was equally determined that this visit not turn into some kind of surrender, a retreat from all he had achieved since his move to France eleven weeks earlier. He had given his word. He had no intention of going back on it. It hurt that Thomas thought he would.

Well, they hadn't known each other long. No. That wasn't true. But they had been together less than a month—much of which had, in fact, been spent apart. They were still learning each other. And apparently what Thomas had so far learned led him to believe Colin was the kind of man who chickened out from a difficult situation and broke his promises.

Maybe because Thomas still thought Colin was a boy, not a man.

"What am I supposed to tell Mason?" Thomas was asking. "What excuse am I supposed to come up with?"

The ready anger was not the worst part, but it still rattled Colin. He was sick, scared, and now in the middle of an argument he hadn't seen coming. He had been expecting, seeking, sympathy, concern, reassurance. In the face of Thomas's disapproval he was ashamed of his weakness.

"Tell him I'm sick. It's true."

Thomas made a sound of disgust. "If you're that sick, you better see a doctor. And then *you* can make your excuses to Mason. I don't have time for this." He clicked off.

Colin slowly replaced the receiver.

* * * * *

He opened his eyes to artificial gloom and a medicinal smell. A hospital room. In the dull light he could make out a tall, motionless figure sitting beside the bed.

Thomas. Recognition should have brought relief, happiness, but something had happened between himself and Thomas. The thought of Thomas was a weight on his heart. The sight of him...

Thomas, gray-faced and weary, asked quietly, "How do you feel?"

Colin closed his eyes. Thomas's large, capable hand covered his, and he didn't have the strength to move away.

He took slow and uneasy stock. He felt cold and still queasy, but the pain in his side was gone. Or was different, anyway. He knew he'd had the surgery. He remembered...well, not a lot. Not about the surgery. He remembered Thomas hanging up on him. He remembered the things Thomas had said. The removal of his appendix seemed trivial compared to the other things he had lost.

It was weird how you could yearn for someone you never wanted to see again.

Thomas was saying nothing, but there was strength and warmth in his touch. He was communicating, but Colin did not want to hear it.

* * * * *

He was released on Christmas Eve into the protective custody of his grandfather, who had flown into Paris the previous evening. Thomas was there too, of course.

Not the Christmas Colin had planned, let alone the Christmas he had wanted. But there would be other Christmases. Though still feeling shaky and weak, Colin tried to stay stoic in the face of Mason's unconcealed anxiety.

"Really, I'm okay now," he must have said a dozen times before they even made it back to his little flat above the boulangerie. "This would have happened either way."

"But at home you wouldn't have been alone." His grandfather, as fragile as a bundle of dried twigs, insisted on helping Colin up the narrow staircase—and Thomas followed close on their heels, ready to head off what must look like the imminent plummet to their deaths.

But they made it safely to the flat, where it turned out Santa and his elves had been very busy. The rooms were fragrant with cooking smells: roasted meat and freshly baked pastries. It was very warm— Colin's heater must have been cranked to maximum for hours on end to achieve that summery temperature. The small kitchen table was piled with delightfully wrapped parcels of food and gourmet goodies. Bottles of wine and cheese and nuts and…just so much stuff. *Bûche de Noël*—a buttercream frosted Yule log on a decorative white platter— and a small herb-braised turkey swaddled in tinfoil, sitting in an old-fashioned roasting pan. Where had they come up with a roasted turkey at such short notice?

There was a little Charlie Brown-sized Christmas tree too, sitting in front of the window that looked out over the gray slate roofs and rain-shiny chestnut trees. There were many—too many—gaily wrapped red, green, and silver packages surrounding that tiny tree.

This was Mason's work, of course, aided and abetted by Thomas, but Colin felt only resignation. His grandfather should not have done all this, and Thomas should not have allowed it, but he understood that the gifts, all of it, were motivated by love. His grandfather was trying to make amends, ironically by doing all the things that had made Colin feel he must put some space between them in the first place.

But…he loved the old man, and seeing how frightened he still was at what he perceived to be Colin's close call, Colin did his best to reassure and comfort. After all, had he made it back to the States as planned, it would have gone pretty much the same way. So he faked hunger for food he had no appetite for and delight in presents that made him feel overwhelmed and cornered.

Thomas knew. Thomas knew how Colin really felt about this. Thomas knew Colin so well—and yet he didn't know him at all. Why did that hurt so much? But it did. And every time Colin looked at Thomas—usually to find Thomas watching him with a serious, hard to interpret expression—Colin had to look away. He didn't know what to do about Thomas, didn't feel strong enough to sort through his troubled feelings. And Thomas knew that too because he stayed very much in the background, hadn't kissed Colin, didn't attempt to touch him except to offer unobtrusive and impersonal help with getting in and out of taxis and climbing stairs.

Colin was grateful for Thomas's understanding—and it made his heart ache.

After their small but sumptuous feast, his grandfather walked around the tiny apartment, studying Colin's paintings. Colin was braced to hear any number of concerns and criticisms. The right teachers, the right training might make the necessary difference. Or…Paris was a dangerous place these days, and Colin spent too much time wandering back alleys and lonely streets, sketching the encroaching shadows.

The words he dreaded didn't come.

When Mason said quietly, "This stay has been good for you, Colin. Good for your painting," it felt like a huge concession. A corner had been turned, a milestone had been passed.

It almost made up for the fact that things were probably over with Thomas.

At last Mason said it was time for him to leave. Thomas said he would see Mason back to his hotel, helping him on with his coat.

"I'll see you tomorrow, my boy," Mason said, hugging Colin very tight.

"See you then," Colin said. He felt Thomas's gaze and looked his way.

Thomas said, "I'll be back in an hour or so."

Colin said—and even now it wasn't easy, "I think I'm just going to go to bed. I'm pretty tired."

Thomas eyed him thoughtfully. "All right."

He hadn't misunderstood, hadn't missed what Colin was actually saying. He accepted it without argument. Colin wasn't sure if he was genuinely glad about that or not.

It felt like days later, though it was only a bit before midnight when Colin woke to the sound of knocking at his door. He sat up and snapped on the light.

He knew who it was. Had been expecting this, had in fact been dreaming of the coming confrontation. An awful dream where he and Thomas said awful things to each other.

But dream or reality, it had to be faced. And now was as good as any time. Colin untangled himself from the nest of blankets and pillows, made his way barefoot across the wooden floor.

Thomas had a key, but he always knocked, always gave Colin plenty of warning. It irritated Colin a little, but mostly because he knew in his heart that Thomas was right. If he woke to find someone in his room, he would experience a moment of paralyzing panic before he recognized, realized that it was only Thomas.

Thomas, who made a point of not interfering with Colin's wandering the streets of Paris at night, was absolutely determined to protect him from a few preventable seconds of terror. Therefore Colin had to suffer the minor annoyance of being dragged out of bed to admit his lover. Which was never really an annoyance. Not even tonight when he was dreading what they would say to each other.

He unlocked the door, opened it, and yes, no surprises. Thomas. Tall, ruggedly handsome in jeans and brown leather jacket, unsmiling.

"I know you're tired, Col, and I know you're not feeling well, so we don't have to talk long. But we do have to talk," Thomas said.

Colin hung on to the door frame. He really didn't feel up to this. He didn't know what he felt, beyond hurt and confusion and disappointment. He knew he didn't want to deal with it now. Knew he was liable to say things he didn't mean.

"Thomas—"

"I know you're hurt. I know you're angry."

Colin sighed and turned away from the door. Thomas entered the apartment, closing and locking the door. The heat was fading, and Colin was too cold and in too much pain to try and sit at the table. He went into the bedroom, climbed into bed, and, braced against the pillows and brass headboard, pulled the blankets up around his shoulders.

Thomas did not remove his jacket. He sat down on the foot of the bed. This silent respecting of the new boundaries eased some of Colin's tension.

"I'm sorry, Col. I misread the situation, and I misjudged you."

Colin nodded. That was pretty much it. Thomas zeroing in on the heart of the matter so fast it was disconcerting. He had yet to work through what he was feeling, and Thomas was already summarizing.

"I didn't listen, and I didn't give you a chance to explain."

"No, you didn't."

"I apologize. Sincerely. I'm very sorry."

And he was. That was obvious. There were new lines in his face, and his eyes were shadowy with regret and guilt. He felt bad. Clearly.

So…all better now?

Colin didn't feel all better. He appreciated the apology. But he still felt…chilled and sick.

Thomas was waiting for him to say something, and he didn't know what to say. It wasn't even that he was still mad. The apology defused a lot of the anger. But there was still this big painful emptiness.

He said, "I don't know. I don't understand—"

Thomas waited. That was one thing about Thomas. He really did listen. He listened to what you said. He listened to what you didn't say. That was part of why he was so good at his job.

Colin's mouth was unexpectedly dry. The words sticking in his throat. "What feels wrong to me is that you think I would do that. That I would give my word and then back out."

Thomas seemed to think his reply over. "I knew you were worried and nervous about the trip. I did think you might come up with a reason not to go."

"To back out. To break my word."

Thomas's gaze was troubled. "Yes."

Colin gave a short, humorless laugh. "And that's why I think this is...not easily fixed. Because you don't know me. The person you think I am is someone neither of us would like."

"*No.* That's not true."

"Yes." Colin's sense of the injustice of it all swept him up again. "You think that I could break my promises to you. You think I could hurt my grandfather like that." He stopped. There was probably more, but that felt insurmountable enough.

Thomas didn't rush to reassure him either. He continued to regard Colin with that dark, troubled gaze. His face was grave.

"You don't trust me," Colin said. That was the full realization hitting him. That was why this hurt so much. Why it felt they probably weren't going to be able to get past it.

"I do trust you," Thomas said. But it wasn't very convincing.

Colin shook his head and stared out the window. Through the glass he could see the moon caught in a net of colored Christmas lights strung through the neighboring chestnut trees. A very old ornament handed down through the generations.

"I do trust you," Thomas repeated. "But I'm also a realist."

Colin turned his gaze back to Thomas. "Which means you *don't* trust me."

"No, Colin. It means that I know everyone has their vulnerabilities, their breaking point. And I thought this trip might be difficult for you."

"Difficult enough that I would break my word and let you and my grandfather down." Colin's resentment, his sense of having been wronged was hardening.

Thomas admitted, "Maybe. That's what this job does, I guess."

Colin shivered, pulled the blankets tighter around his shoulders.

"All right," Thomas said with sudden crispness. "But I'll tell you what. I did think you might panic, but not for one second did I consider that a...a deal breaker."

That surprised Colin. He hadn't considered this angle. And his surprise must have showed because Thomas said with renewed confidence, "I underestimated you. I judged you unfairly. But it did not for one second change my feelings for you, change my certainty that together we have something worth fighting for." He added, "That's the other side of being a realist."

He smiled with a wry diffidence Colin had only seen once before: the morning Thomas had missed his plane, stayed behind to tell Colin he might be falling in love.

Thomas said, "I know you could screw up because I screw up sometimes. Like the day you phoned."

And it should work both ways. Right? Couldn't Colin accept that Thomas might screw up occasionally?

"But that's a big one," Colin protested, still feeling aggrieved, wounded. "If you think I'm someone who could let you down like that—"

Thomas moved—the bedsprings squeaked and pinged—closed the distance, wrapped his arms around Colin. Colin told himself he wasn't sure he wanted to be held, wasn't sure they had reached that stage of negotiation. But the fact was, it felt better with Thomas's arms around him; even if they were going to keep arguing, it felt better to argue like this, in the warmth and safety of Thomas's arms. He could be angry and still find refuge here; that was Thomas's unspoken promise.

Thomas said against his ear, "Sometimes the age difference frightens me. Sometimes I think you don't see me like I really am. A middle-aged guy with a job that takes up too much time and too much energy that should rightfully be yours."

"I don't think that."

"And I worry that one day you're going to wake up and notice that you got the short end of the stick."

"That's crazy."

"I don't think it all the time."

"You shouldn't ever think it."

"But it could be a little bit of why maybe I was too quick to believe you were backing out on a commitment. Because I wasn't sure if it was a commitment I had maybe pushed you into making."

They weren't just talking about the trip back to the States. Colin said, "I wasn't backing out. I'm never backing out. I love you, Thomas." He raised his head, found Thomas's glinting gaze and repeated, "I love you."

From across the frosty, chilly distance floated the silvery chimes of Christmas bells.

BÛCHE DE NOËL

(YULE LOG CAKE WITH COFFEE BUTTERCREAM AND GANACHE)

This is another really complicated recipe—you have to start a day in advance—but it's gorgeous. This one comes from Saveur.com.

INGREDIENTS

FOR THE SPONGE CAKE:

5 tablespoons unsalted butter, melted and cooled, plus more for pan

¾ cup cake flour, plus more for pan

⅔ cup plus 2 tablespoons sugar, divided

4 eggs

Confectioners' sugar, for dusting

1 tablespoon dark rum

FOR THE GANACHE ICING, COFFEE BUTTERCREAM FILLING and FINISHING:

14 ounces 70-percent dark chocolate, finely chopped

1 cup heavy cream

2 tablespoons honey

1⅓ cups sugar, divided

6 egg whites, divided

2 teaspoons green food coloring

24 tablespoons (3 sticks) unsalted butter, softened

1 tablespoon strongly brewed espresso

Cocoa powder, for dusting

Edible gold dust, to garnish (available from nycake.com)

DIRECTIONS

FOR THE MERINGUE DECORATIONS

Heat oven to 200°F.

Place ⅓ cup sugar and 2 egg whites in a bowl set over a saucepan of simmering water; stir mixture until egg whites register 140°F on an instant-read thermometer.

Remove bowl from saucepan and beat with a hand mixer on high speed until cooled.

Place 1 cup meringue in a bowl, and stir in food coloring; transfer green meringue to a piping bag fitted with a ⅜-inch star tip.

Working on a parchment-paper-lined baking sheet, pipe two 1½-inch-wide stars; pipe a 1-inch-wide star on top of each larger star, and then pipe a ½-inch-wide star on top of each middle star to form a three-tiered Christmas tree.

Transfer uncolored meringue to a piping bag fitted with a ⅜-inch-round tip; pipe four 1½-inch-wide mounds to resemble mushroom caps, and then pipe four ½-inch-wide x 1½-inch-tall sticks to resemble mushroom stems.

Bake meringue shapes until dry and crisp, about 2 hours. Turn off oven and let shapes cool completely in oven.

THE GANACHE ICING:

Place chocolate in a bowl; set aside.

Bring cream and honey to a boil in a 2-quart saucepan over medium-high heat; pour over chocolate and let sit for 1 minute.

Using a rubber spatula, slowly stir cream and chocolate until smooth and shiny; let cool at room temperature until set and thick, at least 6 hours or overnight.

THE COFFEE BUTTERCREAM FILLING:

Place 1 cup sugar and 4 egg whites in the bowl of a stand mixer and set it over a saucepan of simmering water; stir mixture until egg whites register 140°F on an instant-read thermometer.

Remove bowl from saucepan and place on stand mixer fitted with a whisk; beat on high speed until meringue is cooled and forms stiff peaks.

Replace whisk with paddle and add butter to meringue; beat until smooth, stir in espresso, and set aside.

THE SPONGE CAKE:

Heat oven to 400°F.

Grease and flour a 13x18-inch rimmed baking sheet, lined with parchment paper, and set aside.

In the bowl of a stand mixer fitted with a whisk, beat ⅔ cup sugar and 4 eggs on high speed until mixture falls back in thick ribbons when lifted from the whisk, about 6 minutes; fold in butter and flour.

Spread batter into an even layer on bottom of prepared baking sheet and bake until golden-brown on the bottom, about 12 minutes.

Place a clean kitchen towel that is larger than the baking sheet on a work surface, and dust it liberally with confectioners' sugar.

Invert cake onto towel; dust with more sugar. Starting with a narrow end of the rectangle, immediately roll cake up into a jelly roll, letting the towel roll inside the cake.

Let cool to room temperature.

THE RUM SYRUP:

Bring 2 tablespoons sugar, 1 tablespoon rum, and 1 tablespoon water to a boil in a 1-quart saucepan over high heat; cook until sugar dissolves, and set aside to cool.

ASSEMBLING THE CAKE:

Once cooled, gently unroll and remove towel from cake. Brush the inside with the rum syrup; allow to soak in for about 2 minutes.

Spread buttercream evenly over cake; reroll cake and set the roll seam side down on a serving platter.

Slice about 3 inches off one end of the cake roll at a 30° angle; cut the other end to make it flat.

Spread the flat end of the angled slice with a little buttercream, and set the slice on top of the cake roll to create a "stump."

Stir ganache until smooth and, using a small offset spatula, spread ganache over cake, leaving the ends of cake, and cut top of the "stump" exposed.

Drag the tines of a fork along the ganache, making markings to resemble bark; refrigerate until chilled.

DECORATEING THE BÛCHE DE NOËL:

Using ganache as glue, place meringue "caps" on top of "stems" to form mushrooms.

Dust cocoa powder lightly over the mushrooms, and sprinkle gold dust lightly over the entire Bûche de Noël.

Place meringue mushrooms and Christmas trees decoratively on and around the Bûche de Noël before serving. (There are videos on how to do this properly—I'd watch them if I were you.)

ALEISTER GRIMSHAW AND VALENTINE STRANGE

STRANGE FORTUNE

In the afternoon they had come upon a series of caves in a red-rock canyon. Enormous, unsettling black and red drawings marched down the length of the cave. The creatures depicted there were nothing Strange recognized, not man nor beast. They made the back of his neck crawl.

Aleister was fascinated by the ancient scrawls—delighted, in fact—and had made extensive notes and sketches in his journal.

By the time Strange dragged him away, the sun had begun to slip from the sky. The sky was clear for the first time in days, though everything was still wet from the biting winter rains.

He would have liked to put greater distance between them and those damned caves, but these lands were unfamiliar and he preferred to face the night with his back against the wall and a goodly fire. Plus Aleister had developed a worrying cough. Which was to say, it worried Strange. If one of them fell really ill or was badly injured, there was no help to be had out here on the wrong side of the White Mountains.

No, not true. If Strange fell ill, Aleister would probably be able to do something for him. Aleister was dosing himself with a horrendously unappetizing juice he'd made from poisonous-tasting berries, continuing to blather away about the caves, cheeks flushed and eyes shining fever-bright. His confidence in the future remained as undiminished as it was bewildering.

"Of course, they *might* offer new information on the former extension of the ancestral abodes of certain clans. I suspect these cliff-dwellers were not a distinct people—"

"Sit closer to the fire," Strange told him. "That wind is like a knife."

"I'm boiling as it is." Aleister smiled widely, eyes shadowy, his teeth very white in the firelight. "Do you know what this night is, Val?"

"I know you'll tell me, Master Sticks and Stones."

If Aleister fell ill, really ill, Strange would be able to do little for him. And the thought of losing Aleister was frankly unbearable. He had been fond of him for some time. He had expected that his feelings would temper, ease into a more casual affection, but if anything, they had grown more fierce, more intense. It was painful to care this much, for theirs was often a hand-to-mouth existence, and death could reach out to grab one or the other at any moment. If something—any harm—came to Aleister—

In the frosty distance something howled. It did not sound like any animal Strange knew.

He glanced at Aleister, who was still smiling. Perhaps he had not heard that eerie howl. "It's the winter solstice."

The longest night of the year. What the fuck could be better than that?

"Well, we've got the bonfire for it," Strange said.

"We've got more than that. I've been saving up for your present."

"My—" But he was speaking to empty air. Aleister hopped up, went to his pack, rifled around, and brought back a handful of…dust. He picked up one of the metal plates that Strange had scrubbed clean in the sand, and let the grains trickle through his fingers while he spoke a soft incantation.

Strange was silent, watching. Was this fever, or was Aleister actually practicing magick? After a second or two, he realized that the dust was, in fact, crumbs. Hardtack crumbs saved carefully for days on end.

The crumbs seemed to jump around on the plate, and then suddenly four small cakes materialized, frosted in pink, speckled with tiny silver candies. The kind of thing that had been rare even before the revolution. The kind of sweet Strange had loved as a boy. And Aleister the only person in the world who knew that.

Aleister laughed at Strange's expression. "They're for you, Val. All four of them." He was beaming his pleasure at this foolish, extravagant gift.

Strange's throat closed so tightly no speck of dust, let alone tea cake, could have passed his gullet. He said, "You're a bloody madman, Grimshaw."

"So they tell me."

Aleister held the plate out to him, and Strange said, "Two for each."

"Oh!" Aleister hesitated.

"Go on, then. Share and share alike."

Looking torn between guilt and delight, Aleister chose one of the delectable cakes. He handed the plate to Strange, who took a cake and bit into what seemed to be a cloud made of spun sugar. The sweetness was almost shocking after months of living on wild game, roots, and whatever else they could forage.

Aleister licked frosting off his lips.

They ate their cakes and passed Strange's flask back and forth. Now and again their companionable silence was broken by one of those long, mournful howls that seemed to issue from behind the giant, silver moon.

"You're cold, whether you know it or not. Come here," Strange said, holding up his cape, and Aleister gave him an indulgent look and scooted over into the circle of his arm. He leaned against Strange's shoulder. His lean, hard body was a warm weight down the length of Strange's.

"Spring is coming," he informed Strange, wiping the last pink stickiness from his fingers.

And only the entire winter still to get through. But Strange did not say that. He said, "Yes. Happy Solstice."

"Happy Solstice, Val."

"Those were the best cakes I ever ate in my life," Strange said.

Aleister smiled and tilted his head to rest against Strange's.

PETER AND MIKE

DON'T LOOK BACK

"When were you going to tell me?" Mike asked. He was smiling, his tone wry.

They had reached the pie and coffee stage of their holiday meal. Parkway Grill was Mike's favorite place to dine—plus there weren't a lot of options on Christmas evening. Mike's parents were visiting his sister in Connecticut. Peter didn't have family—other than Mike. Earlier that day, they'd brunched with Roma and Jessica and thirty other people. It had been fun and festive—but Peter was loving this quiet, private dinner, just the two of them.

"Tell you what?" Peter smiled too, but he was puzzled. Mike's blue gaze seemed a little somber given the mood and occasion.

"The job offer in Boston. You didn't think we should talk it over together?"

Peter's eyes widened. He hadn't realized Mike even knew about the opportunity in Boston. The museum must have phoned. "There's nothing to tell. I'm not taking it."

"You're…not."

"No."

"*Why?*" Mike seemed floored by this news, which was sort of, well, disconcerting.

"Why? Because of…us."

Mike continued to look shocked. Not happy, not pleased. Shocked. "You're not taking this job because of me?"

He was starting to worry Peter. Peter said, "Us."

"Because you're in a relationship with me."

Peter kind of wished they weren't having this discussion in public. And he kind of wished Mike wasn't stating these facts in such a brusque, conversational tone, because they were getting a few glances from other diners. Frankly, he hadn't really expected to *have* a discussion on the subject.

"More because it's not easy to maintain a long-distance relationship with anyone."

Mike shook his head. He said flatly, "You can't make your decision based on that."

"What should I base it on?"

"This is a job you wanted. Right?"

Peter stared, his confusion mounting. This was not the reaction he would have expected. He thought—believed—things were going well with Mike. That Mike was happy. But maybe, after four months, Mike was tired of supporting Peter, of carrying the financial load, of sharing his space. In the beginning he'd said it was no problem, no hardship, and that Peter should take his time finding the right position. And that's what Peter had done, partly because he didn't have a choice. The economy might be recovering, but museum curators were still not in high demand.

"If I—if I lived in Boston, this would be the job I wanted."

Mike nodded like *now* Peter was on the right track.

Peter said, "I didn't realize—" He had to stop because the waitress returned to refill their coffee cups. And because he didn't trust his voice.

There was the usual could-she-bring-them-anything-else? Mike requested the check. The waitress departed.

Peter got control and said quietly, "I didn't realize you didn't want—" He broke off because he wasn't sure how to finish it. He was pretty sure, would have sworn, in fact, that Mike *did* want what they had. What they had and what they were building. But maybe only Peter thought they were building something. It wasn't like they had discussed the future.

Their eyes met, and Mike's frown deepened. He opened his mouth, but the waitress was back with the check.

Mike reached for his wallet—because who else was going to pick up the tab? *Of course* he had tired of being the financial default, and Peter should have realized this—been more conscious of the strain he was placing on both Mike and their relationship.

It hurt, though.

Peter said, "Excuse me. I'm going to get some fresh air."

Good luck with that. The cold night air was scented of car exhaust and the restaurant kitchen. It did not smell fresh. It did not smell like Christmas. It smelled like any winter night in any unfamiliar city. Maybe Boston smelled like this. Peter took a turn around the parking lot. Second time around Mike met him, footsteps crunching dead leaves on the pavement.

"You feeling all right?" Mike asked, offering Peter a peppermint.

Peter declined the peppermint. "I feel blindsided."

"I can see that." Mike peeled the paper off his peppermint. "What's kind of funny is I was trying not to get worked up about the fact you'd decided to take that job without talking to me. And then it turns out you're not taking the job. Also without talking to me."

Peter had to struggle not to say something childish like, *I didn't realize you were so desperate to get rid of me.* He knew Mike didn't want to get rid of him. At least, he thought he did. He was still hurt. Hurt that Mike could seemingly accept—calmly accept—that Peter might be leaving for Boston. That he didn't want to stop him, didn't want to put up a fight for what they had together. In the end he said nothing.

Mike, watching his struggle, said awkwardly, "If I seem ungrateful or like I don't appreciate what you're trying to do, that's not my intent. You did this once. Gave up your life for a relationship. And that asshole let you. You're not doing it again. Not for me. I don't want that. I may be an asshole, but I'm not that big of an asshole."

"I didn't realize I was giving up my life," Peter said bitterly. "I thought it was just a job."

"It's not just a job. It's your career."

Right. And what could be more important than that? Peter drew a deep, shaky breath and said, "I'm cold. We should get back."

Not *we should go home* because plainly Mike's condo was not his home.

* * * * *

The sight of the evergreen wreath on the front door was painful.

Peter hadn't bought the wreath for Mike. He'd bought it for both of them. For *their* home.

"Do you want a drink?" Mike unlocked the door and felt around for the light switch.

"No. Thanks."

The front room smelled like apples and cinnamon. Comforting and homely, but the holiday fragrance made his stomach churn. He felt stupid for decorating Mike's place. Mike hadn't asked for any of that nonsense. The Christmas tree, the fake snow on windows…that was all his idea, and it had been a bad one. He was embarrassed at having presumed too much. He felt unwelcome. The sight of the presents they had opened that morning—nothing extravagant or very expensive, but everything chosen with care and affection (on both sides, he had imagined)—made him want to cry.

However, crying on Christmas was not permissible once you were out of the single digits.

It was only eight thirty, so he couldn't exactly announce he wanted to go to bed. Anyway, it was going to be too weird trying to lie on that mattress next to Mike with all this between them. All this being… apparently not that much. He could invite himself over to Jessica and Roma's place, but that wasn't a very caring thing to do to friends who had already spent the long day hosting a holiday brunch.

"You sure you don't want anything?" Mike asked from the kitchen.

"I think I'll go for a walk," Peter called.

He was two houses down, staring unseeingly at a yard full of mechanical reindeer raising and lowering their lightbulb-lined heads to feast on a dead lawn, when Mike appeared beside him.

"Even *I* can tell something is wrong," Mike said. "Tell me what I did." And the heartless bastard put his arm around Peter's shoulders.

Peter shook his head. Not *No, I won't tell you.* More *I can't tell you—it's too ridiculous.*

"Come on." Mike lowered his head and kissed Peter's cheek. His breath was warm in the cold night. "Talk to me, Peter."

How the hell did women manage to cry and talk at the same time? Because it was pretty much physically impossible, with your throat closed up and your sinuses flooding and your breath jerking in and out, to manage anything like a sentence. Let alone an intelligent sentence.

What he wanted to say was so tangled up and complicated. When he'd finally got his memory back, all of his memory, it had been difficult to accept how alone he was, how *lonely.* He had friends, wonderful friends who made up for the fact that he did not have family. But even that was not the same as having that one special person: the lover who was both friend and partner. Not everyone needed or wanted that, but Peter did. He had hungered for it his entire life. He had wanted it so badly that for years he had put up with the palest imitation. He didn't even know why.

And then Mike had come along. And Peter had really thought the loneliness was over. Really thought that Mike was the guy he would spend the rest of his life with. He was convinced Mike saw it the same way. But now it turned out that once again he had got it wrong. At least in Mike's case there was real affection and caring, but the end result was the same. He was on his own.

Mike's arm tightened around Peter's shoulders. "Have you already turned the job down? Is that it?"

"Not yet."

"Then—"

Peter pulled away. "Until an hour ago, this was the best Christmas of my entire life. Maybe the best day of my entire life. I really did think—"

Into that raw and unsteady pause, Mike said very quietly, "I'm not sure why me supporting your decision to take a job you really want somehow spoils that for you."

"I don't want that fucking job, Mike!" Peter glared at him. "Or I didn't. If we're not going to be together anyway, then I don't know. Maybe that would be the best option."

Mike's head snapped back like Peter had punched him. "We're not going to…"

"You're talking about job versus career, and I understand and appreciate the difference. And I understand that difference should be as important to me as it apparently is to you, but you know what I want more than anything? To be wanted. To be loved. For it to matter to someone if I stay or if I go—"

"You *are* wanted," Mike protested. "You *are* loved, and of course it matters if you stay or go."

"That's not how it feels."

This time there was no pushing Mike away. He wrapped his arms around Peter—not that Peter was fighting him—and whispered, "I don't want you to go. How could you think that? I'm trying to do the right thing, that's all. I don't want to be like *him*. All he did was take from you. I want to give to you. I want to give you whatever you need."

Peter pressed his face into Mike's. "You already do. You already have. Just waking up together this morning... There will be other jobs. I'll get another job. I promise. But I don't want a job that's going to put the entire country between us. It's not worth it to me."

"Then it's not worth it to me either. You think I'm worried about who pays the electric bill? I don't care if you have a job so long as you don't care. All I'm trying to do is show you that you're free to make whatever decision you want."

"I don't want to be *that* free."

"I was never talking about ending things! We could make it work long-distance."

"I don't want to."

"Neither do I," Mike admitted. He shook his head. "Did you really think, even for a minute, that I didn't want you to stay? That the idea of you leaving didn't hurt like hell?"

"You sure didn't show it."

"Didn't I?"

"No."

Mike made a thoughtful "huh" sound. He admitted finally, "Maybe I was trying to protect myself a little bit too."

Peter stared. "From what?"

"From coming in second. Again."

"Never. I've told you how I feel. The only way I'm taking that job is if I'm not wanted here."

After a moment, Mike offered the old wolfish smile. "Let's go home. I want to show you just how much you're wanted..."

WEEKEND IRISH COFFEE

INGREDIENTS

1½ ounces Irish whiskey

1½ ounces Baileys or similar

1 teaspoon brown sugar

6 ounces hot hazelnut coffee

1 dollop heavy cream

DIRECTIONS

Like anything on the internet, you'll find plenty of arguments about how to "properly" prepare an Irish coffee.

Basically you pour the booze in the cup, add the sugar and cream, add the coffee, stir, and taste. If it isn't perfect, add more sugar.

WINTER KILL: ADAM AND ROB

WINTER KILL

"We could toss a coin," Rob said. "Heads my family. Tails yours."

"Let's just go to your family for Christmas." Adam glanced at the clock and set his coffee cup in the stainless-steel sink.

"If we do go to my family, we'll for sure go to yours next year. We'll trade off."

"Yes," Adam said with brisk indifference. He was already on his way out the door. In that charcoal-gray suit, he looked as handsome and stylish as if he was headed for a *GQ* magazine shoot and not a day of chasing bad guys through the mean streets of Klamath Falls.

Rob put down his coffee cup, following Adam down the stairs that led to the garage.

Adam had been working out of the Bend satellite office for the past four months—which was exactly how long they had been living together.

Rob said, "It's probably only fair to go to your family. But I can't deny I'm looking forward to the fun of sharing our meet-cute story with the aunts and uncles and cousins. The adorable tale of how a serial killer brought us together…"

Adam, still in motion, threw over his shoulder, "Sure. Up to you."

Rob stopped midway down the stairs. Adam's mind was clearly not on the holidays. It wasn't on Rob at all. He hadn't even remembered to kiss Rob good-bye. Not that it was a huge deal, but they were both conscious that they held jobs with a higher level of risk than working in, say, a hardware store.

But Adam was preoccupied with work. Not a big case or anything like that. He was just trying to fit in with his new team, his new boss, his new coworkers, his new partner. The truth was, Bend was overjoyed to get him, thrilled Adam had opted for their satellite office rather than Portland, but Adam couldn't see it. He was in high gear all the time. And given the fact that he was by nature an overachiever…Adam giving that extra 110% was frankly exhausting. But Rob got it. Adam had given up a lot—everything—to move to Nearby and be with Rob. Rob was determined to make it as easy for Adam as he could.

Adam jumped in his SUV, hit the automatic garage door opener, and zipped out into the wintry morning. Rob walked slowly back upstairs.

* * * * *

He was digging Jack Elkins' pickup out of the snowy slush and mud when his cell phone rang.

Adam.

"Howdy." Rob leaned the shovel against the tailgate.

"Hey." Adam sounded funny, almost self-conscious. "I think I forgot to say good-bye this morning."

Rob wiped his forehead, squinting at the white sun through the dark branches of the towering pines. What time was it? Two? Three?

"No worries. You can make it up to me when you say hello." He was smiling, anticipating that moment. He definitely preferred their hellos to their good-byes.

"Rob. About Christmas. Whatever you want is fine."

"Same here," Rob said. "It's one Christmas out of all the Christmases we're going to spend. Who cares whose family goes first?"

There was a sharp silence. Had he said the wrong thing? How could promising to compromise be the wrong thing?

Adam said something gruffly.

"What?" Rob asked.

Adam said clearly, "I just want to be with you."

Rob's heart lightened. "Yeah, me too." A sudden thought occurred. "What if we don't go anywhere? It's our first Christmas together. What if we stay home, just the two of us?"

"No, I'm not saying that," Adam said. "You want to see your family, of course." He added in that carefully neutral tone that Rob was getting to know meant he cared a lot, "Unless that's what you want?"

Rob grinned inwardly, but he was touched too. "Hm. I don't know," he mused. "What would we do? I mean beyond cook and eat and sleep and...you know, make snow angels."

He could hear the smile in Adam's voice. "Snow angels, huh?"

"Welllll, unless you have a better idea."

"Oh, I have a couple of ideas," Adam said softly.

BLUE CHEESE, BACON, AND BALSAMIC ONION BURGER

Burgers are definitely Rob's food. The blue cheese and balsamic vinegar is Adam's contribution.

INGREDIENTS

½ medium red onion

2 tablespoons balsamic vinegar

Kosher salt

Pepper

1½ pounds lean ground sirloin

4 ounces blue cheese

4 brioche hamburger buns

Lettuce

Tomato

Cooked bacon slices

DIRECTIONS

In a small bowl, toss together the onion, vinegar, and ¼ teaspoon each salt and pepper. Let sit, tossing occasionally, until ready to use.

Heat grill to medium-high. Gently form the beef into 4 balls. (Don't overwork the meat—this can result in a tough, dry burger.) Flatten each ball into a ¾-inch-thick patty. Using your thumb, make a shallow 1½-inch-wide indent in the top of each patty. Season the patties with ½ teaspoon each salt and pepper.

Place the patties on the grill, indent facing up, and cook until the burgers release easily from the grill, 3 to 4 minutes. Flip and cook to desired doneness, 3 to 4 minutes more for medium. During the last 2 minutes, top with the blue cheese and grill, covered, until gooey.

To do this right, grill the buns until lightly toasted. Serve the burgers on buns, and top with the balsamic onions, lettuce, tomato, and bacon, if desired (and how would bacon ever NOT be desired?).

GHOST AND GENE

FADE TO BLACK

Off-season they were both broke—that was the reality of island living—so Ghost offered yet again to fix that blowout tat he'd carved onto Gene's chest twenty years earlier, and Gene declined yet again for sentimental reasons, but this time Ghost put up a fight.

"Yeah, okay, dude, it's part of you now, but that would be the cool thing about this. I'd be building on the past, but it would be something totally new. It would be about…flying into the future. Together."

That was probably the most romantic thing he'd ever said to anyone ever, and he actually got a little choked up on the word *future*. Because for someone whose life philosophy was based on the conscious decision of living one day at a time—of neither borrowing trouble nor putting off till tomorrow—it was pretty damned close to a vow of commitment.

Terrifyingly close.

Maybe Gene saw it because after a moment he cocked his head like a thoughtful Rottweiler and shrugged. "Okay, G."

He didn't like to call Ghost "ghost," and Ghost didn't answer to Gordon—was deaf to the name—so Gene called him "G," which was funny since it was his own initial too. It was pretty typical of the way they were together. Goofy, sure, but easy. Very easy. In fact, Ghost had never been with anyone as easygoing as Gene.

So for Christmas he replaced that monstrous, evil-looking stapler on Gene's chest with a vintage China Clipper. It was really gorgeous. One of the nicest bits of art he'd ever done. Gene was flatteringly surprised and complimentary.

"Flying into the future together," Gene quoted, preening bare-chested in front of the mirror on the closet door.

Ghost got very red hearing that aloud and in daylight, but Gene kissed all the embarrassment away.

On Christmas Day Gene took Ghost for a private helicopter tour of the island, a long, leisurely flight. The kind of thing tourists paid a lot for. He'd been floored when he'd learned Ghost had never had an aerial view of the place he'd lived in for fifteen years.

It turned out to be a rougher ride than expected—a storm was blowing in from the south—but Gene remained cool and capable, and aside from a bit of queasiness from being tossed up and down in what felt like a tin can, Ghost found the whole experience kind of exhilarating.

As a matter of fact, he found life with Gene in general kind of exhilarating.

Safely back home, they had one of those turkey loaf things with Stovetop Stuffing and mashed potatoes and frozen corn (only not frozen, of course).

They split a six pack of Corona, and Ghost said, "Should we toast to something?"

Gene grinned, gold incisors showing, and clicked the bottom of his bottle to Ghost's. "Here's to our next fifty Christmases together."

"God bless 'em, every one," said Ghost.

JASON AND SAM

THE MERMAID MURDERS

He didn't expect to hear from Sam on Christmas Day.

By now Jason understood enough to know anniversaries, holidays, and family get-togethers were problematic for his...well, what were they exactly?

More than friends and less than lovers.

Any time he thought about it—something he mostly avoided—he was reminded of that scene in *Young Frankenstein* where Frau Blücher declares, "He vass my...BOYFRIEND!"

Except Sam wasn't. Was he?

As a matter fact, Halloween was the last time they'd really talked. Coincidentally, he'd heard from Dr. Jeremy Kyser too. That was after he'd spoken to Sam, though.

Anyway, it wasn't like Jason was sitting around waiting for newly appointed BAU Chief Sam Kennedy's phone call. Those months were pretty damned grueling for Jason too. The part he had played in Massachusetts ended up giving his own career a nice boost. He was flying all over the country to consult with museums directors and art gallery owners.

No one was shooting at him. That was nice.

It was natural enough, given how much they were both traveling, that they hadn't actually ever had time for that now legendary date. In fact, they hadn't seen each other since the summer.

Well, no. It wasn't natural.

But it was partly the job and partly—

Yeah, no. It wasn't natural.

But Jason didn't have anything to lose. He liked talking to Sam, liked looking forward to what they might do when they eventually hooked up again. In a way, there were advantages to not seeing each other. They could talk more honestly, more openly—like to a pen pal or a radio talk-show therapist.

Let's be clear. Jason vassn't renouncing…DATING! His schedule didn't leave a lot of time for anything other than his schedule.

Which pretty much explained June through December. There was no phone call on Thanksgiving and only one very brief call mid-December.

So no. Jason wasn't expecting a phone call from Sam.

Holidays were a BFD at Stately West Manor. Not Jason's favorite thing, frankly. The BFD, not the holidays; he enjoyed holidays. Anyway, he believed in picking his battles. Every year, since time immemorial, his parents had hosted a Christmas Eve party for the movers and shakers of the City of Angels. Attendance, while not mandatory, was strongly encouraged. And being ambitious, Jason understood the importance of networking over the wassail.

When his cell phone rang, he figured it was work. Something about the holidays brought out people's worst instincts. But Sam's number flashed up, and Jason's heart flashed up with it. He excused himself to his brother-in-law the congressman and stepped out onto the terrace.

The chilly—for Los Angeles—night was scented with orange blossoms (the ornamental trees having been artificially forced into bloom) and lit by hundreds of tiny star-shaped lights strung everywhere you could possibly hang a fake celestial body. From the other side of the French doors he could hear a big band version of "'Zat You, Santa Claus?"

"Hey," he said, and he could practically hear the champagne bubbles warming his tone. But he was glad to hear from Sam. No point pretending he wasn't.

"Hey," Sam said as terse as ever. But Jason could now recognize the gradations of terseness, and this level of brevity was Sam practically oozing holiday charm.

"Where are you?"

Sam seemed to hesitate, and for one crazy—and, admit it, thrilling—moment, Jason thought he might be about to say he was actually here in town.

What if this was the night? Light me up with me on top, let's fa-la-la-la-la-la...ahem.

But no. After that odd pause, Sam said, "Vegas."

"Ah. Too bad. What are you doing in Vegas?"

Sam sighed, and it was a weary, weary sound. "The Roadside Ripper."

Right. The night air was suddenly frosty, bitter cold. The Roadside Ripper serial killings were one seriously ugly case, and Jason was very glad he had no part in it, although a lot of the L.A. field office was involved. The taskforce was one of the largest ever formed.

"How's that going?"

"It's not."

In the background Jason could hear the chink of ice and clink of glasses and a lot of too-loud voices. A bar. A Vegas bar on Christmas Eve. Come to think of it, he preferred Stately West Manor.

"You okay?" It wasn't what he meant to ask. But he didn't know what to ask Sam, and the fact was, he did wonder if Sam was okay. He worried about Sam, although that was probably ridiculous—Sam would think it was ridiculous.

"Yeah." Sam sounded different. Almost…soft. "Are you having a Merry Christmas?"

"Sure. It'd be merrier if you were here." Now that was definitely the champagne talking.

Sam laughed that low sexy laugh that Jason so rarely got to hear. "I don't know. I'm not exactly a party guy. I'd do my best to warm you up, though."

"Yeah?"

"Mmhm."

"I'm still waiting for that date."

"I haven't forgotten." A jingle of ice sliding down glass and the sound of swallowing. "So what's Santa bringing you for Christmas?"

And just like that the tone changed. Still warm, still friendly, but the distance wasn't only geographic. It made Jason a little melancholy because he was beginning to suspect that date was never going to happen. Still, there had to be some reason Sam continued to phone.

They chatted for a few minutes, and then Sam said, "I'd better let you go."

And Jason made himself reply cheerfully, "Yeah. It's good hearing your voice, Sam."

There was another of those funny pauses where he thought he was about to hear something important.

"Jason?"

"Yep?"

He could feel his heart thumping with an uncertain mix of unease and hope.

Sam said very gently, "Merry Christmas."

It sounded…like something else. Jason said huskily, "Merry Christmas, Sam."

That little click of disconnect felt like the loneliest sound in all the world.

BLUE MERMAID COCKTAIL

Which is obviously going to be better than a green mermaid.

INGREDIENTS

1½ ounces gin

1 ounce blue curaçao (a bitter orange liqueur)

½ ounce dry white vermouth

½ ounce lemon-lime soda

Crushed ice

½ cup caster sugar or fine salt

1 anchovy

DIRECTIONS
(LOL. REALLY?)

Put ice in your shaker

Put booze in your shaker

Shake your shaker

Pour contents of shaker into martini glass

You didn't think I was serious about that anchovy, did you?

NIGHT WATCH

"I don't do Christmas," Parker said.

"Really?" Henry had answered. "I do."

That's where they were by then. This was the emotional odyssey from April to December.

Anyway, it wasn't even completely true. Once upon a time Parker had done Christmas. He'd had a friendly, affectionate relationship with the holidays, even if he hadn't always given them a lot of time and attention. That was another lifetime. Remembering how hard he'd worked to make up all those missed Christmases for Ricky... Honestly? Nowadays the idea of the holidays turned his heart cold.

At first Henry had tiptoed around Parker's...call them sensitivities. Because he definitely had his weak spots, blind spots, sore spots. He knew it, and he did try to push past them. He appreciated the fact that Henry did not dole out kindness in measured doses. Henry was not a scorekeeper. Nor did he sweat the small stuff. He was a guy who had his priorities straight. Maybe that came from being a cop. Maybe that came from losing the love of your life.

Also, Henry had a built-in bullshit detector like nobody else. Sure as hell unlike Parker who, as everyone knew, was one of the biggest suckers in town. Or he had been until he stopped believing in true love and Santa Claus.

But that wasn't true either. He did believe in true love. He just knew it wasn't for him.

Except sometimes when he was with Henry he thought maybe it was.

Maybe there was an element of guilt to Parker's turning into the Boyfriend from Hell. He'd been working all autumn on an exposé of the investigation of the investigation of the investigation into the death of Police Officer Tori Sykes, and he knew Henry was taking a lot of heat from the, well, heat. He never asked Parker to cool it, never asked him to back off. The only thing he'd ever said was, "Are you sure of your facts?"

Reasonable enough, except Parker was a fanatic about his facts. Sometimes he felt like his facts were all he had left. He'd blown up. That was the first real argument they'd had.

It was not the last.

Once they crossed that line—the line of arguing about one thing when they were really pissed off about something else—it was hard to go back.

But at least with Henry, Parker always knew where he was. And there was something liberating about being able to yell openly and loudly, and be yelled at back, and know he wasn't going to be stabbed for it.

They weren't moving closer, but at least he knew Henry wasn't going to kill him when they broke up. Which they clearly were going to do.

Over Christmas.

"Okay," Henry had said, "I'd like to have Christmas with you, but if you've got other plans, so be it." He'd already assured Parker all he had to do was show up, and Parker had already declined to make the effort, so no wonder Henry sounded like, *Suit yourself, asshole.*

Henry had tried very hard to make it work. And Parker, who probably wanted, needed it to work more than Henry, had barely tried at all.

So Henry spent Christmas with Jared's family, and Parker spent Christmas at home working and pretending it was like any other day.

But it was not any other day. It was the day he had finally managed to push Henry away. And for the first hour or so after he woke up with no Henry in his bed—and no word from Henry as to the next time they might see each other—he was relieved.

Thank God. The pressure was off. At last.

The truth was this had been destined from the first. Parker was damaged goods, and Henry was just too damned nice. So. Big Relief. Merry Fucking Christmas.

Except it didn't feel like relief. In fact, he felt sick with disappointment. Like he'd applied for a job on the *New Yorker*, got it, and then hadn't had the nerve to pick up the phone and accept the position. What was that about? He had never been like this before Ricky. He hated this frightened, angry guy he'd become. But he didn't know how to stop. And if he couldn't stop for Henry, then it was safe to assume this was who he was now.

By lunchtime—which Henry would be having with his late partner's family, who would no doubt be encouraging him to dump this neurotic, unappreciative, loser journalist he'd saddled himself with—Parker was questioning his fatalistic acceptance that his relationship with Henry had always been doomed. Parker had worked his butt off to make things work with Ricky. Couldn't he have at least tried a little for Henry? Given that, unlike Ricky, Henry would have met him halfway. Hell, Henry would have met him on the welcome mat, if he'd ever made any kind of real effort.

It was confusing because he really liked Henry. Everything with Henry had been so…good. When he had let it be. So easy, so right. Too easy. Too right. He couldn't trust it. It terrified him. He always felt compelled to fuck it up. Not consciously. But really, that made it worse. As if he just couldn't help being a total shit to this very kind, very nice, very decent guy who was trying and trying to have a normal relationship with him.

There was no law that said, having messed everything up, he couldn't try to fix the situation, right?

If it just hadn't been for that note of finality in Henry's voice when he'd said "so be it." Like he was delivering the verdict in a trial that had dragged on for months. Which…was probably exactly how it felt to Henry.

Maybe Henry was feeling relief today too. Only in his case, genuine relief.

Henry had mentioned that Jared's family had their Christmas dinner around two, so Parker figured Henry should be safely home by seven. He tried phoning Henry at seven thirty.

His call went straight to message.

"Hi, Henry," Parker said to the machine. "I just want—wondered—hoped." Well, that pretty much covered all of it, and with embarrassing frankness. He pulled himself together and said, "I forgot to tell you Merry Christmas. And I...miss you."

The minutes passed.

Very long minutes.

When Henry was working, he didn't always call Parker back immediately. It was possible he was still at his in-laws. It was possible he'd been called out to a crime scene. It was possible he couldn't hear his phone ringing over the fantastic time he was having wherever he was. It was very unlikely that Henry was sitting at home listening to that message and deciding whether he was going to call Parker back or not.

But as the minutes ticked by, Parker felt more and more convinced that was exactly what was happening. Henry was trying to decide if he was going to give Parker one final chance.

And with each minute that passed, the odds were mounting against Parker.

He felt desperate enough to phone again, but managed not to. He didn't want to scare Henry. He just wanted him to know...so many things. But they were things you had to say in person.

So why not make the effort to drive over to Henry's and tell him everything he'd been thinking and feeling all day? About how he knew he'd been a fool and he wanted another chance. That what they had together, fragile and delicate as a Christmas ornament, was worth... well, deserved not to be dropped on the floor and smashed into pieces, at least.

Okay. Yes. He would do that. He would drive to Henry's and tell him all that. But in the meantime, he waited for Henry to phone because if Henry wasn't taking his calls, this was all beside the point.

But maybe that was the point. To, for once, make the effort without waiting for Henry to do it first.

Parker studied his phone, willing it to ring. The phone stayed silent. So okay. Henry would not sit here waiting for the phone to ring. Parker rose, found his wallet, shrugged on his coat, and opened the front door.

Henry stood on the other side of the security screen, hand raised as though he had been about to knock—or maybe punch Parker in the nose.

Parker said, "Henry?" Henry's hand fell to his side.

"Merry Christmas," he said. Gravely. Very gravely for Henry.

"I was just on my way to your place."

"I was on my way over here when I got your call." Henry was still looking very serious. Not like a guy brimming over with holiday cheer.

There's nothing like an aborted launch. Parker felt off-stride, off balance. He unlocked the screen. Henry had not tried to use his key, which meant Parker's instincts were correct. This was a mess. He pushed open the screen, stepped back, holding the door for Henry.

Henry stepped inside, and Parker caught a hint of Henry's after-shave and his leather jacket.

Henry glanced around as though he hadn't stood in that very room three days earlier. The only concession to the holiday was Henry's own Christmas card perched on the mantel and the remains of a frozen turkey dinner sitting next to Parker's laptop on the coffee table.

"Did you have a nice day?" he asked.

"Not really," Parker admitted.

Henry nodded as though this confirmed something for him.

"I did. I actually had a really nice day," Henry said. His eyes were blue and direct and unsympathetic.

Parker's heart seemed to shrink a couple of sizes, like the Grinch in that Dr. Seuss cartoon. Only in the cartoon, the Grinch's heart grew three sizes. He made himself say, "I'm glad. You deserve to have a really nice day."

As a matter of fact, Henry deserved a lot of really nice days. He deserved for every day to be a nice day because he was a very nice guy.

"Yeah," Henry said. "It made a pleasant change being with people who can occasionally look on the bright side, who aren't afraid to hope or dream or just plan a goddamned vacation now and then."

Henry was not raising his voice. He did not sound particularly angry, but he did sound...unrelenting. Like he had decided on his plan of action. And Parker was pretty sure he knew what that plan of action was.

He nodded because he could not find the words, and even if he had, his throat had closed. Like a steel trap clamping tight. So he nodded again.

"Jared's sister Eileen brought a work friend to dinner. I didn't know anything about it, but he was someone she thought I'd get along with, and she was right. We hit it off immediately. And if I wasn't in this sort-of-relationship with you, I'd have asked him out when we left the house together..."—Henry looked at his watch—"forty-eight minutes ago."

The fact that Henry knew to the minute when he'd said good-bye to this holiday blind date arranged by Jared's sister hit Parker hard. He felt like Henry had punched him in the throat. He literally could not draw a breath. He sat down on the arm of the chair behind him because his legs wouldn't hold him.

It wasn't that he had taken Henry for granted. Not for a single second had he taken Henry for granted. He had known from the beginning, the first time Henry had kissed him, that he was only in remission. That eventually—and sooner rather than later—he would be alone again, struggling to get through the nights and trying to convince himself there was a reason to look forward to the days. Beyond the satisfaction of his work, that is. Because he did, as Henry had pointed out a few times, live for his work.

Which made a certain amount of sense, given that he'd nearly died for it.

Yes, he had always known this day was coming, but that didn't make it any less painful. In fact, despite his preparation, he hadn't really comprehended just how painful it would be. In a funny way, it hurt worse than getting stabbed in the chest. In a funny way, it felt more like a mortal wound.

But the one thing he still had was his pride, and pride made him say, "So I guess it was just as well I didn't go with you today."

Henry laughed. It was not a happy sound. "Right. That's what I'm saying to you, Parker. Thanks for not spoiling my Christmas by having any part in it." He shook his head.

Parker said, "What you're saying to me is you tried for eight months and you're tired of trying. And I don't blame you. You've met someone, and that's... You deserve to be happy."

"That's exactly right," Henry said. "For eight months, I've tried. The problem is, I love you. I really do. And I'd be willing to keep trying forever if I thought there was any point. But I don't think there is. Or I didn't. Until this." He took out his phone, stared at it for a moment, then pressed the screen and held it up so that Parker could hear his own tinny voice sounding as choked and desperate as a kidnapping victim.

"I forgot to tell you Merry Christmas. And I…miss you."

Henry said, "I listened to that three times before I walked up to your porch. I wasn't sure if I was hearing what I wanted to hear—or if you're really trying to tell me that it matters to you that we weren't together today. That it would matter to you if you didn't ever see me again."

"Of course it matters," Parker cried, rising to his feet again. "I don't want to lose you. But I don't know how to do…this. And I know it shows. And I know I'm wearing you out. I'm wearing myself out. I was going to tell you—"

He stopped because suddenly Henry was looking at him like he was a ghost. The Ghost of Christmas Past, or the Ghost of Christmas Future? It was such a weird expression that he actually glanced over his shoulder.

"You're wearing your coat." Henry's voice sounded odd too.

Parker glanced down at himself. "It's cold out."

Henry said slowly, as if he was doing some elaborate computation in his head, "You're still holding your keys. You were on your way out?"

"I was on my way to your place," Parker said.

"You were coming to see me."

"I do sometimes."

"Yeah, but." Henry was still staring at him in something like amazement. "Not after an argument you don't. I wasn't sure you'd even notice I wasn't here."

"I do notice," Parker said wearily. "I always notice. I like it when you're here. I wish you were here all the time. I love you too. I didn't think I ever would again—feel this way. I just…"

"Just what?" Henry was walking toward him, and Parker couldn't seem to tear his gaze from Henry's. He braced for impact.

"Think that I'm not easy to be with."

"That's for sure."

"And you can do better."

"So I've heard. But maybe I like a challenge." Henry smiled, but there was something a little sad in the back of his eyes.

Parker understood. He was never going to love anyone the way he had loved Ricky. Henry was never going to love anyone the way he had loved Jared. But that was okay. It wasn't a competition. Or a test. Whatever was between them had lasted eight difficult months. It was real, and it was tenacious.

Despite the shadows, Henry's eyes were kind again. Warm.

And seeing that light in Henry's eyes, Parker's heart did the Grinch thing once more, expanding three sizes and then another size for good measure.

When Henry reached for him, Parker met him halfway.

THE DO-IT-YOURSELF CLUB SANDWICH

INGREDIENTS

⅓ cup mayonnaise

2 tablespoons Dijon-style mustard

12 slices whole wheat bread, toasted

8 lettuce leaves

8 (¾-ounce) slices of Sharp Cheddar cheese

½ pound thinly sliced deli ham

8 slices tomato

½ pound thinly sliced deli turkey breast

8 slices cooked bacon

DIRECTIONS

Combine mayonnaise and mustard in bowl; mix well. Spread about 1 teaspoon mayonnaise mixture on one side of each toast slice.

Layer 1 slice toast, mayonnaise-side up, 1 lettuce leaf, 1 slice cheese, 2 ounces ham, 2 slices tomato, 1 slice toast, mayonnaise-side down. Spread 1 teaspoon mayonnaise on toast.

Top each sandwich with 1 slice cheese, 2 ounces turkey, 2 slices bacon, 1 lettuce leaf, and 1 slice toast, mayonnaise-side down.

Cut into triangles. Secure with toothpicks. Makes four sandwiches.

FELIX AND LEONARD

MURDER BETWEEN THE PAGES

The clocks were chiming when I landed on Felix's doorstep.

I could hear them through the tall, white front door of the Colonial farmhouse. All fifty-three of them. Ding-donging away. Chiming out the hour in ten long notes.

Maybe that's what was taking him so long to come to the door. Maybe he couldn't hear me over the clocks. Or maybe it was the rain rattling on the windows and roof—and the ragged leaves of the little palm tree plant I cradled in my arms—that deafened him to my knock.

I knocked again and rang the doorbell for good measure. Where would he be on Christmas morning? Hopefully nobody had wrung his scrawny neck while I'd been away.

I was just starting to get nervous when the door suddenly flew open.

"Well?" Felix demanded. His thin face changed. Black eyes narrowing, lip curling. "Oh, it's you."

"Hell, yes, it's me. Who were you expecting?"

"Not you."

"I told you I'd be back."

"Ha!"

"Aren't you going to invite me in?"

His throat jumped as he swallowed. He said haughtily, unpleasantly, "Don't you have somewhere more important to be?"

"No."

His lashes swept down, then flicked up. He gave me a funny, crooked smile. "No?"

"You know I don't."

"I thought they loved you in Hollywood."

"They do. But it's not home, is it?"

"It could be. If you wanted it to be."

"I guess so."

He frowned. "You're shivering, Leonard."

"I'm freezing to death."

"You're not used to our weather anymore."

"I could be. If you wanted me to be."

Felix studied my face. "Hm. Well, maybe you had better come in, then."

I came inside, handing over the little palm tree and the bags of oranges and almonds. "Anyway, Merry Christmas." I took a deep appreciative sniff. "Something smells great."

"It happens that I'm making ham and eggs for breakfast."

"My favorite," I said.

"Is it?" As if he didn't know. As if he hadn't cooked it for me plenty of times. He started to turn toward the kitchen, and I caught his arm, pulling him toward me.

A tinge of color pinked his cheeks. "Leonard, you'll crush my palm tree."

I laughed and kissed him. He closed his eyes and kissed me back, and the oranges and almonds rained down around our feet.

* * * * *

I don't think he believed I'd be back.

Nah. He had to know. Maybe he thought when I did come back, it would be to pack my suitcase and grab my hat.

I don't deny it crossed my mind as that train had clickety-clacked its way over deserts and cornfields, through small towns and mountain ranges, over the rivers and through the woods...

I liked California. I liked the palm trees and the orange trees and the Technicolor blue of those always-sunny skies. I liked the hustle and bustle of movie studios and doing business beside a swimming pool. I liked the money to be made in California.

I liked the fact that nothing shocked people in Hollywood. And that everybody but Hedda Hopper and Louella Parsons minded their own business.

But what Hollywood and California didn't have was Felix Day.

The one thing I couldn't live without.

THE BEST HAM & CHEESE SCRAMBLED EGGS

This one comes from a site called Butter with a Side of Bread. So you know they're on the right track.

INGREDIENTS

6-7 eggs

½ cup diced ham

1 tablespoon water (or milk, but water makes the eggs fluffier)

1 heaping teaspoon Ranch dressing

(Ranch dressing wasn't invented until the 1950s, but buttermilk dressing has been around forever, so I think Felix could still come up with this.)

½ cup shredded Cheddar Jack cheese

Salt, pepper & chives to taste

DIRECTIONS

Heat a frying pan on medium heat. Spray with a bit of non-stick cooking spray and add in diced ham, stirring occasionally.

Crack eggs into a bowl. Add in water and Ranch dressing. Whisk until combined.

Pour eggs into frying pan with ham. Using a rubber spatula, mix gently. Allow to cook, turning eggs occasionally.

Once eggs are nearly cooked, add in half the cheese. Stir to combine.

Remove from heat once completely cooked (time will vary depending on how soft you like your scrambled eggs.)

Top with remaining cheese and serve.

ADAM AND ROSS

A LIMITED ENGAGEMENT

"Tell the story about how you two got together again," someone called from down the long, linen-covered table.

Who?

Marta? Angelique? I couldn't tell who. There were always so many people at this annual Christmas Eve luncheon. Over the years they had all started to look—and sound—alike.

"It was twenty years ago," Ross began, and our guests settled down to be once more amused and entertained by the master. Only Ross could make blackmail and attempted murder sound like the meet-cute opening of a Rom-Com.

They all sipped their wine and listened and laughed in the right places. Everybody loved the story. After all, the course of true love and all that.

No one had gone to jail. No one had gotten hurt.

Well, maybe Anne Cassidy. Hard to know how seriously she'd taken it. Still waters. Anyway, she was a decade underground now.

Strange to think…

Ross had reached the climax of the story and was quoting me. "'You could kill me,' Adam said, 'and it wouldn't hurt as much as watching you marry someone you don't love.'"

Awww, everyone said, as they always did.

* * * * *

"I wish you wouldn't tell that story," I said that night.

Ross, wearing his red silk dressing gown and slippers, was reading the *New Yorker* by the fireplace. He glanced up and smiled.

"It's a great story."

"I hate it."

He laughed. At sixty he was still handsome, still debonair, still charming…still the love of my life. And he always would be.

"Come here, you." He laid aside the magazine, held out an arm, and I joined him beside the hearth, leaning against his chair—at forty-plus I was a bit old for curling up on his lap. I rested my head on his thigh. His fingers gently played with my hair.

He murmured, "There is nothing either good or bad, but thinking makes it so."

I closed my eyes. "*Hamlet.* Act 2. Scene 2."

"Very good." There was a smile in his voice. His fingers, slim and dry and cool, sent little chills of pleasure over my scalp.

"We haven't done so badly, have we? We've lasted longer than any other couple we know. We're certainly happier than any other couple we know."

I moved my head in assent. "Showfolk."

He chuckled. "We're showfolk."

The fire snapped and crackled. Ross was silent, and I wondered if he was nodding off. When I turned my head, he was staring into the fireplace. The flames threw shadows across his face.

"Do you ever regret—" I started softly.

But he smiled again and shook his head. "No. I don't. None of it." His eyes shone in the firelight, studying me. "Do you?"

"I got everything I wanted."

"So did I."

I curled my lip. He said, "I didn't know what I wanted until you."

I turned my head so he couldn't see the tears.

The grandfather clock began to chime midnight. Soft, sonorous bell tones.

One.

Two.

"Make your Christmas wish," Ross said. He sounded indulgent, as he so often did with me. As though I were still that emotional and desperate boy of so long ago.

Over the past year he'd had two strokes. Very mild. You'd have to know him well to ever tell.

I closed my eyes and wished. *Twenty more years...*

DEATH IN THE AFTERNOON COCKTAIL

Also called Hemingway Champagne—Hemingway claims to have invented this one.

INGREDIENTS

3 tablespoons (1½ ounces) absinthe

½ to ¾ cup (4 to 6 ounces) cold champagne or sparkling wine

DIRECTIONS

Pour absinthe into champagne flute. Add champagne until a milky cloud appears, then serve.

ADRIEN AND JAKE

So This is Christmas

Well, baby, I've been here before
I've seen this room, and I've walked this floor
I used to live alone before I knew you
But I've seen your flag on the marble arch
And love is not a victory march
It's a cold and it's a broken Hallelujah

I was humming along with Rufus Wainwright performing Cohen's "Hallelujah" as I ran up the stairs to Jake's office.

"Hey," I said. "I didn't think you were coming back this afternoon."

I stopped in the doorway. Jake stood at the window that overlooked the alley behind the building. I couldn't see his face, but something about the set of his shoulders silenced me. Took my breath away, in fact.

It wasn't defeat exactly. But I got a sense of...weariness that went beyond the physical.

This is actually a deleted scene.

"Jake?"

He tensed, as though he hadn't heard me. As though his mind was a million miles away.

"Yep?"

That glimpse of his eyes froze my heart for a second or two.

He sounded brusque, but that was because…because guys like Jake did not cry. Not when they lost jobs they loved. Not when their marriages broke up. Not when their families wouldn't talk to them.

Maybe he'd cried when Kate lost the baby. He'd never said.

I'd never ask.

He was not crying. His eyes were a little red. It could even be allergies. He probably was genuinely…weary.

Or it could be the result of meeting Kate today. Of course he would feel regret. Wish he'd made different choices. Maybe he was comparing the might-have-beens against the what-he-was-left-withs.

"Everything okay?" I could hear the mix of wariness and worry in my voice.

His smile was twisted, but some of the bleakness in his eyes faded. "Yes."

"You're sure?"

He walked toward me, still smiling that crooked smile. I didn't realize I had left the doorway until I met him halfway.

I slid my arms around his neck; he wrapped his arms around my waist.

He said softly, "I'm very sure."

BLACK ORCHID COCKTAIL

Currently my—and Adrien English's—favorite cocktail.

INGREDIENTS

1 ounce Skyy Raspberry Vodka

1 ounce DeKuyper Blue Curacao

1 ounce DeKuyper Watermelon Pucker

Splash: cranberry juice

DIRECTIONS

Fill shaker with ice. Pour ingredients into icy shaker. Shake it, baby. Pour into martini glass.

JEFFERSON AND GEORGE

JEFFERSON BLYTHE, ESQUIRE

George had been definite. He could not make it back to the States for Christmas.

"You can't ask for the holiday off?" I'd asked. Since George hadn't been home in four years, I thought maybe he could reasonably make that request—and that it might even get a thumbs-up from Corporate. Or whatever code name they used for CIA London. But nope. George declined to even ask.

Which sort of...hurt. We hadn't seen each other since Merry Old E., and that had been five months ago.

Half a year. If we rounded up. Which is the rule in life as in math. Round up.

Was this more of George testing me, of me needing to prove I was really, honestly invested? Or was it George losing interest?

'Coz it felt like George losing interest.

A couple of times I even thought I should ask him outright. *Dude, are we through and you just don't want to break my heart or something?*

In my place, George would have asked outright. And if I asked outright, he'd tell me.

But I didn't ask. I just kept hoping I was wrong. I needed something to hang on to, and poor George was it.

The deal I'd made with my parents was that I'd do a year's apprenticeship with my dad in his architectural firm while I figured out where I was going to go to film school—assuming I could get in anywhere.

I *could* get in somewhere as it turned out. I could get in LFS. The London Film School. I'd applied for the following year. And I'd been accepted.

But was I going? I felt like it kind of depended on George. He hadn't asked, and I hadn't told him.

My parents, of course, believed I'd change my mind about the whole film-school thing. Also the whole being-gay thing, which they attributed to ongoing upset over getting dumped by Amy and being confused and lost and generally…young. They figured I had turned to George because of timing and trauma.

It was the first time I ever heard that fighting bad guys could make you gay, but okay. Interesting take on law enforcement. Anyway, I had my stuff to work through, and they had theirs.

It wasn't as bad as I'd thought, working for my dad. I didn't hate architecture. Not at all. Architecture is a very cool gig, as a matter of fact. It just wasn't how I wanted to spend my life. But as everyone I talked to pointed out, there were worse ways to spend your life, and not everybody got to do what they loved for a living. That was the point of having a hobby.

My dad said the only thing that would really disappoint him was if I deliberately chose something I didn't want for my future because I was afraid to talk to him. Which was a pretty solid 9.9 on the Dad Scale, grading from 1 (deadbeat dad) to 10 (rescues-kid-who-is-not-even-his-own-from-burning-building dad). Very nearly heroic, given how long he'd been planning on me joining the family firm.

The holdup was not my parents. The holdup was George.

And then very casually my mom mentioned that Mrs. Sorocco had said that George was coming home for Christmas.

News to me.

And that sort of hurt too. But was also exciting because…George. On the same continent at the same time. We might talk. We might do something besides talk.

"So you *are* coming home for Christmas?" I asked George the next time we talked.

He swore, and my heart sank. But then he said gruffly, "Damn it. I wanted that to be a surprise."

"It is. I didn't think there was a chance."

"No. Well…it's not like I don't have a stake in this too."

I wasn't *exactly* sure what that meant, but it was probably the most promising thing he'd said yet. About anything.

That was Christmas Eve.

I went to bed that night trying to maintain in the face of my excitement that Santa was bringing me *George*.

Or sort of. Because George literally arrived around two o'clock on Christmas Day and was whisked away into the family fortress.

There was no opportunity for even a brush pass or whatever the hell the spy term was for a chaste hug hello. George waved at my window on his way into Sorocco HQ, and I waved forlornly back. The Berlin Wall couldn't have seemed more insurmountable in those five seconds than Mr. Sorocco's tidy boxwood hedge. The geometric squares of snow-covered lawn and shoveled driveway in front of our separate embassies could have been no-fly zones.

George had dinner at his house, and I had dinner at my house.

Diplomacy? Détente? Defection? I was more confused than ever as I tried to choke down turkey and gravy and mashed potatoes.

"More stuffing?" my mom asked when I'd finally cleared my plate.

I suspected she was being ironic, but the doorbell rang, and I practically knocked my chair over answering it.

George stood on the stoop, framed in twinkling lights and the two potted, beribboned juniper shrubs. The Spy Who Wasn't Sure If He Wanted to Come in from the Cold. He wore a dark overcoat and his most severe horn-rimmed specs. Flakes of snow melted into his neatly combed hair. He looked handsome and serious in a sorry-to-have-to-revoke-your-passport kind of way.

"Hello, Jeffer—"

I heard his *oof* as I knocked the wind out of him with my hello hug. Possibly more of a hello tackle.

"God, George. I can't believe you're here."

Not dignified, I know. But sincere.

"Hey," he said in a very different tone of voice. His arms locked around me, and he hugged me back. Hugged me the way you'd expect to be hugged after you return from deep-space exploration. *"Hey,"* he said again.

"I didn't think you were ever going to get here." I wasn't just talking about arriving for Christmas, and I think he knew it because when I raised my head, he kissed me.

He kissed me like he'd thought he was never going to get there either, and it made up for a lot.

When we broke for air, he drew me out onto the step, pulled shut the door, and led me around the house and out to the backyard and up into the tree house.

The floorboards were dusty with snow, and there were gaps between the planks. I could see the red berries of the holly bushes below. The bird bath looked like an ice sculpture. We hadn't been up here in years. Maybe George thought we were under surveillance. If so, he was right. I pictured the Soroccos and my own parents with binoculars trained out the dining room windows.

Anyway, he shoved a clear space for us and we settled together.

My teeth were chattering—I hadn't had time to stop for my jacket—and George took off his coat and wrapped it around my shoulders, and then wrapped his arm around me for good measure.

"Poor old Jefferson. Has it been tough?" he asked sympathetically.

"It's been h-hell," I replied, snuggling closer. "But not because of my family or friends or anything. That's been...weird, but mostly okay. A lot of it has been good. Better than I expected."

He kissed the top of my head—like he was kissing my five-year-old self—and I said, "George, don't."

Behind the severe glasses, his eyes were guarded.

"You've got to listen to me," I said.

"I'm listening."

"Because this is unfair to both of us, and you're going to wreck any chance we might have."

That expression I knew well. The lordly George of my teens. The George who firmly believed he knew best. Knew everything.

Well, he didn't. Not always.

I headed him off with a quick, "No, listen, George. I know you're doing what you think is best for both of us. You don't want to hurt me, and you don't want to get hurt again. I get all that. But there is no insurance policy for this. Maybe it'll work out for us, and maybe it won't, but it sure as hell won't work out if we don't try."

He opened his mouth again, but I kept talking.

"And this...cooling-off period or whatever it's supposed to be isn't realistic anyway. If this is supposed to be for my sake, then it really doesn't make sense because you've set up a scenario where I can't move on. Because I'm still waiting for you."

"You're not supposed to be waiting for me!"

"But I am, George." I couldn't help the tears that sprang to my eyes. "Because I *love* you. *You.* And until I know for sure it won't work, of *course* I'm waiting for you, of *course* I'm waiting for this stupid, ridiculous, fucking holding pattern to be over!"

"Jefferson." He sounded soft and regretful. "Don't you see that defeats the purpose?"

"What *is* the purpose, George? I don't even know anymore. If you're so sure it's not going to work, that you don't feel enough for me to really try, then *tell* me."

"I *don't*," he broke in.

My heart stopped. I stared at him.

His face twisted, and he said, "*No*, I mean I don't think that. I would tell you if I thought that. I...want it to work. I love you. You know that. I want it to be right. But wanting it won't make it true."

"Yeah, but it's a start." I had to wipe my face. I was so cold, I hadn't even felt the tears falling until I was tasting them. "I don't know why I ever agreed to this because it's the worst idea ever. It's completely illogical. The only way we're ever going to know if it might work out for us is if we actually *try*."

He was silent. Offended that I dared to criticize his stragegy?

"We've already put in half of the year you wanted."

"Five months."

"Close enough for government work."

His head bobbed, acknowledging a point.

"I can't take it, George." I just didn't have it in me to pretend anymore. No more of the cheerful, optimistic, adulting Jefferson of the last five months' worth of phone calls. I could hear the weariness in my voice, and I think he could too. "If it's a test, then I fail. I'm sorry. I just feel like you're coming up with excuses not to be with me."

"I didn't know you felt like this."

I said a little bitterly, "You didn't want to know."

He seemed to be thinking that over. "That's not true," he said finally. Ever the intelligence analyst.

"I can't guarantee anything," I said. "Except that I'm done. And if anyone ought to understand that people aren't predictable, it's a spy, George."

He made a funny sound. Not exactly a laugh. "Maybe so."

I sighed and rested my head on his shoulder. I could feel him thinking. I could practically hear the gears turning.

"Okay, then," he said slowly. "How do you see this working?"

"I want to move to London and start LFS next year. Is that what you want?"

Behind the glasses, his eyes were startled. "Well, yes."

"Is it?"

"Yes."

"If you don't want to live together, that's okay, but I would like to—"

"I would like to try living together," he said. He still looked cautious, like he thought maybe I didn't understand what I was saying.

"You're willing to live together?" I asked, equally cautious.

"It makes the most sense."

"True."

He let out a shaky sigh—as though he'd been holding his breath for a long time. "There's nothing I'd like more."

I raised my head to stare at him. "Well, George, if you were going to give in so easily, what have we been waiting for all these months?"

He was smiling. A sort of silly, sort of self-conscious smile that looked an awful lot like the George I used to know once upon a time. Before he became a secret agent and learned to hide everything he felt. Maybe even from himself.

He said, "I think maybe...this. Maybe for you to see that I was always going to give in the first time you asked—and really meant it."

CHRISTMAS PUNCH

This one is from Martha Stewart.

INGREDIENTS

2 cups chilled pomegranate juice

1 cup chilled cranberry juice (or blueberry-cranberry juice if you're feeling daring)

8 ounces (1 cup) vodka

8 ounces (1 cup) Cointreau or other orange-flavored liqueur

1 cup chilled club soda

½ cup fresh lemon juice (from 6 lemons)

½ cup Simple Syrup for Mixed Drinks

DIRECTIONS

Combine pomegranate and cranberry juice, vodka, Cointreau, club soda, lemon juice, and simple syrup in a punch bowl.

Fill glasses with cranberries frozen in ice cubes, and serve.

Garnish with lemon slices if desired.

ACKNOWLEDGMENTS

Thank you to Johanna Ollila, Kevin Burton Smith, Keren, and Janet.

Happy Holidays to one and all!

ABOUT THE AUTHOR

Bestselling author of over sixty titles of classic Male/Male fiction featuring twisty mystery, kickass adventure, and unapologetic man-on-man romance, **JOSH LANYON** has been called "arguably the single most influential voice in m/m romance today."

Her work has been translated into nine languages. The FBI thriller *Fair Game* was the first Male/Male title to be published by Harlequin Mondadori, the largest romance publisher in Italy. The Adrien English series was awarded the All Time Favorite Couple by the Goodreads M/M Romance Group. Josh is an Eppie Award winner, a four-time Lambda Literary Award finalist (twice for Gay Mystery), and the first ever recipient of the Goodreads All Time Favorite M/M Author award.

Josh is married and lives in Southern California.

Find other Josh Lanyon titles at www.joshlanyon.com

Follow Josh on *Twitter*, *Facebook*, and *Goodreads*.

ALSO BY JOSH LANYON

NOVELS

The ADRIEN ENGLISH Mysteries
Fatal Shadows • *A Dangerous Thing* • *The Hell You Say*
Death of a Pirate King • *The Dark Tide* • *Stranger Things Have Happened*
So This is Christmas

The HOLMES & MORIARITY Mysteries
Somebody Killed His Editor • *All She Wrote*
The Boy with the Painful Tattoo

The ALL'S FAIR Series
Fair Game • *Fair Play* • *Fair Chance (coming soon)*

The A SHOT IN THE DARK Series
This Rough Magic

The ART OF MURDER Series
The Mermaid Murders

OTHER NOVELS

The Ghost Wore Yellow Socks • *Mexican Heat (with Laura Baumbach)*
Strange Fortune • *Come Unto These Yellow Sands* • *Stranger on the Shore*
Winter Kill • *Jefferson Blythe, Esquire* • *Murder in Pastel*
The Curse of the Blue Scarab

NOVELLAS

The DANGEROUS GROUND Series
Dangerous Ground • *Old Poison* • *Blood Heat*
Dead Run • *Kick Start*

OTHER NOVELLAS

SHORT STORIES

COLLECTIONS

Made in the USA
Middletown, DE
22 February 2017